CHOSEN ANGEL

KEEPERS OF THE LIGHT 2

TAMAR SLOAN

V. P. ALLASANDER

KEEPER
CHRONICLES

Cover by Laercio Messias
https://laerciomessias.com.br/

I

GABBY

"I had no idea," mutters Gabby as she stands outside the gates of Mercy Academy in some weird-ass replay of her first day.

She could sense that day was the start of something. She'd been looking forward to it. She'd been overflowing with nervous excitement.

"Yep, no freaking idea," she mutters again.

Even though two months have passed since then, she's still trying to wrap her head around how much can happen in such a short amount of time.

Turns out she's the daughter of an archangel.

And that there are seven evil angels determined to destroy life as she knows it.

Oh, and she's fallen hard and fast for a demon.

Whom she hasn't seen since they defeated the Grigori. Colt's been as MIA as the Grigori have.

Gabby hoists her backpack a little higher. She's not sure which of those unsettles her more. There's been no news of the Grigori since they escaped. No matter how hard she's worked on locating the cowardly bastards, they've remained elusive.

And Colt disappeared as completely as they did. His brown gaze had been shuttered as he'd told her he had some demon business to deal with, then left before she could ask too many questions. She thought he'd be gone for a day, or a week at most. But as the days had progressively accumulated, the uneasiness had grown.

Angels and demons are enemies, their hatred and distrust are as old as time. Has Colt run? She gets the sense he's done a lot of that during his time on Earth. A little part of her can't blame him...even as the thought slices far deeper than she'd like it to.

Knowing she needs to get going—one-month suspension, then the academy had unexpectedly closed for another month, the dean giving some vague emergency building issues—means a two-month unexpected break. On top of everything else, she needs to put her study pants on.

"Hopefully I won't fail classes as spectacularly as I have everything else," she says under her breath, even as she wonders when she started talking to herself.

"You haven't failed," a familiar voice says, "in fact, you achieved what no one else could."

Gabby spins around, her heart shooting up her throat. Colt stands a few feet away, the afternoon light gilding his wine-colored hair, stroking his broad shoulders. Catching in the tangle of emotions shifting in his earth-colored eyes.

"You're back," she breathes, her heart a drum against her ribs. It's demanding that she close the distance between them. Her fingers twitch with the need to touch him.

A part of her wondered if she'd ever see him again. It's certainly what her father told her. He'd practically sneered each time he'd pointed out Colt's a demon. Untrustworthy. The spawn of Hell. Just plain wrong.

Except there's nothing wrong about Colt. He's so...right.

Gabby quickly shakes her head. She has more backbone than that—Colt's been gone for weeks, without a word. "Where have you been?"

He takes a small, almost hesitant step forward. "I'm sorry. The...demon business took longer than I expected."

"I tried to contact you," she says, realizing she just took a step of her own. She stops, another realization hitting her. "You're not going to tell me, are you?"

"I can't." He doesn't move, as if he's waiting to see what her response to that will be.

Dammit. She should demand an answer. Yell and shout that she deserves one. But she's just so freaking happy to see him. And one fact is undeniable.

He came back.

She plants her hands on her hips. "Are you trying to start an argument?"

Colt's lips twitch as his gaze roams the gates behind her. "Well, we're standing here. It would seem a disservice if we don't."

He's referencing the first time they met. The chemistry had been there, even then. It's one of the reasons she'd reacted so strongly. The remaining reasons—the whole she's an angel, he's a demon thing—is something she's not going to think about too deeply.

Not when Colt just took another step closer.

"Or we use it as a second chance," she says, her voice husky.

His eyes flare bronze. "Now there's an interesting proposition," he murmurs.

"This time around, we'd be completely honest about how we're feeling." A step of her own and only a couple of feet are between them. "I'd tell you I've missed you."

"I'd tell you it's been hard being away. Harder than I expected."

Gabby's smile starts somewhere in her heart. "Then I'd kiss you."

"Actually, I'd kiss you first."

Their mouths slowly gravitate toward the other, almost as if in slow motion. Gabby welcomes it. She wants to savor this. Glory in it. It means when their lips finally connect, she lets out a shuddering breath. All the magic of their first kiss there. The instant heat. The delicious stuttering of her heart. The unstoppable wave of passion.

But this is so much more tender. A reconnection. A reaffirmation.

Whatever this is between them, it's very, *very* real.

The faint sounds of chatter and laughter filter through the sweet haze and Gabby pulls back quickly. What is it about this guy that she totally forgets who she is, let alone where she is? "We can't…"

"I've shrouded us. No one can see us," says Colt. He sighs. "We can't be seen together too much."

It's against academy rules.

And celestial rules, apparently.

She nods, but then lifts her chin defiantly. "I told my father about us." Back when she thought there was an us. For a while, it seemed she jumped the gun. But now Colt's back, kissing her. Does that mean there's an…us again?

"I'd wager the great Gabriel didn't appreciate hearing that. Angels don't like demons."

"But I like you," she retorts, a smile playing on her lips. "And he's trying to keep me happy."

"He's been training you?"

"Yes. But I want to be out there, finding the Grigori. The Daniels, the last couple they murdered, were Maya's uncle and aunt."

Colt's lips press together in a tight line. "I'm sorry to hear that." His hands tighten around her waist. "You should listen to your father. The Grigori will be back. They'll want the parchments. And the more prepared you are, the better."

Gabby smirks. "You're agreeing with my father? An archangel?"

He arches a brow. "Maybe your father's agreeing with me."

"Oh wow, Hell has frozen over?"

They smile at each other, and Gabby wonders if he's marveling, just like she is, at how quickly and easily they've slipped into their groove. As if they've known each other for as long as Colt's been roaming the Earth. Or as if they've never been apart.

She chews her lip, knowing neither of those are true. "Will you be leaving again?"

"Not if I can help it." His gaze dips to her lips then back up. "We have the Grigori to take care of."

Gabby steps back, trying to regain some equilibrium. For some reason, that's not quite the answer she's looking for.

"And I'm going to talk to Belphegor about no longer working for the academy," he adds. "I'll suggest providing private tuition to students."

That has the uneasiness settling. Colt's ensuring they have one less hurdle for them to overcome. "Great idea."

He glances over her shoulder, his handsome features hardening a little. "I have to go. The first thing I'm supposed to do on returning is report to him."

Gabby blinks. He had to leave, and he can't, or won't tell her where or why. Yet Colt came to see her first. Learning that is almost as beautiful as the kiss they just shared.

She watches him walk away, eyes roaming over his jean-clad butt as she reflects how much a world can change in a few short minutes. Colt's back. Their connection wasn't her imagination. What's more, he feels it too.

She knows it.

She flicks her curls over her shoulders, wishing there wasn't another realization chasing the first.

Colt spoke of fighting the Grigori when the time comes. Of staying.

But he hasn't promised more than that.

2
COLT

Colt walks away, conscious of Gabby's eyes on him. It's a gentle weight he welcomes. It had been harder than he expected to be away from her. His very soul had rebelled against it. But he had no choice.

He owes Belphegor.

And they wouldn't have won against the Grigori without the might of the demons.

"Skata," he mutters under his breath as he makes his way through the gates and down the drive.

Each day he'd almost called. Just sent a message. Something to nourish the fragile connection between them. But he didn't. Gabby would've asked questions, a lot of them. Her bright, curious mind wouldn't have been okay with non-answers and glib side-stepping.

He had to do it in person. He wanted to make sure whatever's blossomed between them wasn't a trick of his mind. That he could tell her what he could face-to-face, and hope that would be enough.

Of course, he underestimated her. Or maybe he underestimated the power of the emotions that have sparked between them. In all his centuries, he's never experienced anything like it. Didn't even know it was possible. And in the end, they took precedence over why they were forced to be separated. They refused to be denied any longer than they needed to.

And that kiss had scorched his soul in ways even the fires of Hell were never able to.

Resisting the need to go after her and lose himself in her magic all over again, Colt takes a sharp right that will lead him to a side entrance. There's something he should've done the moment he returned, but he just couldn't. He had to see Gabby.

But as he makes his way through the academy, he focuses on what would've been first on any loyal demon's list—the report he needs to give to Belphegor. Colt was asked to track a truck-load of demonic weapons that had gone off the road somewhere along the Mississippi. Just hearing what happened sent shivers of unease rippling under his skin.

It was surprising that humans had attacked a load of weapons that had just left Hell. It was even more surprising that they succeeded.

When he'd arrived at the scene, he'd found human bodies scattered on the side of the busy highway. All dead. The scene had already been reported to law enforcement but demons intercepted the communications, letting Belphegor know who then sent Colt. Once he was there, he'd used his powers to compel anyone there to leave, although it wasn't easy. The trucking company didn't want to leave bodies lying under the care of one person. But Colt's magic had been more powerful than their objections. He needed privacy if he was going to find out what happened.

When he finally managed to take a look at the bodies, he discovered they'd been exorcized. He'd frowned as he'd crouched beside a corpse. Who could wield such power over demons? Did these humans somehow come in contact with spells that could send demons back to Hell? If so, their work had been shoddy. The humans hosting the demons had died as well. A skilled wielder of magic would have saved the possessed human.

But not a lot of humans possessed such skills, those being reserved for witches and, sometimes, Catholic priests who came across such spells. Of course, the movies and television shows have it all wrong. Holy Water and the sign of the Cross have no impact on demons. Those were just showmanship, something humans excelled at.

Whoever had done it had been successful, though. And it turns out, hard to trace even though they'd disappeared with a cache of demonic weapons. As each day had passed, Colt's frustration and impatience grew. There was only one place he wanted to be.

With Gabby.

It turned out that a powerful witch named Iris had wanted to get her hands on the weapons. All so she could exact revenge upon a coven in Dallas that expelled her after she'd started to practice black magic, a type so dark it bordered on necromancy. Colt had put an end to her plans, but that had required close to two months.

That's almost sixty days where he would have preferred to spend time with Gabby, getting to know the badass angel girl.

Something he had never thought he would do.

A demon falling for an angel is unheard of. It's also frowned upon, and why Gabby's father automatically dislikes him. More like loathes him. Colt's lips twitch as he jogs up the stairs, imagining Gabriel's reaction to his daughter's announcement. Angels, especially archangels, don't like demons. Period.

Except perhaps Gabby.

Which may be because she was raised among humans. She

escaped the superior attitude of angels, something both angels and humans can learn from. Even demons, for that matter.

Colt pauses outside the dean's office. Being with Gabby has shown him a new way of thinking. He's had two months to ruminate on it. To see if these feelings would wane with distance and time.

But they hadn't. And he knew Fate was right. His future is irrevocably tied to Gabby's. And he's no longer going to fight it. He now has a new purpose. Protect Gabby. And to do that, he needs to stop the death and destruction that will rain down if angels and demons openly declare war.

And for that not to happen, he needs the Tear closed.

Unfortunately, that's what Belphegor has asked him to keep open. What Colt is honor bound to do.

He knocks and enters as Belphegor calls out. The office is large and opulent, as befitting the dean of a prestigious academy. Belphegor—the dean—sits behind his mammoth desk, tapping his fingers impatiently.

Colt nods differentially as he takes a seat on the other side, even though the dean isn't someone who has the physical appearance that inspires respect. A short and square head sits on top of a short and square body, giving the overall sense of a toad. The fact Belphegor has possessed this body shows the depths of his desire to track down Colt. It should've been for vengeance, but the simmering hostility between angels and demons meant the archdemon needs him.

It's meant a reprieve. But also a debt.

Colt sits and waits, keeping his face neutral as he shoves his thoughts deep. The Dean watches him for long seconds, weighing him, his eyes boring into Colt. He knows Colt is barely an ally, and he's reminding him of that.

"Anything further you have to report will have to wait,"

grinds out Belphegor. "Troubling news has reached me, and I want your opinion on it."

"Yes?" asks Colt as he braces himself internally. Something troubling the archdemon is...unsettling.

The dean sighs. "Another shipment of demonic weapons I ordered brought from Hell went missing a couple of hours ago. Though this cache was smaller than the one before, it still consisted of dangerous armaments, which in the wrong hands could be disastrous."

Colt nods, letting the words sink in. Surely he won't have to leave so soon. He only just got back.

And the connection between him and Gabby needs time to be nurtured. Disappearing without giving answers a second time will certainly not do that.

"I thought I had taken care of the damn witch!" he snarls.

"I don't think that witch stole this shipment," the dean clarifies, sitting on his well-cushioned chair. "This robbery has been committed by someone else."

Colt frowns. "Someone else...but how?"

"Same modus operandi," the Dean explains. "Exorcize the demons and kill off the humans transporting the cache. But my question remains...how are they finding out about the shipments?"

"Maybe they're watching the Tear?" suggests Colt.

"And who has the patience and the resources to do that?" the dean asks.

Colt has no answer to that question. Whoever they are, they seem to be well-funded.

"I think the angels are behind this," snarls Belphegor, crumpling a piece of paper in his fist. "Only they would be interested in whatever we're getting out of Hell."

Seeing the sense in the explanation, Colt wonders which

faction. Is Gabby's father behind this.... Or is it that insufferable obnoxious angel, Samandriel?

He needs to find out.

"And if angels are watching the Tear, they'll want to close it, and soon."

Colt holds himself still even though he wants to shift in the leather chair. It was only a matter of time before the conversation came to this.

"We cannot let that happen," the Dean continues. "So, tell me, Colt, what's the progress on that?"

He shakes his head. "Gabby seems more focused on finding the whereabouts of the Grigori rather than closing the Tear."

The dean nods. "Well, it's best we keep it that way, understand? The last thing we need is a powerful half-angel finding a way to close the Tear and putting us at a disadvantage."

"Of course," says Colt, glad he's known to be a demon of few words. His throat is too constricted.

The dean leans forward, his eyes snapping with challenge. "You say that, but your heart isn't in it. Is it, Colt?"

He holds the archdemon's gaze. He doesn't like lying, unlike many of his kind, but it's necessary at times. "I owe you, Belphegor, and I will honor that which is owed. Just don't expect me to take pleasure in it."

That seems to satisfy Belphegor, because he leans back in his chair. "I'll tell you one thing, this world will be better off without angels in it. They're petty and pesky nuisances neither humans nor demons need. Trust me on this." His toad face hardens. "And someday, you will have to choose a side. You can't run away from your blood any more than I can, Colt. Remember that. And if you think those angels will give a rat's behind to your relationship with that angel girl, think twice."

Colt simply nods. Everything Belphegor is saying is true. Angels will not bless his relationship with Gabby. Demons will demand he take their side. But he doesn't care. He wants none of it. He would rather demons take their wars and the angels their prejudices away and leave him alone. Instead, they're determined to pull him into an unnecessary war with apocalyptic repercussions for every human on Earth.

"I'd like to propose I resign as an instructor at the academy. All this will require focus and time, I can't guarantee I'm available for regular lessons. I suggest I take on private clients, using the academy gym, which keeps me in the vicinity."

Belphegor strokes his square chin. "I see the value in that." His gaze sharpens. "You can move into the old groundskeeper's cottage at the rear of the academy."

Colt nods, conscious Belphegor is keeping him close. But at least he's no longer an instructor here. One less barrier between him and Gabby.

"That is all," grunts the dean. "I'll personally look into this latest robbery and try to find out who's behind this."

Colt nods, thankful that the archdemon didn't ask him to track down the latest perpetrators. It's too soon to reveal his divided loyalties, and being asked to leave again would've done that.

He's not willing to leave Gabby again. Not yet.

Probably not ever.

Once out of the dean's office, the need to see Gabby before he retires to his room is overwhelming. His mind made up, he walks out of the administrative building and makes his way towards the west wing where the student dorm rooms were. It doesn't matter to him whether that evening in settling in or that the Dean has mandated a curfew. He stopped following rules centuries ago. And he wants to see Gabby with every shred of his being.

As soon as he is close to the west wing, he wonders how much Gabby has honed her powers in the time he's been gone.

Tucking his hands in his pockets he stares up at her window, focusing his mind on the curtains on the other side. They twitch once. Twice. He whispers her name through his mind. "*Gabrielle.*"

She appears far quicker than he expected and it has a smile blooming across his face. One of the first since he left her. No wonder this girl, angel or no angel, is so addictive.

Gabby pushes the window up. "What are you doing here?" she whispers.

He extends his arms wide. "Making up for lost time."

She giggles and it's like music dancing across his heart. "What did you have in mind?"

"An impromptu date. What's your favorite dessert?"

"You," she says instantly.

He grins. "It's a given I'll be there. What else?"

Gabby purses her luscious lips in thought. "Choc-mallow brownies."

He arches a brow, knowing she's trying to challenge him. One he gladly accepts. "I'll meet you in the foyer."

"It's a date," she says, her eyes shining.

As he waits among the shadows of the foyer, Colt marvels at how much his life has changed in such a short period of time. How much *he's* changed. He's spent centuries determined to be alone. Refusing to be tied down to any place or person. It's the closest he could come to being free considering he was a hunted demon.

But now...

That existence seems...hollow. Almost like he was waiting. Floating. Until he found a reason to anchor.

And all because of one girl. Gabrielle Heartley. And it doesn't matter that she's the daughter of an archangel. That he's a demon. Or that he's honor bound to do the opposite of what she's promised. He can't stop this any more than he could stop gravity.

He just has to find a way to not betray her.

There's a whisper of movement and she appears. Gabby's changed into denim shorts and a white tank top. It's a simple outfit, yet undeniably sexy. Her lean legs are bare, like her arms, and the rest of her is hugged by material. Curvy and cute, yet sultry and sexy. It has Colt's breath catching in his throat.

She sidles right up to him, placing a hand on his chest. "Where were you thinking of taking me?" she whispers.

Although he'd love to take her to an expensive restaurant, he knows they can't afford to flaunt the rules too much. And curfew is one rule that's strictly enforced. Which means they'll have to make do.

Colt grins. "I'll show you."

He takes her hand and leads her to the curved stairs at the back of the building, then ascends, keeping her close. They're almost silent as they continue up, stealing glances and flashing smiles. Colt continues to the first floor, then the second, and past the third. It's only once they're on the top floor does he escort her down the hall to the far east wing, where he slips through a door.

There's no need to turn a light on, because the small attic-like space is already illuminated by the string of lights criss-crossing over the ceiling. One of the arched windows that grace the steepled corners of Mercy Academy is on the other side, framing dark night. A picnic blanket is spread out over the timber floor, cushions scattered over it. In the center sits a plate of choc-mallow brownies.

"But how?" says Gabby, looking around in amazement.

"I had this planned before I left," he says, conscious his cheeks feel hot. Maybe he's going too fast. Revealing too much. He may have spent hundreds of years alone and drifting, but

Gabby is still young. She probably doesn't want to take this too seriously. In fact, that's probably why she didn't ask too many questions about why he was gone.

"You set this up then kept it like this, even though you had to go away?" she asks, still looking around wide-eyed.

Colt shifts a little. "It seemed a waste. And I was hoping to be back sooner, so I magically sealed the door."

Gabby steps around so she's facing him. "You were planning on coming back," she breathes. "And you brought me here on the first day you returned."

Unsure what the luminous glow in her blue eyes means, Colt just nods. This is too soon. Too much.

Gabby's fingers climb up his shoulders, then twine behind his neck. "I love it," she breathes. "It's perfect."

His breath whooshes out, unknowingly trapped in his frozen lungs. "I'm glad. I don't know much about..." He waves his arm to indicate the room. Romance is as alien as sharing a building with angels.

"That's because you hadn't met me," she says, her eyes twinkling and teasing.

"Essentially."

That has her smile returning, so big and beautiful it eclipses the whole room. Although the urge to rest his hands on her hips is strong, he steps back. He needs to take it slow with Gabby. She has enough intensity in her life right now. He leads her to the picnic rug and she bends over to pick up a glistening square topped with marshmallows.

"And the brownies? They've been sitting here for almost two months?" she jokes.

"Those I conjured once the order had been placed," he says with a smile.

Gabby takes a bite and closes her eyes, pleasure spreading over her features. It's the most fascinating thing Colt's ever watched. "Ooh, these are good." Her eyes flutter open, then drop to half-mast as she lifts the brownie to his mouth. "You try."

Colt is powerless to say no. He takes a bite, noting the way Gabby seems to be watching him just as intensely as he's watching her. He chews, delicious chocolate and chewy marshmallow dissolving over his taste buds. "It's good," he growls.

She pushes up and licks a crumb from the corner of his mouth with the tip of her tongue. "Mm, yes, it is."

Sweet purgatory. She's going to combust him with nothing but her eyes. His hands fall to her hips, his fingers tightening reflexively. Except Colt grits his teeth as he holds her in place and steps back an inch. Then another.

Slow down, he tells himself. She has no real idea who, or what, she's entangling herself with.

So he moves to the window, working on getting his pulse under control. There's an almost silent sigh behind him and then Gabby joins him, a second brownie in her hand. She passes it to him. "Do you need to eat?" she asks, her head tilted.

"Demons do not." His lips twist. "Human bodies do."

Gabby takes another bite, her face melting with pleasure all over again. "Demons are missing out then."

Colt doesn't answer. Not that long ago, he would have argued that. Human needs limit and control demons. But now, he knows they can also bring great...joy.

"Tell me," he says, turning back to her. No beautiful vista can compare against her. "What have you been doing over the past weeks?"

Colt listens and watches, learning everything he can. Gabby tells him about the play Klae is planning for this semester—A Romance Forbidden. He doesn't comment on the title, but he's much more interested when he learns Gabby will be the female lead. He also notes her excitement at reconnecting with her friends, along with the faint frown when she mentions Maya is taking the loss of her aunt and uncle hard. She wrinkles her nose as she talks about training with her father and the unending essays and assignments. He also hears what she's not saying.

Gabby's been working hard. She's trying to be everything for everyone.

He's not entirely sure that's sustainable.

But before he can consider whether he should mention that, something catches his eye. Colt turns back to the window, noting there's something that wasn't there before.

A flicker. The smudge of smoke blurring the sky. Far too much light considering it's night.

Gabby must see it, too, because she steps closer to the window. "It looks like fire, but..."

The flames are green.

Colt says the one word he'd never thought he'd use here on Earth. "Hellfires."

3

GABBY

Hellfires?

What the flock are hellfires?

Even as they run out of the room, Gabby's mind churns. Whatever they are, they're not good. And they're not supposed to be in Mercy City.

She quickly slips into the passenger seat of Colt's car while he takes the wheel, also knowing the questions are going to have to wait. Colt revs the engine of the black Ford, the one that replaced the red sports car that exploded thanks to the barrier she'd placed around the academy. She flushes a little, even though she hadn't known she was the one responsible at the time.

"Come on, Nyx," Colt mutters under his breath. "We need to get to the other end of the city quickly."

Gabby's brows shoot up. "Do you name all your cars?"

He flashes her a glance before focusing on accelerating once they're away from the academy. "This is the first."

For some reason, that has Gabby smiling a little. Colt must like this car. What's more, he's intending to keep it. That's gotta be a good thing, right?

She lets him focus on weaving his way through the streets of the city as he takes every corner with breakneck precision. Gabby holds onto her seat, just as tense herself. The Grigori are behind this. They have to be. Who else would let loose the fires of Hell? They've been quiet too long, and now they're causing chaos. All so they can get the parchments.

And it seems they're willing to burn the city down, one building at a time, to find them.

Colt grumbles quietly as the traffic increases the closer they come to the center of the city. Although it's the tail end of peak hour traffic, it's still busy. The roads progressively become more and more clogged. They progressively move slower and slower.

"Skata," curses Colt as his car comes to a standstill on Main Street. Lines of red lights stretch ahead and behind. There's not even anywhere to turn around and try a different route.

Yet, the fires are still a couple of blocks away. She can sense the tension pouring off Colt and she can't blame him. Although she doesn't know much about hellfires, she gets it's bad. Any weapon from the infernal or celestial plane doesn't bode well for the mortal world. They need to snuff those suckers out.

"Skata," mutters Colt again. "We need to get to those fires."

Chewing her lip, Gabby takes out her phone and scrolls through to find the traffic app. Moving her fingers on the screen in a pinching motion, she zooms in to their location, her eyes scanning the road they're on. Deep red indicates very heavy traffic, bright red indicates heavy traffic, orange indicates medium, and green indicates moving traffic. The road on which they are is colored in deep red, and scrolling up, she sees no sign of the color changing.

Scrolling through the map, she sees a green section a few blocks away. Zooming in, she notes down the address, then looks to Colt. "I think I have an idea, but..."

"Yes?" Colt asks, swiftly turning.

"It needs both of us to work. I can teleport us out of here to a place where traffic is comparably less, and we can drive from there to the crime scene. But the humans would notice a car disappearing." She hasn't been doing this long enough to be able to do both.

Colt's eyes sharpen. "I can create an illusion spell."

She frowns. "It's just that I haven't had much practice with teleportation spells." Only marginally more than illusion spells. "And I'm talking about an entire car."

"You are more powerful than you realize, Gabby," says Colt.

His belief in her is all she needs to give this a try. Shooting him a quick smile, she goes over the teleportation spell her father has taught her. He made her learn it in Adamic, even though the language sounded strange to her ears. She suddenly wishes she's spent more time training with him. Between the play and assignments and trying to find the whereabouts of the Grigori and working with Sierra to decipher the parchments, there hadn't been many hours in the day left over.

"I don't mean to rush you..." says Colt, glancing at the skyline above the cars. The green glow is growing. "The moment we're gone, the people around us will have no memory of us being here. I'll make sure of it."

Damned freaking hellfires!

Gabby closes her eyes, hoping she doesn't hurt herself or Colt. Her father's words echo through her mind. *Magic, when done well, is painless. As easy as breathing.* When done well, being the operative words... She mutters the ancient words, feeling two lines tingle down her back. She'd always been scared by that sensation. She knew it set her apart. But now, they feel like power. Raw, elemental energy.

And the only way they can get to those fires.

Colt gasps, and Gabby's eyes fly open. She gasps herself

when she finds they're on another street with not a car in sight. A sign on a nearby corner says La Roche Street.

She did it!

Colt reaches over and squeezes her hand before slamming his foot on the gas. The car— Nyx—leaps forward with a roar of power, and they screech around the bend.

The moment they do, they catch sight of the devastation they're barreling toward. Smoke and fumes rush upward, an eerie green glow hugging the skyline. Flashing lights puncture the surreal scene as another fire truck shoots past.

Another two blocks and they come to a standstill again. There are dozens of fire trucks parked everywhere and even more firefighters milling around. Their mouths open and close, and although their shouts are faint, the urgency is unmistakable. The fires are out of control.

Gabby and Colt climb out, and she's drawn to the fire like a moth. They rage in shades of monstrous green, undeterred by the water pouring out of the hoses of the fire trucks. Police are also rushing around, along with rescue teams. They usher people wrapped in blankets, the burns on their skin fierce and painful-looking. More first responders are preparing to approach a nearby fallen building, masks on and oxygen tanks ready.

A crowd of people look on from behind the yellow lines and Gabby pushes her way through them, conscious of Colt just behind her. The firefighters manning the trucks look both determined and dazed. There's no doubt they're seeing this for the first time. Heck, even she's seeing it for the first time. The carnage left behind by the hellfire has her wondering how many livelihoods have been lost in all of this. How many lives...

"Ma'am, ma'am!" a police officer calls out to her, breaking her thoughts.

Gabby turns to him, shaken.

"Ma'am, please get behind the yellow lines," he says, slightly pushing her towards it. "Even better, get the hell out of here. It's far from safe."

Beside her, Gabby notes that Colt kneels on the ground, his fingers dipping in the ash. Even as she wonders what he's doing, she shuffles slightly in front of him, obscuring him from the view of the fire fighter.

"Ma'am, please!" the officer insists.

She registers more people have arrived at the site, but this time it's heavily armored bomb squad members trudging slowly towards the site of the explosion.

"The fires seem to have a mind of their own," says one man into his phone. "It's always one step ahead of us."

Their voices are lost as they move on, and Gabby turns to the firefighter in front of her. "Where are they going?" she asks as they make their way toward a broken down building, its cavernous exterior charred black.

The officer clamps his jaw shut, muttering something about reporters.

"That's the epicenter of the explosion," comes a voice from behind the yellow tapes. Middle-aged and portly, he pushes his round glasses up his nose. "Forty-five minutes ago, we heard it, all right. It started on the third floor of that building, and within five minutes, the entire thing fell down." He's pale as his eyes return to the destruction. "There were people who couldn't get out in time. I could hear their screams and shrieks, calling for help. And once the green fire was finished with them, it spread to the other buildings. Only God knows what kind of fires those are. If they can't be stopped..."

Gabby's pulse stutters. "It could spread to the entire city?"

The man nods, swallowing hard.

Curses ripple through the crowd beyond. Then hushed whispers. Then panicked shouts. The crowd disperses as people leave, talking of getting the hell out of Mercy City. Nobody wants to live in a city that would become the next Hiroshima if the green fires aren't stopped. Gabby wonders if she should warn her mother and aunt as well.

"Gabrielle Heartley!" calls out a familiar voice, one she's not exactly happy to hear right now. "Why am I not surprised to find you here?"

Sighing, Gabby turns around and sees Detective Espinosa approaching her. Colt slowly straightens, becoming a pillar of protectiveness beside her.

Detective Espinosa investigated the serial murders they'd tried to stop. But Espinosa has no idea something like the Grigori even exist. It meant Gabby and Colt became her prime suspects. She'd gone as far as accusing them of being Satan worshippers given the ritualistic nature of the murders. After the Grigori were defeated, Colt had found a rash of Satan worship in the city. Seems cults had been popping up since demonic influence started to fester in the mortal world, thanks to the continuous arrival of demons through the Tear. Gabby and Colt had rehearsed their stories, and told the detective they were investigating the murders themselves since they figured the serial murders were occult in nature.

The detective hadn't believed them, but Colt provided enough evidence to implicate a man named Leopold, a head of a Satanic cult who led a congregation in the forests surrounding the city. Given enough evidence, Leopold had been arrested and the detective had to grudgingly let Colt and Gabby off the hook.

Gabby still doesn't know how Colt found out about Leopold and the evidence leading to him, seeing as he left shortly after, and now isn't exactly the time to ask...

She smiles at the detective. "What a coincidence!"

Detective Espinosa arches a black eyebrow. "You going to tell me these fires have to do with the occult as well?"

"Anything's possible," hedges Gabby.

"Just because we can't stop them, doesn't mean it's some hocus pocus magic," snaps Espinosa.

"Unstoppable, green fire," says Colt, arching his own brow. "How often have you come across that?"

She pretzels her arms over her chest. "There's a first time for everything."

"We can tell," says Gabby. "The firefighters aren't winning."

Espinosa's eyes flicker to the green flames in the distance. "They're still looking for a way to contain it."

"That's because they're dealing with hellfires."

Gabby hides her surprise that Colt just came out and said it, instead watching the detective closely. She frowns, then glares at Colt. "Which are?"

"Hellfires differ from regular fires," he explains. "Water cannot douse them because it's unable to remove the fire's heat supply."

Espinosa's frown deepens. "Then how do we contain them?"

This time, the surprise is harder to hide. The detective is taking Colt's words seriously.

"These hellfires run on the same principle as a Class B fire," says Colt. "Smothering can be effective, but since these are so large, that's no longer an option. Still, the fires need to be fought as such."

Espinosa's eyes narrow. "And how do you know about this?"

"I've studied it," he answers with a shrug. "There are reports throughout history of different cults creating green fires, especially in the lore of witchcraft."

"This is also occult then, like those serial murders?"

Colt shrugs again, as if all this is just a theory. "Most Class B fires are red. This one is green, which is why it's called hellfire."

Gabby jolts as something occurs to her. "The fires in Hell are rumored to be green. It was a side note in the original Dante's Inferno," she says, glad she can add to the story Colt's weaving.

"Of course it is," Espinosa remarks, rolling her eyes. "So, how would you douse this fire?"

"Dry chemicals," Colt answers. "Something like ammonium phosphate or pressurized carbon dioxide. They're effective means to extinguish a Class B fire. I think they'll work for these as well."

The detective nods, then speaks into her walky-talky. "It's a Class B fire. Try dry chemicals."

Gabby looks at Colt, confused. Since when did the police take their suggestions so seriously?

Espinosa notices the glance and sighs. "We received a video message an hour ago that a bomb had been placed here on Lambda Avenue. The guy introduced himself as Cayden, said he's a devout follower of Leopold, the one we arrested for the serial murders. Cayden said we've wrongly accused the cult of the murders and they're willing to retaliate through violent means unless Leopold is released. Obviously we didn't agree to the terms—we don't negotiate with terrorists, not even cult members. The mayor was very clear about that."

"So, this is revenge for the arrest?" asks Gabby, reeling.

The detective nods. "Violent extremism comes in many forms." Her cell rings and with a curt nod in their direction, she walks away to answer it.

"Why here?" Gabby asks. "Why now?"

Colt looks troubled as his eyes scan the hellfires. "I don't know," he answers after a while. Then he sighs. "But I do know that far too many troubling weapons have been stolen by a mysterious group in the last few months. I've been investigating them." He shakes his head. "But I never expected hellfires."

Her eyes widen. Maybe she should've asked more questions before being swept away by chocolate eyes and luscious lips. "Why didn't you tell me?"

"I didn't want to trouble you," Colt says. "Weapons of Hell have been coming through the Tear, most likely in response to the growing threat of angels and their damn clones. But many of those weapons are being hijacked by a mysterious group."

Gabby frowns, trying to assimilate this. Not only is the reality of dating a demon starting to sink in, the ramifications of the Tear are becoming apparent. The Tear she promised to close. "How did Cayden get his hands on the hellfires?"

"That's a question I'd definitely like answered," Colt replies. "First, I need to speak with Belphegor and get help to contain these hellfires. Greater demons such as himself can control them."

Gabby turns away from the fires. "I'll come with you."

"No!" Colt says, his calm voice suddenly not so calm.

It has Gabby stopping and suppressing a frown. How many secrets are there between them?

"I mean, Belphegor will only talk about them with me," Colt continues, his face relaxing a little. "He won't open up to you, you being an angel and all."

"But you'll tell me whatever Belphegor tells you, won't you?"

Colt holds her gaze. "I want no secrets from you, Gabby."

The intensity of the words has her blushing, and the flush of warmth starts deep in her chest. That warmth only grows when he presses his lips to her forehead then taking her hand, leads her back to his car.

That sort of emotion can't be faked.

Surely it's enough to overcome whatever differences they have.

4

COLT

Colt strides through the halls of Mercy Academy, disbelief fueling the anger simmering in his veins. Some pathetic demon brought hellfires into this world and armed the cultists with it. He can't help but wonder who thought it was a brilliant plan to hand over infernal weapons into the hands of mortals.

This Cayden guy is seeking revenge for the arrest of his mentor in the most violent means possible. Colt suspects whoever gave him the hellfires knew that too. They handed him a loaded flamethrower. He jams his fingers through his hair as he takes a corner. Somewhere deep inside, he knows he is to blame for all of this. He redirected the police to Leopold even though he was innocent of the serial murders. He did it so the police would no longer suspect him and Gabby. Nor could he tell them of the real perpetrators. The Grigori are a force the police can't handle.

Colt expected the cult Leopold led would seek out ways to free Leopold from the prison, but through the courts. Appeals were inevitable. Never in his mind did he think they would use hellfires to make a point. With these raging green monstrosities, they're now trying to hold the city ransom until their demands are met. They don't care about how many people get hurt in the process.

Although the question remains: who armed them with the hellfires?

A question he hopes Belphegor will be able to answer.

Breaking into a run, Colt makes his way through the length of the academy until he comes to the great doors of the main building, the Assembly Hall on the other side of it. He heads up the spiral stairway that leads him to the second floor, where there's a bridge connecting the main building to the Academy's administrative wing.

He's just reached the start of that bridge when a familiar voice stops him. Cursing under his breath, Colt turns slowly, every muscle coiled, to see Gabriel walking towards him. He keeps his hands by his side, not presenting as a threat, even as he watches every twitch on the archangel's face.

"I hear you took my daughter out of the academy grounds, demon," snarls Gabriel.

"I'm sure she'll tell you all about it in good time," Colt says coldly.

"Where did you go?" snaps Gabriel.

Colt doesn't answer. Does the archangel know that he took Gabby to Lambda Avenue? Does he know about the hellfires?

Gabriel takes a step closer. "Did you take her to the hellfires?"

"You've heard," observes Colt.

"Of course, I have!" the archangel spits. "Did you take her there?"

Colt has no intention of lying to Gabby's father. At the same time, there's a muscle twitching just below the archangel's eye. "Gabby is free to make her own choices as to where she goes."

Gabriel moves fast. Faster than Colt expected.

He flies at him and pins him to the wall behind him. "I don't know what you demons are playing at, but trust me when I say this, Colt Grayson," he snarls, "when I find out why infernal weapons are in human hands, I'll wreak havoc on your world."

Colt struggles under his tight grasp, but Gabriel tightens his hold on his neck, satisfaction flaring in his cold eyes. Colt stills as pain shoots down his spine and his air supply is cut off. The intent to kill is clear on Gabriel's face. And no doubt he's going to use the hellfires as the excuse to do it.

Even though this anger is really rooted in the fact his daughter has chosen a demon as her partner.

Gabriel growls as his hands clamp tighter, cinching the noose around Colt's neck. He knows he has to fight. If he doesn't, he'll die. He just wanted to give Gabriel a chance to change his mind. To save Gabby the stress such a fight will cause.

Colt holds Gabriel's hard, silver gaze as he locks his muscles. There's no more time. His strength is waning. He's going to have to hurt Gabby's father.

Before he can move, a force clashes into Gabriel, shoving him away. The archangel stumbles, reaching as far as the stairs before he rights himself. Colt drops the fists that had instinctively shot up to protect himself as Gabby stalks to his side.

"Leave him alone!" she snaps at her father. "He's not responsible for those hellfires."

Gabriel walks back, fury festering in his gaze. "But his kind is!" he spits. "All demons want is death. Why else would they create weapons capable of such destruction!"

"And the clone army is what?" Colt retorts. "A peacekeeping force?"

Gabriel's eyes flare again, and he moves forward, but Gabby steps in between them.

"Enough!" she snaps, her voice louder. "Both angels and

demons are the cause of the upheaval. If you want to help humans, then this isn't how to do it."

Gabriel breathes deep. "Fine, but if demons are behind the hellfires, daughter, trust me, there will be nothing that can stop me." He glares at her. "Not even you."

He spins on his heel and disappears into the next corridor.

Colt waits until the sound of his footsteps wane and turns to Gabby. "Merci," he says. "He was quite...angry about the hellfires."

She winks at him. "We both know that anger was less because of the weapons and more because I'm dating you."

His lips hover on the cusp of a smile. He does love the fire in this girl. "He takes overprotective father to a new echelon."

Gabby giggles. "Maybe it's an archangel thing."

"How did you come here so quickly?" he asks, tilting his head.

She takes a step closer. "I wanted to finish the date properly." She presses herself against him. "With a kiss."

Unable to resist the sweet lips that are angling up toward him, Colt kisses her. Passion flares quickly, scorching his skin, burning him just as fiercely as the hellfires burning Mercy City. Eager to consume him.

Except he can't. He can't forget himself like he did when he first arrived. Gabby thinks they're in this together. That she can trust him.

And yet...

He can't fully commit to Gabby until he knows he won't betray her.

He steps back, smiling ruefully. "I need to find Belphegor."

Colt braces himself, unsure whether he has the strength to fight this if she closes the distance between them again.

But Gabby nods, sighing. "Yes, you do," she says. "There

was another reason I came looking for you. The hellfires have spread to Maria Avenue."

COLT STRIDES DOWN THE HALLWAY. If the hellfires have spread to Maria Avenue, then they're moving fast. If they aren't stopped, the city may cease to exist tomorrow.

Belphegor needs to stop this.

Colt reaches the dean's office a few moments later and he pushes through the door, finding the Dean looking out the window, deep in thought.

"You've heard of the hellfires?" he asks, not bothering with a greeting.

Belphegor turns around. "Yes, I have," the archdemon answers. "They're spreading faster than I expected."

"Yes, a cult is behind it. A Satanic cult."

Belphegor grunts. "I thought stolen weapons were a threat. But this is far more of an issue."

That's not what surprises Colt. "How are they even using it?" he asks. "Just like the weapons, hellfires answer to demons alone. It is our magic."

"That's no longer the case," the dean says, letting out an exasperated sigh. "Recently, Hell has been devising weapons that could be used by anyone. The Great Lord's plan was to arm humans with enough weapons so they could be influenced into creating a scenario that demanded the attention of the angels."

Colt's limbs go cold. "Thus leading to a war and the prophesied apocalypse..."

Belphegor nods. "But that was supposed to happen at the right time. Such weapons let loose now would spoil our surprise. I would love to know who's been stealing them but our leads keep drying up. Everything we do reaches a dead end."

"And what about the hellfires? I didn't know they were also stolen."

Belphegor's toad face contracts with tension. "They were stolen, Colt, but not from the caches that came out of the Tear."

"Then from where?" Colt asks cautiously.

"From here at the Academy," admits Belphegor, clenching his jaw. "Some time before we confronted the Grigori."

"What?" Colt demands, working to keep his voice under control. "How?"

"I don't know how they got to know about my personal stash of hellfire, but they stole enough to level a country."

"Skata."

"I've been trying to search for them, and I believe that some of it was used in Lambda Avenue. Not all of it though."

"But even that some is enough to bring this city down," says Colt, his gut twisting. "Tomorrow everything will be reduced to ashes if we don't do something."

"True," the Dean agrees. "But it's not that simple, I'm afraid. These hellfires are a bit...different. Modified. They grow more sentient as time passes."

Colt rubs his brow. "I don't understand." How could hellfires be modified?

"The hellfires you learned about in Hell were just like normal fires, one's demons could control and quell. But Hell has experimented and infused the ability to think into the fires. This hellfire you see right now has developed sentience. They have become deadlier than ever."

Colt suppresses another string of curses. No language is foul enough to convey how he's feeling. Heaven and Hell need to stop experimenting and creating evolved weapons. Hellfires having a sentient mind does not bode well for anybody.

"Can demons control them?" he asks, looking for some way forward.

Belphegor twitches, as if he's suppressing his own feelings. "To control these hellfires, demons would have to cut the bonds between the heat supply and their sentience. Except the fire will see it coming."

"But there has got to be some way!" bursts Colt. "Don't tell me we can't do anything."

"Hellfires could be neutralized by an opposite kind of fire," says Belphegor heavily. "But we don't have access to that kind of weapon."

"What kind of fire?" Colt asks, though he thinks he already knows the answer.

"Celestial fire."

A fire just as deadly as hellfire itself. One demons cannot wield. And that no angel has remembered how to conjure in centuries.

Except for Gabby.

She used celestial fire to make the Grigori run when they faced the once powerful guardians of Eden. Colt spins on his heel and strides out of the dean's office. All solutions lead to Gabby, it seems.

Although the question is, can Gabby conjure such a fire again?

She'll have to. Everything depends on her to quell the hellfires that threaten to devour the city that's as close to home as he'll ever have.

Colt heads to the girls' dorm rooms, ignoring the words of protests coming out of the Matron's mouth as he stalks past her. The Matron is new, he suspects placed here by Gabriel to keep an eye on his daughter, and she guards the hall to the girl's dorm rooms like a gargoyle.

He knocks on the door with a couple of short raps. A groan

sounds on its other side. And then a couple of brisk footsteps. The door opens inward and reveals a sleepy Kalisha. Her eyes widen the moment she sees him standing outside her room.

"M-Mr. Grayson?" she stutters.

"May I speak to Gabby, please?" he asks, as if this is a perfectly normal occurrence.

"She's asleep," Kalisha remarks, pointing behind her.

Colt's surprised to find the girl's right. Gabby's nothing more than a lump beneath her duvet. She didn't even wake to his knocking. Her exhaustion must have overwhelmed her.

"Could you wake her up?" he requests. "It's urgent."

"And risk certain death?" asks Kalisha, rolling her eyes. "I don't think so. But I'm happy to take a message and pass it on once she wakes up."

"This cannot wait," he says, trying not to get impatient. "You'll need to wake her."

Kalisha folds her hands against her chest. "Interrupting beauty sleep is sacrilegious." She turns to look at Gabby. "I can't interrupt it any more than I could prayer."

Colt huffs in frustration. He's about to insist when Gabby's second roommate appears. Maya's the adopted daughter of the Daniels, the last family the Grigori murdered to find the parchments leading to the location of the seven black stones. And for some reason, she doesn't look happy to see him.

"What're you doing here?" she demands, stepping out and forcing Colt to take a few steps back. "Gabby's been working hard for weeks now, she needs her sleep."

Colt narrows his eyes. "I need to speak to her. It's a matter of urgency."

Maya stalks forward a few more steps, widening the gap between Colt and their door. "And what information can't wait until the morning?" she asks, crossing her arms.

Colt frowns. The girl seems angry. A lot angrier if she's

willing to speak in such a manner to a previous instructor of the academy. "Because the news cannot wait." He keeps his face stern. "And I am not beholden to tell you anything, Maya."

"I wouldn't believe it anyway," she snaps. She glances over her shoulder where Kalisha is watching her, eyes a little wide. She drops her voice. "I know the truth. You're the one who killed my aunt and uncle."

Colt's nostrils flare. "I didn't kill your uncle and aunt, Maya, trust me when I say that—"

"And you brought Gabby into this! You made her an accomplice," she spits.

"You are out of line," he growls.

Maya shakes her head furiously. "And then you blamed that Leopold guy," she hisses.

"That Leopold guy, as you call him, heads a Satanic cult that is way over their head."

"What utter rubbish!" Maya retorts. "Leopold heads a group of Wiccans. And you blamed them for the serial murders, to get the cops off your back."

"That's preposterous, Maya, and you would do well not to accuse me of it."

"Is that a threat?" Maya asks, eyes widening. There's a sliver of fear in her eyes for a brief moment, making him think about what he said. He curses. He should have watched his tongue.

"Not at all," he answers, calming down. "But I am not involved in the serial murders. And maybe you don't know about the Wiccans as much as you think. They are a Satanic cult."

"They're not!" she insists, the fierce light back in her eyes. "One of my cousins is a part of it, and she told me how her group's leader was framed for the serial murders."

He sighs. Leopold had been framed, sure, but he's no innocent. His followers are now holding the city ransom even as they speak, using hellfire—a dangerous weapon they stole from Belphegor himself.

Colt opens his mouth to tell Maya this conversation is over when the Matron bustles down the hall, a burly security guard on either side of her. "That's him. He's out of bounds, and after hours, no less."

Colt grits his teeth as he allows one of the men to grab his wrist and yank it behind his back. He could easily fight them off, but that would mean outing his demon powers or causing a ruckus. Although he almost changes his mind when Maya's eyes gleam with victory. She's happy that he's been caught. Her animosity towards him goes deep.

Kalisha comes running forward. "Maya!" she calls, aghast. "You called the security on him?"

Maya shakes her head. "I didn't!" she says. "The Matron did."

"Matron, please," says Kalisha. "Mr. Grayson came to meet Gabby as he has something important to tell her."

"The rules say otherwise, young lady," the Matron says in her shrill voice. "No man is allowed inside the wing at this hour of the night. It doesn't matter who it is and for what matter. He should have given the message to me instead. I tried to stop him, but he kept going. I had to call security."

"Fine," growls Colt. "I'll leave."

"I'm taking you to the dean, Mr. Grayson," the Matron says. "He'll know what to do with you."

Colt allows the security guards to lead him away, knowing full well there will be no consequences from the dean, but a voice stops them from behind.

"Colt!" Gabby calls as she runs out of the room and then stops as she registers what's going on. "Matron, I called him here, then went and fell asleep. Technically, he didn't break any rules since he came upon my request."

The Matron bristles as if that's not any better. "That may be, but he's not supposed to be here in the girls' wing, Gabrielle, and you would also do well not to invite the opposite sex here from now on."

"I apologize, Matron," she says, trying to look contrite and failing. She turns and heads to her room, head hanging. Just as she's about to enter, she glances over her shoulder. "Meet me in ten," she mouths.

Colt suppresses a smile. He shakes off the security guard's grip. "I'll make my way there myself," he growls.

Turning around, he strides away, finally allowing the smile to bloom. He's not sure, but he thinks he hears Gabby giggle.

5

GABBY

It takes longer to leave her dorm room than Gabby would like. Kalisha was worried and asked a gazillion questions as to why Gabby was meeting a previous instructor in the middle of the night. Especially when it looks like Mercy City is about to be put in a state of emergency thanks to the out-of-control fires.

And then Maya had almost been...angry in her demands that Gabby stay. She'd been insistent Colt can't be trusted. That he was lying to her. No matter what Gabby said, that Colt is a good guy, that he wouldn't lie to her, Maya wouldn't listen.

All feelings of frustration and confusion disappear when she sees Colt standing in the shadows, leaning against the wall of the academy. His shoulders are hunched. His hands are jammed in his pocket. His chin is resting against his chest. She's never seen him look more...human.

"Colt?"

He looks up, and just the fact that she got this close without his awareness is enough to make her concerned. He wouldn't barge into the girl's dorm rooms in the middle of the night, ignoring the Matron, without good reason.

Then again, he probably expected her to be awake still. Or to wake up when he arrived. Gabby flushes a little. The past couple of months have been intense. The hunt for the Grigori, training with her father, catching up on her studies after her suspension, even preparing for Klae's play. Now the hellfires... Gabby's head hit the pillow with the intention of faking sleep until Colt texted or something. She never heard Colt coming to the door and talking to Kalisha and Maya.

"What's up?" she asks.

He pushes away from the wall, the shadows hugging his tall, muscled form, as if they don't want to let him go. Gabby knows the feeling. Even now, when he looks every bit the dark demon, a shiver of attraction slips down her spine. The need to kiss away all his troubles is overwhelming.

"It's you, Gabby," he says. "You're the one who can stop the hellfires."

She does exactly that. Stops. "Me?"

"As it turns out, celestial fire is the only thing that can quell the hellfires."

Gabby blinks, as if that can make the information easier to absorb. It never occurred to her that her powers could be the answer to the hellfire problem. Especially considering she doesn't know how to whip up celestial fire. Sure, she'd conjured it before and driven the Grigori away, but she has no idea how she did it. Her father had spoken at length about it afterward, whenever he got her to train with her, but that hadn't helped her repeat the process.

She hasn't conjured it since.

"But Colt, I don't know how. The last time I did, it was out of desperation."

He takes a couple of steps forward and places a reassuring hand on her shoulder. "Good thing we're just as desperate," he says. "Hellfires will destroy this city if they are not stopped. If you can't conjure celestial fire in time, Mercy City will become ash by tomorrow."

She huffs out a half-laugh. "No pressure, huh?"

"Absolutely none," he says, his barely discernible lips twitching.

Anxiety fills her, making her mind spin and gut churn. Can she really conjure celestial fire again? The fate of the city depends on it. She draws in long breaths, trying to get her focus back.

"We have to try," she concedes.

"We have to succeed," says Colt grimly.

Gabby's lips twist. Yep, absolutely no pressure. "We'd better get going then." The sooner they get there, the smaller the monstrous fires will be.

Colt's hands slip down her arms and grip her hands, squeezing. "There's an old saying. It's not the size of the hellfire in the city, it's the size of the celestial fire in the angel that counts."

The laugh that tumbles out this time is far more genuine. "Wow. That's a very specific saying that amazingly fits this exact scenario."

"Pure chance," he says, a hint of teeth flashing. "Now, we need to get back to the city."

Gabby nods and they run back toward his car. Only one thought fills her mind as she climbs in and he roars back out of the academy gates.

It's *finding* the celestial fire in the angel that's the issue.

COLT TAKES her to Marie Avenue rather than Lambda Avenue. There's not much left of the latter thanks to the hellfires. The monstrous green flames have taken on a more aggressive form and started to devour whatever's in their way. The moment it touches anything, it crumbles to ash.

It has Gabby balking at the wanton destruction the cult has resorted to in the name of revenge. Guilt gnaws at her. It was Colt, and her, who implicated Leopold. At the time, it seemed like a perfect solution. Leopold was far from innocent. He was a violent man, and some of his cult members indulged in ritualistic sacrifices that resulted in mysterious disappearances.

The guilt is burned away the moment she sees the destruction of Marie Avenue. Houses, shops, what used to be a small park, all gone. There aren't even skeletons of buildings still standing. All that's left behind is scorched ash, flattening what was once a variegated line of angled roofs and rounded trees.

The closer they get to the hellfires, the angrier Gabby becomes. They might have imprisoned Leopold for a crime he didn't commit, but the bombing on Lambda Avenue was a choice that the cult made. A choice that Cayden made. She wants to hunt the man down and punish him. To scream in his face that this is so deeply wrong.

But there's something more pressing right now. They have to leave Cayden to the police. Her focus needs to be on the hellfires and stopping the destruction they've wrought. And for that, she needs to conjure celestial fire. Her father told her it was something only a few angels have done in the past. And only once in modern times. By her.

Colt pulls over even though the tall, flickering flames are yards away. The road is empty seeing as there aren't any fire trucks here. They'd seen their blue and red flashing lights as they raced to a new front of the fire. As if they'd have more chance with that than the relentless wall of flames they'd just been battling.

Gabby walks forward, trying to instill a confidence into her steps she's not feeling, Colt close beside her. The street is deserted even though the fire front seems to be progressing the other way...against the wind. All the surrounding suburbs have been evacuated. This fire is too fast. Too unpredictable.

"I've cloaked us," Colt says under his breath. "Just in case."

Gabby nods, glad it's one less thing she needs to think of. She doesn't need anyone seeing her do the almost-impossible. Or worse. Fail.

Breathing deep, she focuses inward, imagining a fire in her head, a fire that replicates the energy she felt when she conjured the flames of Heaven. She doesn't know whether it will succeed, but it's the only way that makes sense. She imagines the golden flames that had danced around her hands, glorious and impossibly bright. Blazing like the sun. It had shot up her arms, exploded across her wings, swallowed her whole body. It had been what had the Grigori running.

But as Gabby looks at her palms, they stay the same pale, human color. She clenches her hands, as if that will help. Nothing.

"Gabby," Colt says quietly.

"I'm trying, okay?" she huffs.

"No, look."

She glances up, and stills.

The hellfire has changed direction again. And it's now coming at them like a furious, green firestorm.

"It's trying to attack us?" she asks, horrified.

"It knows you're a threat," mutters Colt. "You need to be quick."

"Fuck," she mutters.

She closes her eyes and tries again, picturing the golden fire. She tries to connect with the unlimited power it had brought with it. There's a flicker in her veins. A jolt through her bones.

Then nothing.

"Fuckity fuck," she snarls.

"You can do this," says Colt, his voice weighed with grim determination.

He hopes she can do this, Gabby thinks to herself. She opens her eyes and gasps, discovering he's wanting her to win for a whole new reason.

The hellfires have moved faster than she thought possible. It's already covered the yards that were between them, leaving its trail of flattened ash behind. Now, she can feel its heat, scorching and infernal. As it swallows the next house along Marie Avenue, she could swear it's laughing at her. That twisted, jeering faces are flickering amongst the shades of iridescent green.

"Well, we have another desperate moment," observes Colt and she admires his cool demeanor, despite the circumstances. "And no, I'm not leaving you."

Gabby's mouth snaps shut. He's stopped the thought just as it was being born. It's logical that Colt should try to at least save himself. There's no point in him staying here, crossing everything in the hope she'll save not just their asses, but everyone else's.

He turns to look at her, the fierce determination in his eyes just as compelling as the fire getting inevitably closer.

She's not sure whether he knows that by staying here, she's now even more driven to do this or not, but there's no time to ask. She's not letting those freaking flames anywhere near this hot, surprising, amazing demon.

Gabby raises her arms, no longer thinking or visualizing or wishing. She just *feels*. The need to protect. The desire to prove herself. The overwhelming drive to stop this.

Energy, as pure and powerful as light, courses through her. Around her. Awaits her command. Then, a ball appears in her hand, golden and fiery. Satisfaction seeps through Gabby. She can't wait to see what it can do.

The flames dance on her palms, growing with every heartbeat that passes. Her brow deepens as she brings her hands together, combining the two into one massive entity. Her wings unfurl behind her, majestic silver and white filling her peripheral vision. Drawing a scream from the depth of her lungs, she hurls the ball of pure celestial energy towards the spreading hellfires.

Gold meets green, their flames twisting and coiling as if one is trying to get the upper hand. The hellfire flares fluorescent green as if it's mustering a surge of power, but it makes no difference. The celestial fire overcomes it like a wave of wrath, swallowing the green and extinguishing it. It never stood a chance against the golden light of good.

The celestial fire continues on, erasing the hellfire as it explodes over the fire line. Gabby hears shouts of excitement come from several locations.

But it isn't over yet.

Celestial fire is as deadly as hellfire. She's not sure how she knows this, but the truth is as bright as the golden flames themselves. The celestial fires could wreak a similar level of destruction if they're left unchecked. Gabby closed her palms and, upon instinct, mouths some words in a language she doesn't understand. Even though she has no idea what she just said, the celestial fires stop in their tracks and vanish in puffs of white smoke.

Dropping her arms, Gabby finds she's breathing hard. She did it!

And yet, the newly found silence reveals something else. The wails of sirens. The faint cries of children. The deafening destruction the hellfires wrought.

She turns to Colt. "We have to stop this from ever happening again."

He nods solemnly. "Right now, we need to get back to the academy."

Before they're seen.

Shoulders drooping, Gabby's about to turn toward his car when he envelops her in his arms. "You did it, Gabby. That's the part that counts here."

He holds her tightly and she finds she's holding him with just as much emotion. "What a date, huh?" she says, her face tucked into his neck.

"It's memorable, that's for sure."

She loosens her arms even though she's not ready to let him go. She's not sure she ever will be. "We'd better get back."

Colt looks down at her, the night caressing the handsome lines of his face. "Let's at least finish it on a positive note."

Before she can ask what he means, even as she secretly hopes it's a kiss, Colt has her heart soaring in a completely different way.

They launch into the sky, his black wings beating the air in powerful strokes.

Gabby smiles as she holds on tight. She could unfurl her own wings again, but she doesn't want to. If she does, Colt might let her go.

And with everything going on, with everything that's still to come, she's not sure she can do this without him.

6

GABBY

Gabby sleeps most of the day. In fact, she doesn't wake until early evening, and even then, it's a struggle. She sits up, shoving her riot of blonde curls out of her face. For some reason, she's surprised to find she's alone, even though it's probably dinner time.

She falls back onto her bed with a groan. She missed all her classes, which will now mean more catching up to do, and exams aren't too far away. Her stomach rumbles, reminding her she hasn't eaten all day. Her bladder is stridently reminding her it'll win if she continues to ignore it. And yet, her brain is debating whether it's really ready to wake up.

A quick trip to the bathroom and she sees what she'd missed in her groggy return to reality. A note is on the floor, having probably fallen from her bed. Picking it up, she sees there's a message written in bold, flamboyant black.

Orientation Celebration, You are cordially invited to the Hall of Dreams at 8PM tonight.

Orientation? Hall of Dreams?

Both don't make any sense. Gabby looks around as if she's going to suddenly find she's not alone. Who left the note here?

Isn't it a bit late to celebrate orientation? And she's never come across anything called the Hall of Dreams at the academy.

She's not exactly wanting any more mysteries in her life right now.

Kalisha and Maya still haven't returned, although Gabby doubts either of them left the note for her. Kalisha is more of an announce-a-party-at-the-top-of-her-lungs kinda girl, while Gabby's not even sure Maya's talking to her right now. Gabby focuses on the note again and turns it over and around. It only has writing on one side, the other side is blank. Peering a little closer, she sees the paper is quite fragile and almost see-through. And then for the first time she sees something small written on the top right corner.

Icarus.

Gabby's read a lot about Greek mythologies, especially after joining the ranks of the Percy Jackson fandom. As per the Greek legends, Icarus was the son of the master craftsman Daedalus who was rumored to have created the Labyrinth. A Labyrinth that still exists somewhere beneath the earth and would lead into Mount Olympus, the home of the Greek Gods.

Both father and son attempted to escape with the help of wings Daedalus constructed from feathers and wax. Ignoring his father's instructions, Icarus flew too close to the sun. His wings burned as the wax melted, and he fell to his death.

Although it's a cool story—apart from poor Icarus—Gabby's not sure how it relates to the slip of paper she's holding. An invite to some party in a place she's never heard of. Is there something about Icarus's death that can help her decipher the invitation?

Icarus' wings melted as he flew too close to the sun.

The sentence repeats itself in her mind, caught on a loop. That is, until an idea dawns. With a smile dancing over her lips, Gabby conjures a small fire in her hands. She absentmindedly notes the flames burn bright red on the edges, with deep gold at its center. She holds the paper over the fire, and it bursts into flames, the fragile white morphing to charred black. Tendrils of smoke waft into the air, but instead of just rising to the ceiling and dissolving, they wind together, almost folding over each other. Within seconds, they form vivid, intricate images.

At first, she doesn't recognize the images, even as they envelope her, creating a new reality. But then she realizes the walls are familiar. The halls. The soaring ceiling. She's standing inside a map of the academy! A three-dimensional one, no less!

Then she finds she's moving, floating, as something pulls her through the corridors, passing doors and rooms. She slows as she approaches two large doors, three words above it in gilded, ornate writing. Hall of Dreams.

And then there's another pull, as an invisible force pulling her upward. Gabby cries out, now not so sure she's willing to just be whisked around. But despite her struggles, the pull won't release her. She's soaring straight up to the ceiling. Her wings release unexpectedly, unlocking their majestic silver glory. She catches sight of a stairway, one that's familiar somewhere, and then everything's black.

Gabby finds herself in front of a frowning, grouchy dog-statue. The celestial hound! She slaps her forehead, realizing where the Hall of Dreams is. The note is an invitation to the orientation of the supernatural club her father has founded here at the academy.

The images fade around her as soon as she comes to the realization. The fire in her hand dims and vanishes in a puff of smoke. Everything around her returns to normal, but when she looks into the mirror, she sees her wings are still out. She tucks them inside again even as she realizes how easy it's become to manipulate them these days.

Checking the clock, she gasps. "Dognabbit!"

She only has an hour to get ready. What the flippity-flock is she going to wear? Her eyes widen.

Especially considering this is another chance at a date with Colt.

GABBY'S only ten minutes late when she walks into the courtyard that's the home for the cranky-hound statue. Colt's already there, just as she knew he would be. Punctual is programmed into his code of honor. It means she nervously wipes her hands down the skirt of her minidress a second before she steps through to the courtyard.

Funnily enough, she didn't pack many dresses that would suit an occasion such as a welcoming party...to a supernatural club. But she did bring this cute little number, wondering when she'd ever get to wear it.

Turns out meeting the demon you're seriously crushing on for a date deep in the bowels beneath the academy is just the occasion. All black, the mini dress has a fitted corset-like bodice and a flared, bell-shaped skirt that stops above her knees. Matching black unattached sleeves, a black choker, and strappy heels complete the ensemble. It's cute, a little goth, and hopefully knock-your-wings-off sexy.

But the moment she enters the courtyard, Gabby stops, all her nervousness disintegrating. Colt's in the center, not close to the statue, but also not next to the door, as if he's wondering whether he should change his mind. And in a dark charcoal shirt and black slacks, *he's* knock-your-wings-off sexy. The top button of his silky shirt is undone and the sleeves rolled up, revealing that strong neck and tanned forearms. His shoulders look deliciously broad, narrowing down to delectably lean hips.

What's more, he's looking at her like she's the most tempting morsel he's ever seen. His chocolate eyes are so hot they're a smoldering bronze that take her breath away. Gabby makes her way toward him, feeling sexy as hell. She doesn't stop until she's slipped her arms around his shoulders and fitted herself against him. The sensation is like coming home and finding Heaven.

"Sheyn," Colt says quietly. Reverently.

Gabby's noticed Colt's tendency to speak in other languages. "What does that mean?"

"It's Yiddish for beautiful. Predivno in Bosnian could've worked. Or sundara is Nepali. And yet none of them describe what I'm holding."

Gabby feels like her heart is floating somewhere in the stratosphere. "How many languages can you speak?"

"A few well, a lot at a basic level. I've been on this Earth a long time, Gabby."

Could there be anything sexier than a guy saying you're beautiful in multiple languages? "I find that fascinating," she admits. She grins. "Like, has there really been any better invention than sliced bread?"

"This dress," he says with a grin.

Gabby inhales, drawing the very essence of this demon deep into her lungs. "First date, take two," she murmurs.

"Or second day, second date."

That has her smiling. "I can't wait for day three." Along with day three hundred and three thousand-million-gazillion, but she doesn't say that out loud. Things are still so new with Colt. He's only just got back. They still have the whole angel-demon-archenemies thing to navigate.

And what better way to start than bringing Colt as her plus one to her welcome party?

Stepping back, even though she could stand in his arms and die happy, she indicates toward the grouchy hound. "Ready?"

"Always," he says simply. "But have you thought through what it means, bringing me here?"

"More or less," she says, wrinkling her nose. She has no idea how this could turn out, but she does know she wants Colt there. That she wants everyone to know they're together. For them to see that even though he's a demon, she trusts him.

As if to prove exactly how much, she walks over to the statue and places her hand on it. "Apertum," she says quietly but clearly. The statue scrapes back, revealing the stairway below. She looks over her shoulder. "You're underestimating how far I'll go to have a dance with you," she says huskily.

His eyes flare to molten bronze. "A dance it is."

THE DOORS to the Hall of Dreams are just like Gabby had seen whilst enveloped by the smoky 3D map that had magically appeared when she burned the paper. She steps through, holding Colt's hand. Nervousness, uncertainty and a great big dose of pride are doing a washing machine impersonation in her gut. She has no idea what tonight will bring, but she's damned proud to be doing it with Colt by her side.

Inside, the hall is large and rectangular and impressively ornate. The ceiling is carved with everything from cupids to centaurs, the walls are covered in intricate gold leaf wallpaper, and the floor is a polished marble. A chandelier arches fragile arms, dripping in glittering surely-they-can't-be-diamonds, casting soft, glistening light everywhere.

Yet, to the left is a very modern-looking bar and dance music is pumping from somewhere. And the students standing around are wearing the slinky dresses and open-collared shirts you'd expect at a club. Once again, this secret space beneath the academy perfects modern meets ages-gone-by.

Gabby takes another step forward only to find Colt hasn't come with her. She looks over her shoulder, noting his wishful glance in the direction of a quiet corner. "Oh no you don't," she warns.

"I won't be far away," he promises. "Your first entrance should be without me."

"How do you say bullshit in any of your languages?" she asks archly, but then presses her lips together. Is she being selfish by wanting Colt by her side? Is she asking too much? "Sorry. I just wanted you there when I had to see my father."

Colt's eyebrows hike up. "Your father is the last person who wants me here, Gabby. He hates all demons." He watches her closely. "And I thought you've been spending a lot of time with him."

Gabby moves a little closer, keeping her voice down. "Except I've lived my life without him, all these years thinking he abandoned me and my mother. And now he suddenly pops up, just as everything else happens—hellfires, ritualistic murders, the Grigori rearing their head after all these centuries. He arrived at a time where there's a truckload of upheaval."

"And now demonic weapons are being stolen from our caches."

She nods, noting that must be on Colt's mind for him to bring it up. Then realizing he hasn't told her much about it. "You're going to tell me about that, aren't you?"

He nods, his eyes suddenly inscrutable. "I told you, I don't want any secrets between us."

Gabby hesitates, unsure why those words don't completely reassure her. But before she can ask any more questions, there's a voice behind her. "You must be Gabby?"

She turns around and sees a black-haired girl dressed in crimson red walking up to her. "Yes, I am," she replies.

The girl extends her hand. "I'm Sabrina," she says brightly.

Gabby shakes her hand, already liking this girl's energy. "Like the witch?"

"Not quite, considering what my venom can do to a person."

"Your venom?" Gabby asks, now curious.

"You're a werewolf," observes Colt.

"Grr," Sabrina growls good naturedly. "Although only on full moons."

Gabby smiles, admiring the easy way Sabrina accepts her supernatural side. She supposes everyone in this room is probably the same. The news had torn Gabby's life apart. A life she wanted to be normal. Yet, a life that's brought Colt into it.

"Anyhoo, I was asked to escort you to the podium," says Sabrina. "Your father wants to announce you to the world."

Gabby hides her surprise as she follows Sabrina through the crowd. Her father wants to go public. She's not entirely sure what that means. As they weave through the crowd, Gabby wonders what each person is. More werewolves? Witches? Are cupids or centaurs actually a thing? She's so attuned to Colt that she notices the subtle way his nostrils flare as they pass each person. He's breathing in their aura.

Can angels do that?

Of course, we can do that.

Gabby's so used to the voice inside her head, she's no longer startled. The angelic part of her—her Grace—likes to pop up every now and then with a nugget of information and then sink into the obscurity of her sub-consciousness.

You could learn how to sense auras. All you have to do is tap into—

Except, they're now at the steps leading up to the podium and Colt steps back. "You're coming, too," she hisses at him.

But he shakes his head. "Nobody wants a demon up there," he whispers.

"I don't care what anybody—"

"No, Gabby," he says resolutely. "It will cause more problems than it's worth."

The music stops and the silence suddenly feels oppressive. Full of responsibility and expectation. "Fine," she huffs. There's one thing she wants to show these people and that's a united front with Colt. Arguing isn't going to achieve that. Turning around, she walks up the steps, finding her father a few feet away, smiling widely.

Not used to the broad grin on her handsome father's face, she doesn't stop him as he pulls her into a tight embrace. All it does is make her feel more suffocated. Her father isn't openly affectionate. She hadn't realized she was glad of that fact until now.

He releases and turns them both so they're facing the throng of people. "Welcome, everyone, to this celebration," he says, his voice vibrating over the crowd.

The entire hall quietens in response, so many eyes stopping to watch her.

"This is Gabby, my daughter," he says proudly, his hands holding her shoulders tight. "And I'm pleased to announce that today, she's being inducted into this club."

There's an enthusiastic round of applause, even the odd hoot of excitement. Gabby relaxes a little, the warm welcome washing over her. These are her people. They know who she is and accept her for that.

Her father raises his hands, and everyone turns silent again.

"I started this club because I wanted all supernatural creatures to have a safe space. A place to come into their own. A place they don't have to hide because of ignorance or fear."

Gabby keeps her smile in place as she listens. Her father's echoing her sentiment about having found somewhere to belong, but for some reason, a faint tingle of uneasiness is climbing up her spine.

"But this is also a place to hone your skills and powers," her father continues. "We are at a very important crossroads, and fate has granted us the opportunity to shed aside all the differences and stand together against monsters and demons."

Gabby can see concerned eyes turn towards Colt and she no longer wants to be up here. She's inadvertently presented a united front—with her father!

"A Tear has been opened," her father says solemnly. "And demons pour through it into our world each and every day. We must prepare ourselves."

Murmurs shift through the crowd as brows crease and contract. Gabby has to work not to frown herself. Prepare themselves for what?

"But enough talk of these things," her father says, raising his voice. "Tonight is a time for peace. Tonight is a time for celebration! "

Hoots and claps fill the room as people return to whatever they were doing before Gabby's father's speech. A few eyes are on her as her father leads her down the podium and toward a quiet space behind it. "It is done, daughter," he says, clearly a proud parent. "You are now a member of this club. One I established just for a moment such as this."

Gabby doesn't know how to respond. She's just been reminded he founded the club to rally the supernatural factions on Earth against his war on demons. Just like she was reminded angels don't do anything without an agenda, and everything they do has a cost attached to it. This little party also has a price. She's not here because he's excited to see his daughter. She's just as much a pawn as anyone else.

Neither does she think this is ever going to make up for his abandoning her and her mother all these years. She only accepted him in her life because she wants him to teach her how to control her powers. She's going to need them when the Grigori raise their ugly-ass heads again.

When she doesn't say anything, her father's smile dips a little. "I see you brought Colt as your plus one."

"Yes, I did," she says, raising her chin. "And I told you if you try to come between us I'd—"

"Yes, I know," he huffs. "You'll have nothing more to do with me."

Gabby nods. "As long as we're clear."

Her father opens his mouth to speak, but a loud scream echoes from beyond the large doors of the Hall of Dreams. Gabby breaks into a run, Colt appearing beside her as she follows the terrified sound.

A smaller door across from the hall is wide open, and her father rushes past Gabby as she steps through. She stops as her own scream lodges in her throat.

Sabrina is standing in the middle of an empty room, staring at a lifeless body nailed to the wall.

Colt's hand falls on her shoulder as Gabby stares, her gut churning and her mind reeling. The woman is clearly dead, a bloody wound seeping on the side of her neck.

"Stand back! Stand back!" her father instructs as more students try to enter. "Unfortunately, the celebration will have to end early. You all need to leave."

Gabby watches the students nod despite the fear and confusion on their faces. They turn and start ushering those behind them to leave. One even comes in and wraps an arm around Sabrina, taking the pale girl out.

Gabby's father sighs, his somber gaze on the dead woman. "It is unfortunate that this had to happen tonight," he says. "I knew her. She was a good angel."

"I'm sorry," Gabby murmurs. "Especially with the way she was killed." In cold blood, and then pinned to the wall for everyone to see.

Her father's hands clench. "The knife that made this wound is of Heaven's make, and only angels can wield such weapons."

"So, she was killed by an angel?" she asks, for some reason not really shocked.

"Yes, he was killed by an angel," her father growls. "And I suspect I know who."

Gabby frowns, finding that she's pressed herself closer to Colt. She knew there were angel factions, but they hadn't gone as far as killing each other. Until now.

Colt stiffens. "Samandriel."

7
COLT

Samandriel. The same deranged angel who kidnapped Colt. The same insane celestial who warned him to not go anywhere near Gabby.

The same despicable bastard who allied himself with the Grigori.

Ever since the Grigori were defeated, Samandriel disappeared. They searched for him, but he was nowhere to be found. For a time, Colt wondered if the coward had scampered off to Heaven, but had quickly discounted the idea. Samandriel wouldn't risk going back and being held accountable. Although he's crazy, unfortunately, he's not stupid.

Most likely, Samandriel's off on an international trip with the Grigori, planning their next move, figuring out a way they can get their hands on the parchments Gabby managed to secure. It's clear that as long as they breathe air, they'll be after those seven stones.

Those pesky seven stones Fate warned him about.

Those evil stones Gabriel called the obsidian.

An epitome of darkness that only insane minds would want.

Colt studies the unfortunate angel crucified against the

wall. Why would Samandriel do this? Is he trying to send some kind of message? A warning? Although questions flood his mind, answers escape him.

This also means that although Samandriel has fled, his followers are still here. The other angel faction still exists at the Academy. Although who they are, is another unanswered question.

Slowly, inevitably, anger suffuses Colt's blood. Samandriel had struck closer. What if this angel had been Gabby?

A shudder so violent he can't contain it ripples through his body. Gabby glances up at him, clearly having felt it. "Colt?"

He doesn't answer. Fear as he's never felt before locks every muscle. Yet, the need to take Gabby away from all of this has adrenaline shooting through them, desperate to run.

"Colt?" she asks again, looking concerned. "Is everything okay?"

No longer wanting to be in this room with the dead angel and Gabriel, Colt spins on his heel and walks out. The Hall is now empty, although the music is still playing. For a change, it's not that awful electronically altered, autotune-dependent rubbish. It's an older song. A little slower, with strings blending into the rock ballad.

"Colt." Gabby comes up behind him. "You need to tell me what's going on."

He turns around, words climbing up his throat. Words he can't say, no matter how much he wishes he could. So he tells her the truths he can. "Things are happening too fast," he says on a sigh. "The serial murders, the Grigori, the hellfires, and now this." He waves his arm toward the room beyond the Hall, where Gabriel is no doubt trying to clean up the mess as quickly as possible. "And the weapons of Hell being stolen."

Gabby glances over her shoulder, then looks back at him,

chewing her lip in thought. "You think this is connected to all that?"

Always perceptive. He admires that trait as much as it makes him uneasy. "The Grigori and Samandriel and all those angels answering to them haven't given up. And yes, I think they have something to do with the theft of the weapons."

Gabby holds still as she waits, her blue eyes simmering with far more than curiosity. She's waiting to see whether he'll tell her what demons are up to. Whether he trusts her.

Little does she realize it's Colt she shouldn't trust.

And yet, there's nothing he won't do to keep her safe. Which means she needs to know. "Weapons are being imported into the world through the Tear. And then the caches that were being transported have been hijacked and stolen" He sighs. "A lot of dangerous weapons have gone missing, and the robberies haven't stopped."

"And you think the Grigori are behind those?" she asks.

He nods again.

"But why? What would angels such as the Grigori want with weapons from Hell?"

"I wondered the same, but I believe they've been arming people with the weapons to create chaos. Like the hellfires. Who else would want this city burned?"

Gabby looks at him thoughtfully, a faint frown creasing her brow. "Then we need to find out who's stealing the weapons."

Her use of *we* strikes Colt deep and hard. He realizes that by giving her this information, Gabby's falling under the illusion more and more than they're working as a team. Although that's what his soul cries for, he can never forget who or what he is. A demon. One under the yoke of Belphegor.

Colt takes a step back. He's walking on a knife edge as he balances between his honor and his heart. The last thing he wants to do is for Gabby to be hurt by the war inside of him.

Her gaze sharpens. "Where are you going?"

"I thought I'd do some research," he says, a sliver of the truth. He needs to find Samandriel before he hurts Gabby. Colt waves a hand to encompass the empty Hall. "The party's over, unfortunately."

"Haven't you heard the saying, the party's not over until Gabby gets the last dance?" she says, propping a hand on her hip.

He finds himself almost smiling, despite it all. "No, I can't say I have."

Gabby closes the distance he created, weaving her fingers through his. She looks up, a sultry heat smoldering in her blue eyes. "May I have this dance, Colt Grayson?"

Yes.

Ja. Oui. Sì. Noib.

It doesn't matter what language he says it in, including ancient Enochian, the answer will always be the same.

Yes.

Wordlessly, Colt places his right hand on Gabby's hip while joining her other hand with his left. He's danced before with women. The baroque period was full of dancing. So were the sixties. But he knows this will be different. Special.

Soul searing.

He changes the music with his mind, and a slow, earthy tune filters through the Hall. Gabby smiles with delight and Colt's insides melt in a way he's never felt before. Seamlessly, he guides her around the floor, although it's not the flow of music that guides him. It's his heart.

Gabby moves with unconscious grace, so close he can feel the warmth of her skin, feel her sigh. Her eyes never leave his and Colt finds himself inevitably, helplessly falling into the sweet, seductive pools of emotion. For the moments where they hold each other and move around the Hall, there is no dead angel in an adjoining room. There are no hellfires. No weapons escaping Hell. No Samandriel, no Grigori.

There's only a demon and an angel, holding each other. Dancing, chest to chest. Smiling, heart to heart.

There's a ripple of power, as if their auras just blended. It sends hot and cold shivers skittering over his skin, but Colt welcomes it. Whatever comes with Gabby, he'll face gladly. No matter the consequences.

He blinks as three words form in his throat. Surely not...

They haven't even defined their relationship. Are they boyfriend and girlfriend? Are they exclusive to each other? And yet there are so many feelings. So many emotions. All ones he thought were copyrighted by the mortal world.

Although, it seems the mundane doesn't hold the patent on love.

Colt executes a slow spin, smiling even wider when Gabby's right there with him. Their bodies are seamlessly in tune. When one moves, the other follows, doing whatever's necessary to maintain the heat that's progressively growing everywhere they touch. The hand on her hip instinctively moves up, pressing into the small of her back and her eyes flare with awareness. His blood ignites and he presses her closer, tucking her head under his chin before he does something foolish. The need to kiss her, to explore these emotions is undeniable.

Is it really love that he feels for Gabby?

Many books had spoken of love transcending boundaries. But Heaven and Hell? A demon who believed he wasn't even capable of these emotions, and the daughter of an archangel? Colt's seen some impossible things, but this would have to top it.

Or is it just a crush or an infatuation or whatever synonyms mortals have for more fleeting emotions?

No, this could not be love, he tells himself, trying to be a little more level-headed. It's too early. They've gone on two dates, and neither have ended well. He likes her. He revels in her company. The girl makes him happy. He would also go as far as saying she has the potential to change who he is. He feels like he's a better person around Gabby. But love? That's a powerful emotion. And word...

There's a sudden clattering of feet down the steps and someone bursts into the Hall. Alarm instantly replaces the relaxed joy that had infiltrated his muscles.

Klae comes to a comical stop, arms flailing and all, as she realizes only Gabby and Colt are in the room. "Ohmigod, I'm so sorry. I thought I was late for the party!" She flushes. "Did I get the day wrong?"

"No, it's fine," Gabby assures her. "The party ended early."

"Oh, that's too bad," says Klae, her face filling with excitement again. "I had an idea for the next play and I just had to write it down. It's going to be amazeballs. I'm going to call it One Murder Please."

Gabby blanches. "Ah, the party finished early because an angel was murdered, Klae."

The girl pales, her acne standing out in stark relief. "That's terrible."

Colt steps away. As much as he wanted that dance to go for as long as time itself, reality has invaded in the form of a clueless, excited golem. A dead angel isn't far away.

"Why don't you tell Gabby all about it?" he suggests as he makes his way past Klae, already missing the sensation of Gabby in his arms, but a new determination weaving its way through the sinews and tendons of his body.

Gabby sends him an unimpressed glance, aware he's just tied her up for at least thirty minutes. Maybe more, judging by the glee on Klae's face. He winks at her, maintaining the pretense that this is all light-hearted.

That is, until he leaves the Hall. Then his eyebrows slam low. The edges of his lips tip down. Klae's animated voice follows Colt as he strides down the corridor. He bows his head, making a promise.

He will keep Gabby safe, no matter what.

Right now, that means finding Samandriel.

And ending him.

8

COLT

Colt makes his way to the rear of the academy, intent on combing through any book he can get his hands on to see if he can learn anything about Samandriel or the angel he killed, and the privacy of his small cottage is just the pace to do it. He's just turned a corner when a note floats down in front of him. Colt stops and snatches it from the air, already suspecting what it will say.

The pale slip of paper only holds a few sharply angled words.

Meet me in my office.

The note incinerates, not even leaving a puff of ash or smoke to indicate it ever existed.

Colt sighs. Belphegor wants to have a word with him. He wonders what it's about. Has the archdemon learned something important?

Knowing he can't say no, Colt makes his way to the dean's office with heavy feet. He has enough to deal with at the moment. He reaches the dean's office and knocks lightly. When there's no answer, Colt knocks a little louder.

Still, no response. No sounds of movement within the office.

Frowning, Colt wouldn't put it past Belphegor to be one of his tests to see whether he'd come running when summoned. Just to make sure, he tries the doorknob, surprised when it twists in his hand. Belphegor must be inside. There's no way he'd leave his office unlocked. Colt carefully pushes it open, wary as to what the archdemon is playing at.

Yet the office is empty. And in complete disarray.

Chairs are overturned, papers litter the floor, and books are scattered on the desk. There's no way Belphegor would leave the room like this. It means something else has happened here.

Another break in.

Colt enters more fully, now wondering if something has happened to Belphegor himself. A quick circle of the room reveals he's alone, though. There's also no scent of any aura, angel or demon. A ruffling noise tickles his senses and Colt spins around, alert and ready to fight.

Belphegor struts in as if he's much taller than he actually is. "Apologies. I was caught up with a student. They can be so needy—"

His words are cut off as he registers the mess his office is. "What the heaven happened here?" he demands, now moving around frantically and assessing the damage.

Colt remains where he is, noticing that Belphegor hasn't insisted on an answer. Instead, the dean is rushing around, opening and closing drawers and scanning the room with frantic, shrewd eyes.

He's looking to see if anything's been stolen.

Belphegor straightens, letting out a long breath. "As far as I can determine, nothing seems to have been stolen. The question is what the bastards wanted." His gaze sharpens. "And why my security alarms didn't go off?"

"The intruders disabled it?" suggests Colt.

"Except there were both human and demonic alarms. Now,

I know human alarms could be worked around but demonic ones, especially those invisible and as complex as I divined? I hardly think so."

Which means whoever came in here was determined and powerful. "What's so important here that they broke in?" asks Colt, even as he wonders whether Belphegor would tell him the truth.

The dean shrugs. "Perhaps they thought I had more hellfires."

"And do you?"

"Yes," Belphegor answers, "but I doubt they'll get their hands on it. After the last time, I stashed the last few I had at a more secure place. One that is not easily accessed and protected by blood magic. No one can get to it but me."

"So, what's in this office?" presses Colt. "Why would the room be trashed like this?"

"Like I said, they might have been looking for the hellfires," the Dean answers, beginning to sound irritated. "But that's not why I wanted you here. And you'd do well to remember, Colt, that in this relationship, I ask the questions."

Colt tenses, curious as to what Belphegor might be hiding in this office, but conscious he won't get anywhere by asking more questions. He doesn't want an annoyed archdemon.

"Then why am I here?"

Instead of answering, Belphegor walks to the window, staring at the lawns that sprawl beyond and Colt stills. Every time he's come here, the archdemon has always stood by the window. It could not be just a coincidence. For some reason—call it a gut feeling or instinct—he wonders if Belphegor has hidden something in the lawns. It's possible the hellfires are deep underground beneath the expanse of emerald green.

"I heard an angel was murdered on the Academy's premises," says Belphegor. "I assume you were there?"

Colt grits his teeth. News can certainly travel fast, but how does Belphegor know about the murder when Gabby's father would have worked hard to cover it up?

Belphegor glances over his shoulder, his toad-like face folding into a smile. "I have eyes and ears everywhere, Colt. Something else you're best off not forgetting. Now tell me, what do you know of the murder?"

"It appears you've already been appraised," says Colt, conscious he's hedging.

The dean turns to face Colt completely, his eyes shrewd. "We all know demons aren't allowed in that place, and yet you were given entry. Because of Gabby."

Colt nods. The dean's words were a statement, meaning he doesn't technically need a response.

"And an angel was found dead there, correct?"

Once again, Colt doesn't answer, but his eyes seem to give away something because the dean turns back to the window and closes it. The cool breeze that was wafting in stops.

"Pinned to a wall, stabbed with angelic blades," he muses. "Now I wouldn't put it past them to blame demons for this."

"I don't think they will," says Colt. "Their main suspect is someone we know and fought not too long ago—Samandriel." He spits out the name, wishing he could do the same with the bitter taste on his tongue.

"That goat's ass!" growls the dean. "I should have killed him when I had the chance." He makes disgruntled noise even as he closes his eyes.

Colt waits, wondering what Belphegor's thinking over. He can feel the archdemon trying to probe his mind, even as he mulls whatever scheming is festering inside his own.

"Angels killing angels," Belphegor continues. "And they aren't blaming us demons, you say?"

"No," says Colt, not offering more than that. He wishes he

hadn't divulged as much as he has, but such is Belphegor's power. The price of lying to the archdemon is just too high. For centuries, Colt had been freed of it, and he's realizing how good it had felt. Now, he's trapped again. Nor will it be easy to get out of the archdemon's hold over him.

"And that Samandriel fellow is behind all of this," says Belphegor, a smile spreading across his features. "I think this creates an opportunity."

Colt holds himself still as he waits. If Belphegor sees an opportunity in this, that isn't going to be good for anybody. A part of him doesn't want to hear it.

And yet, he needs to know.

"What opportunity?" he asks.

"We could use this to pit Gabriel against Samandriel. This way, the angels battle it out and lose focus on us demons." Belphegor's smile grows, lighting his eyes. "And we can continue with our grand plans."

"Which are?"

The dean curls his lips wide. "To find a way to open the Gates of Hell, of course!"

Colt has to work hard to suppress his horror. "But that would let out every one of—"

"Yes," the dean agrees, excited. "It would let every demon out. One by one, the levels would be peeled away, and the world would be full of every imaginable Sin there is."

The utter shock of the archdemon's plan shakes Colt to the core. "But it can't be done," he says. "The Gates cannot be broken. They are absolute."

"There could be ways," the dean tells him. "Ways we haven't come close to finding yet. Ways I think—" Belphegor stops, his eyes narrowing. "You owe me, remember?"

Colt locks every muscle, knowing he's being reminded of his loyalty. Yes, he does owe Belphegor. He asked the archdemon for his help in dealing with the Grigori and saving Gabby. Now, he's beholden to him.

And Belphegor wants him to foil Gabby's plans to close down the Tear for good.

Now he knows why.

"This plan would mean a full-scale war," says Colt in a low voice.

"Yes," Belphegor says, hissing the word with enthusiasm "The apocalypse will come to Earth."

"And you want it to?" It feels like acid has filled Colt's stomach.

"Of course," snaps the dean. "The orders come from within the Cage itself. It won't be long now and He will influence the events in this world. The tendrils of His power strengthen every second the Tear is open, creating a slow but ever-increasing rift in the fabric that divides Hell and the mortal world. We believe the rift will lead us to the Gates and those that are given the responsibility of protecting them."

"This war will have a huge cost," says Colt, not quite believing he's hearing this. "Humans will be exposed to all kinds of monsters."

"I know. It's time they understand. They were gifted with free will and look at what they've done. They have played God in this world and created chaos and utter destruction. And look what the oppression of angels and their skewed faith in them has achieved. When we demons are finally out, when the Sins spread throughout the world, they will come face-to-face with reality itself. They scorn us demons, tell us we are evil, but we are just extensions of their conscience. A part of them that wants them freed from the clutches of angelic oppression."

"But—"

"No buts, Colt!" snaps Belphegor. "You're either on our side or theirs. Your job is to ensure that you put a stop in Gabby's plans to close the Tear. I don't care how you make it happen, only that you do." He leans forward, his eyes burning with promise. "If the Tear closes, I will be severely displeased."

Belphegor straightens again, puffing out his square chest as he waves a hand in dismissal and turns back to the window.

Although he's seething with frustration, Colt bows his head and exits. No matter how much it chafes, he needs to appear subservient to Belphegor.

That is, until he has a plan.

One that's eluding him right now. Colt owes the archdemon, and such promises come with a blood debt. He either betrays Gabby or pays for it with something he holds precious, something Belphegor gets to choose.

Either way, Colt's in a lot of trouble. Closing the door behind him, he walks toward his cottage, troubled.

As he walks, his mind is a desperate merry-go-round. He needs to find a way out. He owes Belphegor a favor—stopping Gabby from closing the Tear. He can't go back on his word.

But he vows to find some other way to stop the rift that will lead straight to the Gates of Hell. And he has to do it before Gabby finds a way to close the Tear.

He has to. For his sake.

And Gabby's.

9

GABBY

"So, tell me about this play, One Murder Please," Gabby says to Klae, resisting the desire to follow Colt.

He needs time to think. She sensed his frustration and anger, even sadness. And all of them were tinted with guilt. They'd failed to save the seven families the Grigori murdered. Then an angel was killed. Heck, he might even blame himself for letting Samandriel escape from his grasp.

Colt wants to make things right.

He just hadn't realized they need to do it as a team.

Klae's eyes shine with excitement as Gabby leads her out of the Hall and back above ground. "It's quite fascinating, really," she says, a small skip in her step as they ascend the steps.

Klae's obvious enthusiasm, even in the face of everything that's happening, tells Gabby she's done the right thing by giving this sweet, strange girl her time and attention. Especially after Klae was willing to fight alongside them against the Grigori.

Gabby suppresses a shudder as flashes of Klae's broken body after one of the ancient angels tried to kill her rise in her mind. Klae had risked her life. She'd almost died. She owes her this much.

Ever since Klae told her she was a golem, Gabby had researched exactly what that is. According to lore and legend, golems are built entirely of clay, given life by a witch's spell. Usually, golems are controlled by their creators. That had Gabby wondering who controlled Klae. And could her creator call on her at any time, taking control of her?

Klae wouldn't answer those questions, though. She wouldn't even disclose who her creator is, saying all that was a dark past she didn't want to revisit. Undeterred, Gabby had done some digging. Although there was little information, her aunt Sierra found for her a strange but heavy tome that listed information about all the different supernatural creatures that exist in the world. It had one full section on golems and their history.

According to the book, golems are an experiment aimed to replicate the experiments that the forces of Heaven when they created the first man Adam. The golems first came into light when the followers of Judaism bought control of them from the witches. Ever since, golems have been protecting Jewish communities worldwide. Most golems operate in secrecy, doing whatever they can to protect the community. Rumor has it that Dr. Viktor Frankenstein also managed to create a golem of his own, but it turned out to be monstrous and evil.

The book also told her that most golems were killed and destroyed by Adolf Hitler and his Nazi men during the Holocaust. Ever since then, no golem had been seen or heard of.

Yet there was one right here, in Mercy Academy.

Klae. It's possible she's a golem who survived the whole thing. It's possible she doesn't want to talk about it because the Holocaust was part of her dark past, which is why she avoids too much questioning.

Yet Klae is bubbly and sweet. Despite being a loner and the victim of bullying, she never loses her temper, never has a bad word to say about anyone. Although Gabby shudders to think what would happen if she did. She'd seen Klae in action. She's the ultimate shape shifter, but one as strong as the Hulk.

"With a title like One Murder Please, it sounds like a crime story?" asks Gabby, bringing herself back to the present.

"It has a little bit of everything, actually," says Klae, not seeming to care where they're walking as Gabby makes her way to the rear of the academy. "The cool part about it is it takes elements from mythology."

"Sounds intriguing," comments Gabby, conscious she's scanning the hallways. Surely Colt came this way?

"Well, it's the story of a female investigator," Klae nudges Gabby, "as in you, investigating the murder of a young girl after she found something...dark. It's kind of a supernatural mystery thriller, but with a touch of romance."

The word dark has Gabby turning her full attention to Klae. "What does she find?"

"That's where the mythology comes in," Klae says, dropping her voice. "Although some of the records I found suggested this actually happened a long time ago."

"So, it's historical fact?" asks Gabby, now definitely intrigued.

Klae shrugs. "There's no way to be sure. For the play, I put together a story from my research, then embellished it for a little more drama."

Gabby stops. "Tragic ending or a happy one?"

"The real story has a tragic ending, but I converted it into a happy one. The audience doesn't really like tragic endings to the stories, and given that there's romance in this one, I thought a happy ending was better."

"Good call," says Gabby, unsure why she feels relieved. "So, what exactly is the story about?" Maybe the mention of a girl finding a dark object is purely coincidental.

Klae's eyes light up again. "Well, the girl who was murdered lived some time after the Crucifixion. She was murdered after she found something—a black stone, radiating an aura. She thought it was connected to the Resurrection. The dark stone began to influence her and she started doing bad things. She was murdered in cold blood and whatever the object was, a group of men stole it."

"A black stone, you say?" Gabby asks, frowning.

"Yes," Klae answers, nodding. "The black stone was said to be evil and influenced people to do very bad things. The group of men who investigated the murder found what the dark stone was. They called the stone the—"

"Obsidian," finishes Gabby.

"Yes." Klae beams, Gabby's insight only seeming to make her smile wider.

"And?" Gabby prods, unsure why this is such an exciting story. Klae knows seven families were murdered trying to find the obsidian.

"Divining the stone to be evil, they called upon angels to help. And an angel named Uriel did come to help them. He said the stone could not be destroyed, so he broke it into seven pieces and buried them in secret locations. He noted the locations on divine parchments, and then handed them over to the patriarchs of the seven prominent families. These seven families lived on through generations in secrecy."

"Until the Grigori killed every last one of them." Gabby slumps against the wall, heaving a sigh.

Klae nods in understanding, although she still doesn't look as pained by this as Gabby. "But in my story, the ending is a little different. The protagonist—you—finds a way to ensure the obsidian's powers stay in control."

"And how do I do that?"

"I'm not terribly sure," Klae answers, now looking a little subdued. "The angel Uriel broke the stones, but he didn't break the power, but maybe dividing the power itself could make the obsidian's influence lessen."

Gabby nods thoughtfully. "Thanks Klae, it sounds like an awesome...play.

"Thanks, Gabby," says Klae, unable to hold her gaze as if she's still not comfortable with praise. "I thought it might help, you know, give you hope that this can all turn out okay."

Gabby's heart softens and she engulfs the shorter girl in a hug. "You're a good friend, Klae."

Klae squeezes tight but then quickly releases Gabby, her cheeks the brightest red so far. "Anyway, that's another day's problems. Our first play is only in a few days!"

"Of course," says Gabby, trying to smile once more. "We'd better get some sleep."

Klae looks around. "In the back gardens of the academy?" she asks cheekily.

It's Gabby's turn to flush as she realizes she'd been unconsciously leading them to where Colt might be. "I, ah, forgot to tell him something."

"Sure you did," says Klae, giggling. With an ungraceful twist, she walks away, still giggling.

Gabby watches her leave, chewing her lip. Klae's new play is supposed to help her realize there has to be a way forward. A way to take the obsidian out of the equation.

But the more she thinks about it, the more she wonders if she could have done more to save the seven families in the first place. If she'd accepted being an angel, could she have protected them? Would they still be alive?

Guilt chewing at the edges of her gut, Gabby heads down the hall even though she's not supposed to be in this part of the academy. She needs to find Colt. She needs to be held, reminding her she's not alone in this.

But Colt's not in his cottage.

And a few minutes later Gabby confirmed he's not waiting outside her dorm room.

An hour later, Gabby discovers he's nowhere in the academy.

He'd disappeared. Again.

SEVERAL DAYS PASS and there's no sight of him. And Gabby looked everywhere. He wasn't running his martial arts classes or out for his morning run. She'd even tried to ask the Dean, but Belphegor had glared so hard she expected him to burst into flames. Or for herself to. Seems the rift between angels and demons is going to be a major hurdle. It didn't help that her father kept muttering about demons being unreliable and that they couldn't be trusted.

But even as the number of days grew, even as it hurt more and more to not have him near, Gabby's trust in Colt never faltered. So she tried to keep busy. Rehearsals for the play had really intensified now that the first show was only minutes away.

Klae's nervous excitement had steadily grown. So had everyone else's. It was good timing in some ways. It meant the shadows under Gabby's eyes, the fact she kept glancing over her shoulder, or the fact she wasn't really hungry could all be easily explained. Despite that, she ensured she didn't ruin Klae's play by letting her emotions get in the way. She made sure she gave her best during every rehearsal.

Yet, the whole time, all she wanted was to see Colt. Touch him. Know he's okay.

That they're okay.

Gabby pulls in a slow, deep breath as Kalisha fusses over her eye makeup. "I've gotta say, girlfriend," she says, dabbing on a thick layer of eyeshadow, "you are one heck of a canvas for a girl to work on."

"Thanks," says Gabby, smiling wanly. "I cleansed this morning just for you."

"That's m'girl," says Kalisha. "Now purse your lips for me."

"Kalisha!" a girl cries out a few moments later. "My mascara has smudged."

"Only if you repeatedly rub it," she mutters under her breath then quickly rushes over. The play is about to start any minute.

Klae enters the room, flushed even more than usual. "All's good in here?"

The handful of people in the room taking part in the small play nod or shout a loud "yes" depending on where they are on the freak-out meter. Gabby pulls up a smile with her now red lips and nods, hoping she can pull this off. Her mind is elsewhere.

With a demon who is flock-knows-where.

Klae walks further in, her face looking as if she's about to step out on the stage. "I just wanted to say, I know this is our first play together, but I know we'll ace it. I'm confident you won't let me or this academy down. So, let's rock the stage, guys, and keep our fingers crossed the audience likes, no, loves it."

Another round of loud hoots followed.

"Awesome," Klae claps. "Let's go break a leg!"

The other students in the room rush out, excited and

nervous at the same time. Gabby can hear their hearts pounding.

And so is her own. But hers has a new beat. Colt. Colt. Colt.

"You all right?" Klae inquires, the concern clear in her voice.

Gabby nods. "Yeah, don't worry about me." She shrugs, the truth unwilling to be ignored. "I was just wishing Colt could've been here, that's all."

Klae looks confused for a second before a wide smile splits her face. "He's here, Gabby," she says. "Seated on a front row seat not far from the teacher's section. He said he's been looking forward to this."

Gabby closes her eyes and takes a deep breath. Colt's here. He came back. Which, of course, she never doubted for a second. She opens one eye, looking at Klae. "He's here?" she confirms. "Really?"

"Really!"

Gabby's own smile blooms across her face and man, does it feel good. Her shoulders drop and it suddenly feels like they've been pulled up in their tense position since the moment he left. "Well, that is good news," she remarks, ending her words with a bubbly giggle.

"You really do love him, don't you?" Klae playfully winks at her.

Gabby feels her cheeks go hot. "Ah, it's a bit early for the L-word, Klae. I just like him...a lot."

"Of course you do!" Klae giggles.

"He's hot and I like his company, okay?" Gabby asks, pushing up from her chair and smoothing her costume. "He just has this...way about him."

"And to think that he annoyed you once upon a time," Klae teases.

"Oh, he still annoys me," Gabby remarks archly. Like his tendency to disappear without a word.

"And yet you light up like the sun at the mention of his name. Sure sounds like I—"

"Don't say it!" says Gabby, walking past her. "We have a play to rock, remember?"

Klae raises her hands in mock surrender. "Fine, fine. But only because you need to stop blushing. I need fair cheeks on my protagonist, not tomato-colored ones."

Gabby sticks out her tongue. "Of course, Director."

They giggle and quickly move toward their places. Gabby's only taken a few steps before her smile fades. She's about to perform in front of an audience for the first time. It's a play for academy residents to attend only, although it was being recorded for family and friends, but what will people think of it? Of her?

And most importantly, what will Colt think?

The moment the curtain lifts, Gabby slips into character. The play passes in a blur. She recites her lines by rote, wishing she could see past the bright lights into the crowd. Everyone plays their part seamlessly and the finishing line comes far faster than she expected.

The moment she delivers it, the crowd bursts into applause. Whistles fill the air along with shouts of "Encore! Encore!" Even Klae is so caught up in the enthusiastic response that she comes out onto the stage, bowing with the rest of the cast.

But all the excitement is muted for Gabby. She can't celebrate. Not yet.

The lights drop and she can finally see the crowd. Squinting, her gaze shoots straight to the staffing section. She finds him instantly, his very presence a magnet to her senses.

Colt is standing not far from the other teachers, a little taller than most, definitely more muscular. Undoubtedly in his own category of delicious.

Their gazes meet. Hold. And don't let go.

Gabby's not sure how much time passes, but it feels like a second. And a lifetime. Too long. Not long enough.

Then, he turns and leaves.

10

COLT

Colt tried to stay away from Gabby. He really did.

It's the best thing for both of them until he finds a loophole in his deal with Belphegor. Going back on his word meant a life of being hunted, for both himself and Gabby. Because Belphegor was smart enough to know that hurting Gabby means hurting Colt. Neither of them would be safe.

And yet, the Tear could not be allowed to remain open. More demons pouring into the world means more chaos, and that would undoubtedly grab the attention of more angels. War would be inevitable. Then there's the matter of hellish weapons entering the mortal realm. The war would be one of epic proportions. One that no being, human, angel or demon, has ever seen before.

So Colt had remained in the shadows. He found he couldn't leave the academy—the need to keep Gabby safe was too strong. Yet, he didn't let her see him.

Of course, he hadn't been cloaking himself or hiding from Klae, so she inevitably found him. And insisted he attend the play. It was Gabby's first and she deserved to have his support.

That, and Klae had pointed out that if he didn't attend, she'd tell Gabby Colt hadn't actually left the academy.

As Colt settles into his chair and the curtains lift, he concedes he couldn't have stayed away. The chance to see Gabby, for a full hour without the need to skulk like a...demon, was too tempting.

She's flawless. Her face is animated, sad, laughing, angry as she lives the life of her character. There's only one part that Colt hates with every fiber of his immortal being, and that's during the final scene when Gabby presses her lips to the hero's. He knows it's just acting. He knows she doesn't melt into the boy with the bobbing Adam's apple, but he still finds his hands clutching the armrests so hard one of them cracks.

Colt has to consciously unclench his jaw and unwind his fingers, knowing he's drawing enough attention just by being here. Throughout the entirety of the play, he could feel Belphegor's eyes on him, watching. And waiting. Apart from a polite nod of acknowledgement when he first arrived, Colt ignores it. He needs to keep the dean onside. For now.

Then there was Gabriel, disguised as MR. Davenport. He also stared, probably plotting how to banish him to Hell. What would the archangel do if he knew Colt was sworn to betray his daughter? The punishment would be as swift and vicious as Belphegor's will be if Colt doesn't honor his word.

The unholy kiss finished, Colt tunes out his personal audience. The final line is delivered and the crowd erupts in applause. He's the first to stand up, everyone else in the room quickly following as he claps the loudest.

Gabby's a natural. A brightly shining star. A vessel of unlimited potential. Her masterful acting is proof she can be whatever she wants to be.

The lights finally drop a little, indicating it's time for the cast to leave, but the moment they do, Gabby's eyes start scanning. Colt freezes as he realizes what she's looking for. No, who.

Him.

Within a heartbeat, her blue eyes find him. And capture him.

In that moment, everything inside him falters. His knees weaken, his muscles all but dissolve. His strength is gone as his body admits what his mind won't. He doesn't want to leave. In fact, his heart is pounding against his ribs, demanding he go to her.

The world around him fades away, and Gabby's now wearing a brilliant white dress. She walks toward him, scarlet roses and white lilies scattered over the carpet. Colt breathes in deep, wanting that scent to be part of him for the rest of his days. A soft smile graces Gabby's face as she steadily, inevitably, comes closer. He barely registers the girl behind her, one who reminds him of Sierra, holding a cushion with rings. All he sees is the beautiful young woman who stops in front of him, her face alive with happiness and soft with tenderness.

Two words echo through every shred of his being.

"I do."

But as Gabby reaches out to take his hands, darkness envelops the achingly beautiful vision. It spreads quickly, swallowing the peripheries, then others. Then Gabby herself.

A bark of laughter pierces the blackness as a form takes shape. Belphegor.

"You're destined to betray her," the archdemon chuckles, obviously taking great glee.

Betray. The word is like a hellish arrow impaling Colt's heart. The vision fades, leaving Colt standing in the theater, shouts of "Encore! Encore!" filling the air.

Heart painfully beating, he turns on his heel, drawn to the shadows he's always moved in. He wraps them around himself along with the guilt, working hard on making himself disappear. He risks one last glance over his shoulder before leaving the room and finds Gabby is making her way down the stairs of the stage, a determined frown on her face.

"Skata," he mutters, extending his stride.

Out in the hall, he walks even faster. Registering the corridor is empty and holds no convenient alcoves or hiding spots, he quickly enters the first door he finds. It turns out to be a storeroom for costumes, a strong smell of mothballs clogging his throat. Wrinkling his nose, he pushes back into what looks like replicas of dresses from the Victorian era.

Footsteps echo down the corridor a moment later, proving he was right. Gabby did follow him. They start off sharp and purposeful, but they slow almost instantly as she must register that the hallway is empty. Then they stop a few feet away from the storeroom he's holed up in like some cowering human.

How far he's sunk...

He's not even sure he would've gone to these lengths to hide from Belphegor back when he was being hunted. Then again, he wasn't worried about hurting Belphegor like he is with Gabby. Colt shakes his head. Things were much simpler then. Run or die. Now he can't stay.

And he can't leave.

There's silence for long, breathless seconds. Colt imagines Gabby has her hand on her hips as she scowls, frustrated that he slipped through her fingers. But then he scowls, too. Unless she can sense him...

"Gabby! What are you doing?" Colt recognizes Gabby's roommate, Maya's, voice.

"Maya!" says another female—Kalisha. "Now isn't the time to—"

"Now is definitely the time to discuss this," snaps Maya. "You're chasing him again, aren't you?"

"I don't know what you're talking about," says Gabby, managing to sound indignant. "I needed a bit of air."

"You're lying." Even tucked among the layers of material and lace, Colt can hear the fury in Maya's voice. "You came out here looking for *him*."

"His name is Colt," says Gabby evenly. "And even if I did, it's none of your business."

"It most certainly is when he's the one who murdered my aunt and uncle!"

"I'm so sorry, Gabby." This time it's Kalisha speaking, sounding like she's deeply uncomfortable with what's happening. "Maya, now isn't the time—"

"No! He has her under his spell or something. I know it!" Maya gasps. "He practices black magic, doesn't he?"

"What? No!" says Gabby.

"Maya," pleads Kalisha. "Now you're talking crazy."

"No, I'm not. I know it sounds unbelievable, but why else would someone as smart as Gabby fall for someone so dangerous and evil? Haven't you heard how brutally my aunt and uncle were murdered? Their skin was peeled off their chest! Just like all the other victims." Maya takes a step, probably closer to Gabby. "The police may have believed his story that Leopold and his cult did this, but I don't. Colt is nothing but a liar. Leopold had nothing to do with any of this."

"Colt is not a liar," grinds out Gabby, surprising him.

Warmth floods his chest at the fierceness in Gabby's tone. She's defending him.

Then ice quickly suffocates it. He's the last person Gabby should be trusting.

"I'll find out the truth, Gabby," vows Maya. "They were like parents to me. They deserve the truth."

There's a strangled sob and then Gabby and Kalisha are

making sounds of comfort. Footsteps sound as they must lead Maya back to the theater.

Colt waits for long minutes, making sure the corridor is silent before he opens the door. He fully intends to go back to his cottage and spend more sleepless hours trying to figure a way out of this, one where Gabby's life isn't at risk.

But he's barely taken a step when a finger spears through the open doorway, straight into his chest. "Oh no, you don't," Gabby says in a heated whisper.

He's too shocked to object, letting her push him back into the storage room until his back is against the racks of clothes and Gabby closes the door behind her. "How..." he asks.

"I muted my footsteps," she says smugly. "A little trick I learned using my magic."

His clever angel.

"You left me, again," she says, clearly angry. "And this time, I want to know why."

"I—"

"And don't give me that secret demon business. We're in this together, Colt. You need to start acting like it."

He blinks, awareness of their proximity, the fact there are no prying eyes, climbing into his consciousness. He's spent days away from Gabby, and now she's here, close enough to kiss...

Colt clears his throat. "I've been here. I just think it might be better if I stayed away a little more."

Gabby angles her head. "How do you say 'bullshit' in any of your countless languages?"

"You either don't understand, or don't want to see it, Gabby. Me being involved makes this far more dangerous for you."

"So, you're protecting me?" she asks, placing a hand over his chest. Beneath, his heart is thundering against his ribs, wanting more of her touch.

"Of course. I don't want to see you hurt."

"Leaving me hurts."

The words are said simply. Softly. With an aching mix of courage and vulnerability.

Colt gives into the need to hold her, wrapping his arms around her. Gabby fits herself against him with a sigh. "This is hard, Colt. All of it. Every choice we make makes a difference for countless lives." She looks up at him. "But it's easier together."

Why is it that when he's holding her, anything seems possible? "You make it very hard to stay away, Gabrielle Heartley."

She pushes up so her breath tickles his lips. "That's the idea."

Giving in to the building passion, Colt kisses her. Their mouths meshing is like coming home and like nothing he's ever experienced before. His fingers tighten on her waist, clutching her. His tongue can't help but sample her sweetness. He groans. She moans.

They're creating their very own version of fire right here, between them.

Gabby pulls back a little, and he likes the way her breathing has picked up. "Don't leave again without telling me, okay?"

In the same with this angel is a woman of contrasts, the words are both a soft plea and a stern order.

Colt nods. "I won't," he promises. She's right. They'll solve this quicker together. And once again, she's not prying. Not asking too many questions. Gabby's trying to navigate this angel-demon dichotomy their relationship straddles. He owes her that much.

And this way, he doesn't have to stay away.

"Good." She smiles. "Tell me. If you haven't left, what have you been doing?"

"Trying to track Samandriel," he huffs. "With no luck. So, I started to investigate the robberies of the Hell weapons. Especially the stash of hellfires. Again, no luck there either. All traces mysteriously wiped out."

Gabby's brow wrinkles in thought. "And you believe the Grigori are behind it?"

"That's what my gut tells me. Although it doesn't add up. Robberies there, and then the hellfires in the city. What's the connection?"

Gabby rests her forehead against his chest, still thinking. A moment later she looks up, eyes alight in the gloom of the storeroom. "We focus on the weapons then! We find the weapons, we find the Grigori. Or at the very least, Samandriel."

"Except we haven't been able to trace the weapons," he points out. "Otherwise, Belphegor would have found them by now."

"My guess is there will be more weapons coming through the Tear, though?"

His eyebrows shoot up. "You want to follow the cache and see who steals it?"

"Yep."

"It won't be as easy as that," he warns. "No one has succeeded in finding the weapons."

It's Gabby's turn to smile. "Well, they haven't met me."

Colt grins. His clever angel. He leans down to kiss her again, losing himself in the magic that only happens when he's with her.

Yes, he should stay away from Gabby.

Yes, the promise to Belphegor still stands.

But by working together, they may be the only two who can stop this.

II

GABBY

Gabby stretches her arms up high, trying to untwist all the knots down her back. They've spent days pouring over everything Colt has on the weapon robberies, and they're getting close. She can feel it.

She notices Colt watching her movements and she makes sure she arches a little more, curving her back and exposing a sliver of abdomen beneath her t-shirt. He stops breathing and the air around him heats.

But he doesn't move.

Her demon's holding back.

She suspects it's for the same reason he's disappeared twice. The same reason secrets lurk in the depths of his chocolate eyes. And she has yet to learn why.

But he keeps coming back. He's here now as they sit in the small room on the top floor of the academy where they had their first date. Looking at her like she's wearing far less than a shirt and mini-skirt. And he's doing everything he can to find those responsible for stealing the weapons of Hell.

For now, that's enough. Gabby knows this is complicated. That Colt is navigating centuries of existence that she has no idea about. Of course, because he won't tell her, but there will be time for that. After they solve who's behind the robberies...

Colt clears his throat. "Maybe they're watching the Tear? How else could they know about the shipments?"

"Maybe," agrees Gabby, trying to focus on the words rather than his lips. She yanks her gaze back up. "What if the demonic weapons have some kind of signature? An aura that someone could trace?"

"Possible," says Colt thoughtfully. "But humans have been attacking. They can't trace using that signature."

"Iris was involved in the first one, right? She's a witch, so she might have picked up on the demonic energy, then sent the humans she hired to the location."

Colt rubs his chin. "True, although I'm also interested in how they got the exorcism spell. Priests keep it secret. And only a few witches have it. Exorcism takes dark energy, and witches rarely attempt it unless they have to."

"Could the cults have it?" Gabby asks, once again trying to understand how all this is linked. "If the cult you spoke of could steal hellfire from here, they could be involved in the other robberies as well?"

"There's no evidence suggesting Leopold had anything to do with removing the hellfire from Belphegor's stash," Colt answers. "Besides, the cult members wouldn't know about the hellfires. It's a closely guarded secret among us demons. I think they were given it. By Samandriel. Not many people knew that Belphegor had taken demons from the Academy with him to help us, and the robbery happened around the same time we all were distracted by the fighting off the Grigori. But how did he know about the other demon weapons coming out of the Tear? And why go so far as to hire a witch and humans to steal the weapons? Angels would fare much better in a battle against demons."

Gabby sighs. Colt's right. There are too many questions that they don't have answers to. What connects Samandriel to the cult members and the hellfires? What connects Samandriel to the robbers? And how did anyone know what was coming out of the Tear?

Colt leans back, stretching out his legs and she can't help but notice their muscled length. "How are your studies going?"

Her mouth twists. "They're kinda not." The first semester's coming to an end, which means exams are looming. Trying to figure all this out along with studying has been a tall order. Before Colt can say anything, she smiles. "I saw Klae today. She wants you to take on a role in next semester's play."

Colt sits upright, looking horrified. "Definitely not! I'm happy to provide music for the play, but I will not act in it. I am not an actor."

Gabby narrows her eyes at him. "Haven't you spent hundreds of years acting?"

Colt has leapt from century to century pretending to blend in. And this play is about the obsidian, although she's going to keep that quiet for now. The idea of him playing opposite her means more time spent together. Colt's character grows close to the protagonist as he finds a new purpose in life. Gabby likes the idea of that...

"That's different. Lying and acting were a matter of survival."

"But you're so good at it," pouts Gabby.

Although she's teasing, she notes the way Colt shifts uncomfortably. He obviously doesn't like talking about this. And yet, she's not willing to back down, even if she's not entirely sure why.

"Come on," she cajoles. "Please? Do it for me?" She flutters her lashes as she extends the pout.

Colt groans. "Now you're not playing fair."

She grins. "I never claimed I would." She sidles closer. "Please? We'd have fun."

His face softens in a way that makes her heart clench. "Very well. But this is the only one. No more after this!"

Gabby giggles as she nods. The next play is a whole semester away. Who knows where things will be between them, then?

Colt pushes to his feet and holds out a hand. "Come on. You'd best get back to your dorm before the Matron starts wondering where you are." His brow wrinkles. "And you should study."

Gabby takes his hand and pulls herself up. Colt goes to release her but she holds on, stepping until their bodies are flush. "Thank you, Colt. For being so generous. And considerate. And amazing."

He shakes his head. "Gabby, I'm none of those—"

She presses her fingers to his lips. "Are you disagreeing with the daughter of an archangel?"

His mouth tips up, brushing warm air against her finger. "One thing I am not is a fool."

"Good," she murmurs, her mind quickly turning to Colt-induced mush. It's so hard to think straight when he's this close.

But he steps back, looking a little pained. "You need to study. Your mother won't be happy if you don't do well after the suspension."

Gabby's face twists, not liking that he's right. "Fine. But only because you have no idea exactly how terrifying my mom actually is."

Colt steps away and walks to the door, holding it open. "While you do that, I'll see what else I can find out about the location of the Tear."

Gabby stops right in front of him. "But you'll tell me if you're leaving?"

"Yes, of course," he says solemnly. "You were right, Gabby. We're better off fighting this together."

"Damn straight," she says sassily.

Colt hesitates, something flickering in the depths of his eyes, but then he quickly turns to leave. In a blink, he's gone. Gabby remains where she is. She needs to wait a few moments before she follows, so they're not seen together. As she stands there, she chews her lip.

Colt saying they need to work on this together is a good thing. It's what she wants. Then why does she feel uneasy?

She closes the door behind her softly and makes her way down the spiral staircase, trying to untangle the feelings inside her. Is she feeling miffed because she wanted him to kiss her? For these feelings to be just as impossible for him to say no to as they are for her?

Making her way to the dorm rooms, she sighs. Patience isn't her strong point. Maybe Colt just needs more time. He's been alone for so long, navigating their relationship wouldn't be easy.

Yet as Gabby reaches her room, she hesitates with her hand on the doorknob. Or is there another reason that Colt's holding back?

Maybe his feelings aren't as strong... Do demons even feel love the same way humans or angels do? She shakes her head. She's starting to sound like her father. Especially considering she's determined not to be like him—influenced by bias and hatred.

Pulling her shoulders back, she opens her door. Colt needs time. And to see exactly how amazing they are together. And maybe some more kisses—

"There you are," cries Kalisha the moment Gabby steps through. "The library closed ages ago!"

Gabby closes the door, suddenly worried. "Is something wrong?"

Kalisha plants her hands on her hips. "Yes. Very wrong. My two academy besties are barely speaking."

Gabby registers Maya sitting on her bed. She scowls and looks away. Gabby's tried to make peace with her. Maya helped her when she was having the blackouts, the last thing Gabby wants is animosity between them. But each time she tries to broach the subject, Maya simply walks away, not even bothering to give lame excuses anymore. She's just too hurt after the loss of her aunt and uncle. And too angry because she believes Colt is behind it all.

"I'm kinda tired," says Gabby, which is the truth. Studying, practicing spells with her father, and trying to spend time with Colt are taking their toll.

But Kalisha has her determined face on. "I think we need to go out. Get away from this place. Have a little fun."

Maya crosses her arm. "Exams are almost here—"

"And we've been studying our hot asses off," says Kalisha. "A couple of hours of fun will do us all good."

Gabby can't help but note the pleading in Kalisha's eyes—already made up with vibrant silver glitter. She stops any objection that was forming and glances at Maya. Maybe some time away from the academy would be good...

"I miss us just hanging out," she confesses. "Maya? What do you think? If we go now, we'll be out and back before curfew kicks in."

Maya grudgingly looks over. "Will Colt be there?"

Gabby shakes her head. "No. He's busy."

"Plotting more death and mayhem?" mumbles Maya.

"No more talk of stuff like that," orders Kalisha. "Tonight we celebrate our awesomeness!"

Gabby finds herself giggling. Maybe this is just what she needs. A bit of good old, normal fun.

No worrying about the Grigori. Or the Tear. Or demonic weapons loose in the world.

Or why Colt is having such a hard time being with her.

WHEN KALISHA DRIVES them to a little place blasting loud music called Urban Legend, Gabby realizes she really was determined to have fun, which would explain the glitzy eyeshadow. But she's also conveniently forgotten they're underage.

They make their way up to the bouncer, who looks at them suspiciously. "ID, please."

Kalisha whips out her card and flicks it to him between two fingers. The bouncer scans it and grunts. "Yep. All good."

Gabby almost rolls her eyes. Of course, Kalisha has a fake ID. She's obviously assumed Gabby and Maya do, too...

Gabby flicks her hair over her shoulder—as if that makes her look older, somehow—as she passes her own ID to the bouncer. A cursory glance is all it takes to be returned to her. "No can do."

Beside her, Kalisha's shoulders visibly sink. She was obviously looking forward to a chance to mend the rift in their friendship group, and Gabby can't blame her. It's something she wants, too.

So she leans forward and passes the bouncer the ID again. Her father's been teaching her how to influence people. She's only used it to encourage others in the library to study, so she's hoping she can pull this off. "I think you should check it again."

The bouncer arches an unimpressed brow, looking like he's about to refuse, when he takes the card.

"You must've read it wrong," Gabby says calmly. "We're all twenty-one."

The bouncer's eyes drop to the card and he blinks. "Oh yes, you are, too." He passes it back. "Sorry, bad math."

"Thanks,"—Gabby's gaze drops to his name badge—" Andrei. You're the best."

He flushes as she steps back to let them through. Kalisha loops her arm through Gabby's giggling. "You're quite the charmer, aren't you?" she whispers.

"I'm sure people say that about Colt, too," mutters Maya as she follows them through.

As they're swallowed by music and brightly colored flashing lights, Gabby ignores the jibe, even though her smile falls away. Tonight's fun-factor is looking questionable.

Kalisha releases Gabby's arm and spins around. "That's enough, Maya," she half-shouts thanks to the music. "Gabby's trying, okay? Can't you just let it go for a couple of hours?"

Maya's face flushes red. "No, I can't! Did you know Gabby was considered a suspect in my aunt and uncle's murder? That Leopold was framed? How can I let it go when justice hasn't been served?"

"We don't know the entire truth, Maya," says Kalisha, dropping her voice. "Maybe Gabby was there to help your aunt and uncle. Maybe they fled from the cops because they thought they'd become suspects, which is exactly what happened. And maybe Leopold is guilty. Who knows? Gabby's a nice person. She wouldn't get caught up in this stuff."

Maya clamps her mouth shut and Gabby has no idea what to say. Kalisha's right, for the most part. Apart from Gabby not actually being involved in all this...

Maya's gaze flickers to Gabby, looking thoughtful. Gabby holds still, hoping this is the breakthrough she's been hoping for. Being back on good terms with her roomie would be amazeballs.

A siren pierces the air. "Out! Everybody out!" shouts a panicked voice.

The people in the club surge forward as the music abruptly stops. Now, screams become the new backdrop. And Gabby quickly realizes why.

Fire.

Green fire.

It dances on the stage beside the dance floor, people running in every direction, their eyes wide and mouths wider. There isn't even a chance to blink before it leaps for the wall, then explodes like a green grenade up it. It's only a matter of time before the club is consumed.

"Hellfires," gasps Gabby before she can stop herself.

"What?" says Kalisha, clearly shocked. Beside her, Maya's face is back in a scowl.

Gabby doesn't get to answer because they're quickly hustled out of the club. Jolting into action, she ushers Kalisha and Maya back toward the door, ensuring anyone else in her orbit joins them. The bouncer runs past them with a fire extinguisher.

The crowd bottlenecks as it reaches the door and a girl wearing a silver top and leather pants trips beside Gabby. She quickly catches her by the elbow. "Here, let me help you." She hauls them up before panicked feet trample the person. The girl smiles in thanks but the movement of people sucks them out the door before she can say anything.

Outside, Gabby grabs her friend's hands and drags them to the other side of the street. She watches as people pour out, smoke already tainting the sky. She wishes she could say they're safe, but she saw firsthand the way the hellfires had spread on Lambda Avenue. They needed to be stopped.

And yet, the only way to do that was with celestial fire. But how? She can't do that with Kalisha and Maya watching. Maya's suspicions would only be cemented. Who knows what Kalisha will do?

Except she has no choice. She can't let the hellfires spread again, destroying everything in their path.

Fire trucks make their way toward the burning building, their sirens echoing through the hazy air. Yet they won't be able to stop the monster engulfing the club. Gabby takes a step toward it, only for Kalisha to grab her hand.

"Where do you think you're going, girlfriend?"

Gabby swallows, unsure of how to say this. "Listen, Kalisha, I need to tell you—"

But a white ball of light stops her. Gabby watches, astounded, as it drops onto the club and suffuses it in a silver glow. An angelic glow. Glancing around, Gabby sees Moroni, her father's lieutenant, standing beside one of the fire trucks, firefighters rushing around him as if they have no idea he's there. Turns out they can't see the silver glow, either.

"We've got it under control!" one of them shouts.

Moroni nods to Gabby, his gaze somber. Seems there's more than one way to deal with hellfires...

"What were you about to say?" asks Kalisha.

"That we need to get back to the academy," says Gabby, snapping her attention back. "Curfew will be in effect soon."

Kalisha looks at her for a long second before nodding. "Good idea. Looks like tonight is a bust, anyway."

Maya crosses her arms. "I'm not ready to go back," she says grimly. "I want to visit my aunt and uncle."

"What?" says Kalisha. "Are you crazy? You would never break curfew!"

"I want to see them, okay?"

Kalisha shakes her head, even her stubborn wild streak not willing to challenge the golden rule of curfew. "But—"

"Tonight has kinda sucked, and seeing them always made me feel better." Maya throws her hands up. "You know what? I'll walk there myself."

Kalisha and Gabby glance at each other. "Okay, Maya, we'll all go," Gabby calls after her. Although she doesn't think this is a good idea, especially after her suspension, she also wants to show her friend she understands her grief.

"Thanks," Maya says grudgingly, then changes direction and heads to Kalisha's car.

As they climb in, Gabby wonders if this is Maya's way of punishing her some more, but she quickly pushes the thought away. When did she become so suspicious?

St. Bernard's Cemetery is on the eastern side of the city, beyond the suburbs. Gabby has no idea why the Daniels' were buried here when there's a much larger cemetery close to their house, but she doesn't ask. The edges of Maya's lips have tugged down lower and lower the closer they get.

The moment they pull up to the shadowy cemetery, Maya jumps out of the car. Without looking back, she walks briskly through the gray tombstones. Gabby follows, Kalisha keeping close to her side.

"Is this fog normal?" she whispers loudly.

Gabby glances down, wondering if it's making Kalisha's feet tingle, too. "I'm sure it's cause the air is cooler down there or something."

"Or it's the Shadow People that I was telling you about in

the car," mutters Kalisha. "They obviously start on your feet first."

Gabby rolls her eyes. Kalisha regaled them with the stories her grandmother told her as a child the whole way here. Gabby worked hard to tell her there's no such thing, even as she wondered if she should research them.

"Come on, Maya's a girl with a mission."

Kalisha stays close as they work to catch up, walking as if she's on tiptoes and glancing around repeatedly. Maya suddenly takes a left and stops near two large tombstones. Gabby slows as the faint streetlights dotted around illuminate the names of Maya's aunt and uncle.

Maya falls to her knees, not caring about the fog or the moist soil as her head drops. Gabby holds still, her heart aching for her friend. No wonder Maya's so fixated on their murders. She's desperate to understand her loss.

The Grigori would pay for this grief.

Maya stands up and walks a few steps to the right, standing in front of another double tombstone. Gabby glances at Kalisha questioningly, wondering who Maya's paying her respects to, but Kalisha just shrugs.

As if she noticed their confusion, Maya glances over her shoulder. "These are my parents' graves."

"Oh, honey!" gasps Kalisha, taking a step closer. "They're buried here too?"

Maya nods, wiping away at her wet cheeks. "They died when I was five. I don't remember much about it, only what I learned when I investigated it a couple of years ago." She turns to face Gabby, holding her gaze. "They were murdered."

"I'm so sorry," says Gabby softly. She had no idea, but even more is making sense now.

"Their killers were never found," continues Maya. "The most information I've gotten is from a Detective Kane. He told me he believes they were killed by a secret sect of people because my parents had seen something and were planning to expose them."

"That's awful," says Kalisha, her voice soft with compassion.

Maya wipes away another sheet of tears from her cheeks. "Yeah, it is. I reached out to a contact of my uncle and got access to the case files." She draws in a shuddering breath and straightens her shoulders, obviously working hard to keep herself together. "I found signs and symbols the cops never told me about that were found at the crime scene. I researched the symbols. They were definitely supernatural. Everything suggested the murders weren't done by something human."

Kalisha's suddenly looking nervous again. "What do you mean? Of course the murderers were human."

"Strange symbols? Ritualistic killings?" snaps Maya. "And now green fires?"

Gabby stills, unsure about what to do about the connections Maya's making.

Maya takes a step forward, her hands now clenched by her sides. "The supernatural is involved." Her angry gaze turns to Gabby. "And Colt's involved."

Gabby shakes her head, wishing it hadn't come back to that. "No, he's not," she says, gently but firmly. "He had nothing to do with the deaths of either your biological or adoptive parents." Maya's scowl is back, but Gabby has to make her see. "The accusations need to stop, Maya."

"He really has done a number on you, hasn't he?" spits Maya. "You believe everything he tells you, never questioning a thing. Are you really that blind, Gabby? Because I don't believe for a second that he's telling you the whole truth!"

Maya's shouting by the time she finishes. She stands in the

shadowy cemetery, her eyes fierce with anger and breathing hard.

And yet Gabby can't defend Colt. Not without telling Maya and Kalisha the truth about who he is. It would probably only fuel Maya's hatred even more.

Not to mention her words...sting. Gabby *is* trusting Colt. And it's highly likely he's not telling her the whole truth.

As the seconds stretch out, Maya spins back to her parents' graves, covering her face with her hands. Kalisha shifts uncomfortably, probably clueless on how to fix this, and possibly wishing they were anywhere but the graveyard in the middle of the night.

Confusion and frustration and unwanted uncertainty clash and crash within Gabby, quickly becoming a riotous storm. Having no idea what to do with any of it, she spins on her heel and walks away. She doesn't want to say anything she regrets.

She's only walked a few yards when she stops. Maybe the truth is the only solution. Maybe Maya and Kalisha need to know what's happening behind the veil of their reality.

Gabby turns around, only to see a dark figure rush at her. There's an exploding pain across her temple, instantly dropping her to the ground. Her head hits the moist ground and her body suddenly feels disconnected. Pain is the only thing she can feel.

Streams of mist move across her fading vision as she watches the dark figure run toward Kalisha and Maya. They scream as it picks them up, throwing them over its shoulders, then dashing away as quickly as it appeared.

"No!" Gabby tries to scream the word, but nothing comes. Not even a whisper.

Then blackness.

12

COLT

Colt paces in his small cottage, chafing that it's only a few strides from one end to the other. The news is playing in the background, although he's hoping for a reprieve from any developments.

They haven't unraveled what's going on with everything that's happened so far.

He's visited every location where a green fire had been reported. It turned out many of them were false reports—no doubt phoned in by the cult to divide firefighting resources. It had wasted his time as much as theirs. Just another reason he's no closer to any answers.

Colt sighs as he drags his fingers through his hair. He wishes he was still with Gabby. Somehow, this all seems achievable when he's with her. Then again, the more he spends time with that delectable angel, the harder it is to keep his mind and heart separated. Yes, they need to work together to solve these mysteries, but he must remember it's safer for both of them if they don't become any more involved than they already are.

He's just not sure how possible that is...

"And we have breaking news," says the reporter who's just appeared on the TV. "A new fire has been reported at the popular Urban Legends club. Is this another of the terrifying green fires that recently destroyed entire streets? We'll keep you posted."

Colt moves back to the television, eyes narrowing as he scans the images flitting across the screen. All that's showing now is a plume of black smoke some distance away, then personally recorded footage of someone trying to escape the club, their cell phone jostling at odd angles as screams filter through. Another false alarm?

Probably.

And yet... Colt moves closer as the erratic footage flicks over a mass of blonde curls. Surely not.

A voice can be heard in the background. "Here, let me help you."

Colt's out of his room before the sentence is finished. He knows that voice. He won't ever forget it, no matter how long he lives. Gabby was at the club.

The Matron's reading a magazine at the desk positioned in the hall and Colt moves so fast the pages flutter. She straightens as she looks around at the sudden gust of wind, but he's already slipped into Gabby's dorm room.

Gabby's empty dorm room.

"Skata," he mutters.

He leaps out the window and unfurls his wings, taking off into the night sky. His heart thunders with each beat of his wings as he tells himself it appeared Gabby left the club in time. Still. Hellfires are deadly. And the only way they know to put them out is with celestial fire. Gabby may be safe, but she might be at risk of exposing the truth about herself.

Colt lands not far away in an empty alley then runs toward the club as his wings retract, his heart knocking against his ribs.

He rounds the corner to find fire trucks filling the street and barricades stopping him from getting too close. Yet Colt doesn't push past them. The fire's out.

He wrinkles his nose as he registers a smell that he can't place. It's not celestial because he would've recognized that after Gabby's spectacular show of power. Then what is it? Is there another way to extinguish hellfires that Belphegor doesn't know about?

Firefighters swarm around, illuminated by flashes of red and blue. A handful of people appear to have been hurt in the evacuations, but there doesn't seem to be any significant injuries. Colt scans the area carefully along with every face in the vicinity, but Gabby and her friends aren't here.

The band around Colt's chest loosens a little. Perhaps they've returned to the academy. Deciding there's only one way to find out, he turns to return to the alley. He's just reached the mouth when a voice reaches from behind.

"Demonic weapons have started a scourge on earth, Colt Grayson."

Soft but steady footsteps approach and Colt turns, muscles poised, to find Gabriel's right-hand-angel approaching him. His eyes hold the same white light Colt noticed when Gabriel is angry.

"Angels are not going to sit quietly if this continues to create chaos," the angel warns.

Colt frowns as he tries to remember the angel's name. What was it?

Horoni?

Coroni?

Ah yes! Moroni! Founded on moron, which seems fitting if he thinks a threat of war is going to scare Colt.

"I have nothing to do with the demonic weapons, friend," he says mildly, unwinding his posture as if to prove how little a threat he thinks Moroni is. "Don't taint all demons with the actions of a few. Then again, you angels have always been biased to our kind."

"Because you're abominations!" snarls Moroni. "Demons were Lucifer's way of creating a species that is nothing but a corrupted version of us angels. It was like he was giving us all the middle-finger and reminding us of his superiority. Not that it did him any good. Now, he's vilified as the Devil. Satan. Goat-headed evil. Shame such brilliance was wasted just because he entertained ideas that had him rebelling. And he failed in that too."

"Did you come here to give me a history lesson that is well known by angel and demon alike?" asks Colt, his lips twisting in a mocking smile.

"No," snaps Moroni, taking an ominous step forward. "I was reminding you why your kind is so hated. Your filth has corrupted Hell. You will not spread that taint to the human world. Stop bringing demonic weapons in and stop arming devil-worshiping cults with them. The last thing this world needs is a full-fledged supernatural war."

Colt angles his head. "If the demons are bringing weapons from Hell, angels are partly to blame." He narrows his eyes. "An army of angel clones is a significant threat to demons *and* humans. It's like you want to bring on the apocalypse."

The mention of angel clones brings a grimace to the angel's face.

Moroni slices his hand through the air. "That's enough. Not every angel out there wants an apocalypse. But that doesn't mean we will allow demon weapons to come through and corrupt humanity." He indicates toward the burned club with a sweep of his hand. "People are suffering because of filth like you."

"Or like you," Colt says quickly. Quietly. But with conviction.

Moroni strides forward until they're face to face, his eyes blazing with silver rage. "I would kill you for your insolence alone, but I've been ordered to see you come to no harm. I don't know how wise Archangel Gabriel is in this, but I assume it's because of his daughter. Or I would smite you here and banish you back to the bowels of Hell from which you come from."

Colt's lips curl into a wide smirk. "How that must grate. That an angel seeks to protect a demon."

Moroni's fists clench so tight the tendons stand out on his forearm. "You're not honorable enough to stay away from Gabby," he spits. "Such a relationship is an—"

"An abomination?" Colt suggests.

Moroni growls under his breath.

"Have you considered extending your vocabulary," asks Colt mildly. "Let me help—atrocity, disgrace, outrage, monstrosity, violation, anathema, bete noire. Did you need more?"

Moroni steps forward in anger, almost bringing them nose to nose. He looks as if his wings will unfurl any moment. Colt doesn't back down. "Not only will you defy the orders of an archangel if you attack me, you will reveal the existence of angels," he reminds him coldly.

The angel's nostrils flare as he draws in a furious, frustrated breath. He bores his eyes into Colt, trying to tell him without words exactly how much he thirsts for his death.

"Good angel," says Colt, deciding against patting Moroni's chest. One touch and the angel will detonate. "Now, if you'll excuse me, I'm going to ensure Gabby's safe rather than have useless arguments."

"As if you haven't coordinated to meet her at the grave-yard," snarls Moroni.

Colt tries to hide his surprise, but he obviously fails because the angel curls his lip. "You thought we wouldn't find out that's where you're organizing your secret trysts? A graveyard is exactly what I'd expect from a demon."

With a hot look of disgust, Moroni spins and walks away. Colt's eyes follow his retreating figure until he vanishes around a corner. So, Gabby had gone to a graveyard. Why?

He strides to the end of the alley and launches into the sky as he mutters a cloaking spell. The only reason he could think the girls would go to a graveyard is to see Maya's family. The question is why.

THE THICK MIST coiling along the ground muffles Colt's footsteps as he stealthily creeps around St. Bernard's Cemetery. He realizes he's holding his breath, almost as if he won't let himself breathe until he finds Gabby. He doesn't find her nearly as quickly as he'd like, but the moment he hears faint female voices, he angles in that direction.

Within seconds, he recognizes Gabby, then Maya and Kalisha. He lets out a slow exhale as his chest loosens. She's safe. In a graveyard in the middle of the night, but safe.

Tucking himself behind a tree, Colt notes that Maya's standing in front of a double gravestone. One that belongs to her parents. He hears her talk of their death and being adopted by the Daniels, and how she had begun to suspect their deaths had a supernatural cause. Is Maya getting close to the truth? Or is her grief-stricken mind desperately clutching at straws?

Colt holds very still as something tugs at a distant memory. But then Maya spits his name and he discovers she's once again blaming him for the deaths of her family. And just like last time, Gabby defends him. But even as the words reveal her loyalty,

Colt feels guilty for putting her in such a position. Their relationship is impacting Gabby's friendships. He also knows the toll the secrets and lies could take.

Colt made the mistake of forging a friendship many years ago with a freckle-faced young man. He'd had some good times with Peyton during his years in Cambridge, England. They'd played chess, no matter how many times Peyton lost, sought out the finest scotch to sample, and competed at who could play the fastest ditty on the fiddle.

But then Peyton found out Colt was a demon. He'd freaked out and moved away the next day. Although he'd never shared Colt's secret—probably too scared he'd be thrown into an institution—he'd wanted nothing more to do with him. Colt had learned friendships weren't worth the disappointment.

Which is why he understands Gabby's predicament. Keeping secrets from best friends isn't easy, but sometimes it's necessary. Especially when it concerns the existence of the supernatural. Peyton's reaction was a modest one, but who knows how Kalisha and Maya would react if Gabby told them the truth?

Gabby seems to be thinking something similar because rather than respond to Maya's accusations, she walks away, her back looking like it's molded from steel. Colt carefully makes his way toward her, wanting to comfort her, when a dark energy overpowers him and he stumbles to the ground. Pain surges through him. He tries to get up, but it's as though a weight has been slammed onto his back.

The dark figure weaves towards Gabby and hits her, too. She drops to the ground, wrenching a groan out of Colt. Every shred of his being wants to go to her, but he's trapped under an invisible weight. The figure scoops up Maya and Kalisha and disappears into the night.

And just like that, the weight is lifted.

Colt's instantly on his feet, stumbling toward Gabby. He falls to his knees beside her, registering her pale face. Her chest flutters with a fragile breath and relief surges through him

"Gabby," he says, conscious she could still be seriously hurt. "Gabby."

For a moment, she doesn't respond. But then a pained groan slips past her lips and her eyes flutter open.

"Thank Lucifer," murmurs Colt, pressing a kiss to her forehead.

"Colt," she gasps, her hands flying to his shoulders. "W—what..." She looks around frantically. "Maya! Kalisha! That thing, it took them. We have to get them back!"

Gabby scrambles to her feet, swaying the moment she's upright. Colt wraps his arms around her and pulls her against him, liking the way she instantly unwinds. "We'll find them," he promises. "We'll get them back."

But even as he says the words, he knows the promise may be an empty one. He looks around the graveyard as he holds his angel. He didn't sense the dark figure. Nor did he recognize it. He's never heard of a supernatural creature like it before. Once again, they're in uncharted territory.

He sighs, pulling back to gaze at her sweet face. "I think we should involve the police."

Gabby's brow wrinkles. "This was supernatural. I don't see how humans can help."

"We can have them search the city," he points out. "It could be faster."

"I don't know," hedges Gabby. "I loathe putting more humans in danger."

Colt smiles, tucking a wild strand of hair behind her ear. "Some humans are more capable than we give them credit for."

"You're talking about Detective Espinosa, aren't you?"

He nods. "She could start a search for Maya and Kalisha."

Gabby nods thoughtfully. "You're right. The more people searching for them, the better."

Colt releases her, even though he doesn't want to. He takes his cell phone out and dials. "Detective, there's been an abduction."

13
GABBY

Gabby's head throbs as she watches Detective Espinosa walk around the area, scribbling in her notepad like she has been since she arrived twenty minutes ago. Whatever the dark figure was, it was definitely supernatural. A human punch couldn't have knocked her unconscious.

At least as an angel, she heals quickly. She just wishes the ache would hurry up and dissipate. Although concerned Colt is kinda nice...

He hasn't been more than a few inches away from her since she regained consciousness, a sexy, hovering presence who keeps brushing her arm or her shoulder. Gabby isn't even sure Colt's aware he's doing it, but she revels in every caress. He cares, and that's what counts.

Detective Espinosa approaches them, looking thoughtful.

"Thank you for coming so quickly, Detective Espinosa," says Gabby. It was a relief to know the search for her two friends is being taken seriously.

The detective waves a hand. "Please, call me Riley. I see you more than I see my dog some days."

Gabby nods, although she's not sure what it means that they're now on a first name basis with a police investigator. "Maya and Kalisha are my roommates. We were here as Maya wanted to visit the graves of her relatives."

"At this time of the night?" Riley frowns.

"Yes, Maya was insistent, especially after the hellfire incident back at the club we were at."

Riley scribbles some more notes. "So you're calling the green fires hellfires, still huh?"

"Seemed fitting," says Colt. "They're giving you hell, aren't they?"

Riley grunts an agreement. "So, you came here right after the fire at the club?"

"Yes," answers Gabby. "Straight after."

"And you," Riley turns towards Colt, "were you with them as well?"

Colt shakes his head. "No, I arrived only moments before the attack happened. I was hit on the head as well before the person moved to Gabby and her friends."

"I'll need a complete picture of what happened from you guys," the detective says, crackling with efficiency. "So, Colt, you were attacked first?"

Colt nods, then gives a succinct summary of what happened. "I tried to get up, but whoever hit me got in a good one."

Gabby slips her hand into his. All of a sudden, she wants to be the one soothing his hurt

"So, the kidnapper leaves you two and just grabs the other two," muses Riley. "This could mean they were the real targets. Any idea why?"

Gabby shakes her head. "No clue."

Riley sighs as if she was hoping not to hear that. "I'll need your friends' details."

"Kalisha Williams and Maya Daniels."

The detective's shoulders tense. "She's related to the seventh family the serial killer targeted?"

"Yes, they were her aunt and uncle who adopted her when she lost her parents as a child," says Gabby.

"So, this kidnapping, it might be connected to the hellfires and the serial killings?"

"It's possible," says Colt, watching the detective closely.

Riley scrawled some more notes. "I'll need access to the dorm rooms and any personal belongings they may have. I'll ask our cyber division to track their cell phones and to be on the lookout for them. Meanwhile, it would help if you guys are able to provide me with any kind of description of the attacker."

Gabby looks at Colt and then the detective, trying to recall the fragmented images. "No, I didn't get a clear view. He wore black."

"He?" Riley asks. "How do you know it was male?"

"The build of the person, the way he moved." Gabby shrugged. "But I could be wrong."

Riley turned towards Colt. "Did you get a good look?"

"I didn't see anything," Colt said. "I was attacked from behind, although I also saw he was in black."

Riley flips to the next page in her notebook. "If Maya has no family, then I doubt this is a ransom attempt," she muses, almost talking to herself. "And if this is related to the recent murders, then someone may want Maya dead."

"What?" gasps Gabby.

"If the kidnapper wanted to kill Maya, wouldn't he have done so here?" Colt points out.

Gabby's gaze shoots back to the detective as she desperately hopes she'll agree.

"Possibly, he might have wanted to leave no witnesses."

"Then why kidnap Kalisha?" adds Colt. "He could have knocked her unconscious, just like he did us."

"Maybe he wants something from both of them then?" Riley argues.

"But why?" whispers Gabby. "They've never hurt anyone."

Colt wraps an arm around her shoulders. "We'll find them."

Riley looks between them, tapping her pen on her notebook. "I'll need Kalisha's family information, too. And I'll set up a tap on their phones. In the meantime, I suggest you two return to the academy. I'll contact you if I need anything else."

She turns away without waiting for an answer, already dialing a number on her cell phone.

Colt takes Gabby's hand and tugs her away. He leads her down the path, quickly changing direction to the rear of the cemetery once Riley can no longer see them. As the lights become sparse and then end all together, Gabby looks at Colt. They're nowhere near the parking lot.

"Ah, how did you get here?"

Colt's teeth flash in the dark. "I flew."

There's a whoosh as his wings unfurl and then he's lifting her into the air. Not to be outdone, Gabby expands her own, and they ascend in a slow pirouette. She holds onto Colt's powerful biceps even though she doesn't need to. Because oh, does she want to.

The ground disappears and they're quickly swallowed by silent night. "You're beautiful," murmurs Colt.

Gabby's heart feels like it's hyperventilating and holding its breath all at once. This is why she's willing to trust Colt with her heart. Why she's holding onto her barely-existent patience. Because he makes her feel like this.

He floats back. "We need to get back to the academy."

The regret in his voice has her smiling. How amazing would

it be to fly together with no place they need to be? No responsibility tugging them back to reality?

One day, she vows to herself. And it'll be freaking beautiful.

Turning, they separate as their wings beat in unison. Almost instantly, the wind is whipping at Gabby's face as they fly through the night. Beside her, Colt is magnificent. Strong. Unconsciously graceful. Casting appreciative glances her way. He seems to be reveling in this as much as she is.

Gabby grins, injecting a little more speed so that she moves half a body length ahead. Colt quickly catches up, but she does it again. When he levels out with her the second time, his eyes are narrowed with suspicion. She winks at him, then with a mighty beat of her wings, shoots forward.

The sound of Colt's chuckle trips over her skin. She hears the thud of his wings compressing air and then he launches past, twisting in the air to throw her a grin on the way past. Giggling, Gabby rockets after him, unwilling to be left behind. They soar through the sky, darting and chasing each other, breathless laughs tumbling over each other. Both fighting for first, but neither caring who is. They're winning just by being here.

Their little race means they get to the academy sooner than Gabby would like, and as her feet touch ground on the other side of the gates, she feels reality grounding far more completely than gravity ever could.

Detective Espinosa, no, Riley, thinks Maya and Kalisha could be murdered. That is, if they haven't been killed already.

And it's Gabby's fault.

It's clear they were kidnapped because Kalisha and Maya are associated with her. Maya's already lost her adoptive parents because Gabby didn't stop the Grigori in time. And now her friend is going to lose her life.

"Gabby?" Colt asks quietly beside her. "It'll be fine. We'll find them in time."

Gabby shakes her head. "You don't know that."

"No, I don't," he sighs. "But I can be pragmatic. Whoever took Maya and Kalisha did so because they wanted something. If they were going to kill them, they would have done so back at the cemetery. They didn't care about witnesses—they left us behind."

Gabby nods slowly, desperately wanting to believe him. "That makes sense."

He steps forward, pressing a kiss to her forehead. "I need to report to the dean."

Belphegor. The archdemon that Colt answers to, even though she never thought he'd be someone to answer to anyone. She lets out a breath, working on calming her fears. "Okay. I need to tell my dad what's happening."

Colt nods, even though she can feel him tense. They both have to go update opposite sides. Sworn enemies. Century-old adversaries.

Urgh.

He steps away and blends into the darkness almost instantly, reminding Gabby that hiding has been something Colt's done ever since he arrived on Earth. Shaking her head at the weird thought, she starts walking down the gravel drive-way. Two of her closest friends have been kidnapped. Right now, the focus is on getting them back.

"Gabriel," she says under her breath. "I need a word."

Gabby keeps strolling down the dark driveway, wondering how long it will be before her father responds to her summons. She hasn't used the skill he taught her not long after they started training together. Exactly how important is she to her Very Important Archangel father?

"You called, daughter?"

Gabby blinks as he materializes to her left, striding toward her. He rarely maintains the head of security persona when they're alone, instead going for the well-built, square-jawed, golden-haired Gabriel that all other angels know. Maybe he knows how intimidating he looks.

Gabby lifts her chin. "I have news."

"About the hellfire at the club? I heard."

Of course, Moroni would've updated him. Her father speaks again before she gets a chance.

"I suspect Colt is involved," he says, his voice hard. "He is a demon, after all."

Gabby has to stop herself from clenching her hands. "Colt is not behind the demon weapons coming out of the Tear," she says tightly. "Your accusations stem from prejudice and hostility, rather than evidence or fact."

"It's a fact that these weapons are coming out of Hell and being doled out to the cult members, though," he snaps back. "Hellfires are burning the city, something the world has never seen before. Did you know how many fires Moroni had to put out tonight? And yes, I know you and your friends were at one of those sites. What in the name of the Holy Trinity were you doing there?"

"Enjoying myself," says Gabby, trying not to sound defensive. "Taking a break!"

"Gabby!" her father barks angrily. "You've already been suspended once. Disregarding the rules again is an unnecessary risk. The academy won't be so lenient this time."

"I was just trying to cheer Maya up," she says, refusing to feel bad. Her father doesn't get to come into her life after nineteen years and lecture her.

His jaw tightens. "There's a war going on, Gabrielle. And it's no longer constrained to this Academy. Even now, angels are battling demons in the city. We know they're behind the hellfire attacks."

"Demons are not—"

"Stop defending demons!" This time, her father is almost shouting as his eyes blaze silver. "You're an angel, for God's sake, so behave like one!"

"I'm also human," she retorts. "A part of me I'm far prouder of."

Her father stiffens. "Gabrielle," he warns in a low voice.

She takes a step back. "I think we're done here." The last thing she wants to tell him about is Maya and Kalisha's abduction. He'll probably blame that on Colt, too. "I'm tired and I want to go to bed."

Impossibly, her father stiffens even more. The great Archangel Gabriel was just dismissed. Gabby suspects anyone else would discover what a good smite would feel like right now.

He leans forward, the line of his jaw looking like a shard of marble. "Your emotions are blinding you, daughter. We've detected demonic aura at the hellfire sites."

With that, he spins on his heel and strides away. Gabby stares, finding she's breathing a little hard. Her father always pushes her buttons. Seems he also knows just what to say to get under her skin.

When there's a flutter of wind behind her, she spins around, wondering if Colt's back already. Except it's not black wings with crimson tips contracting behind a man's shoulders, but white wings with glittery silver tips.

It's an angel. And not one she recognizes.

He remains where he is, long, pale hair brushing his shoulders. "If you want to see your friends alive again, follow me."

It's a trap.

Probably, acknowledges Gabby. And if her Grace is saying

that about another angel, then the likelihood is even higher than that.

But she can't afford to say no. Maya and Kalisha's lives are at stake.

Gabby takes a step forward, about to agree to the deadly proposition, when a ball of black fury drops from the sky.

Colt lands on the angel, fists a blur as he pummels him.

Gabby rushes toward them. "Stop! Colt!"

To her surprise, he does. He stands, yanking the bloodied angel to his feet and holding him by the shirt. "He's one of Samandriel's," growls Colt.

Gabby's eyebrows hunch down. "But that means…"

That Samandriel has Maya and Kalisha.

14

GABBY

The prick.

That damned, crazy-assed Samandriel is behind the kidnapping.

All this time, Gabby assumed Samandriel retreated to some festering corner of the globe to nurse his psychotic ego. But now, one of his men is standing before her, a smirk climbing up the face that's already healing.

"You want Maya and Kalisha?" he sneers. "All you have to do is follow me."

Colt shakes him, barely contained fury rippling through his body. "Or you could just tell us and save me having to beat it out of you."

Gabby places a hand on his shoulder. "I think we should see where he's going to take us."

The muscles under her palm tense so hard they feel like rock. "What?"

"We can't afford to lose the lead, Colt. Nor do we have time to interrogate this slime ball."

"I heard she was smart," says the angel.

Colt hesitates and Gabby knows she's asking a lot from him.

Letting this angel go is a risk. And there's a good chance he's leading them to a trap.

Colt yanks the angel close, growling in his face. "You hurt her, I end you."

With a disgusted shove, he pushes the sneering angel away. It's all the asshat needs, because he launches into the air, his pale hair gleaming.

"It's a trap, Gabby," says Colt in a low voice, watching the angel put some distance between them.

"We've had no leads on Samandriel," she points out. "This guy could lead us straight to them."

Colt sighs. "Of all the reckless, foolhardy things to do right now," he mutters as he leaps into the air, his wings unfolding.

Gabby wants to kiss him for his unconditional support and she's about to say as much when the angel turns around. He throws his hands out, a bolt of white lightning shooting straight at Colt.

Colt twists midair, the electrical charge narrowly missing him as he curses.

"Okay, now I'm pissed," growls Gabby. She pulls her hand back and furiously throws a fireball at the angel.

The angel isn't as quick as Colt, and the orb of fire clips his wing. He spirals to the ground, feathers singed. Gabby can smell the acrid scent from here. But he quickly rights himself, flapping like a lame duck as he climbs back up into the air.

Colt goes to move, but Gabby holds him back. "We need to let him go," she says urgently.

"Yes, listen to the angel," the minion goads. "Like a good little demon."

Gabby glares at him. He's testing her patience as much as Colt's. "Go now before I change my mind. One more move like that and I'll end you myself."

"An angel defending a demon," he says in disgust. "Things are worse than I thought."

He turns and resumes his flight, his flapping ungainly and his movement choppy thanks to his injured wing. Gabby and Colt launch into the air, keeping close as they follow at a distance.

Mercy City glitters below as they fly high, traversing streets and suburbs. They follow the angel for long enough for Gabby to start wondering if this is *too* reckless. Maya and Kalisha might not be waiting at their destination. Or Samandriel. And Gabby's dragging Colt into this, without a clue of their welcoming committee.

Before she can consider changing her mind, the angel drops down and Gabby sees they've followed him to a soccer stadium on the outskirts of the city. A large oval stretches out below, the expanse of green almost black.

Gabby and Colt touch ground several yards away from the angel. He strides to a door leading inside the stadium, not looking over his shoulder as he speaks. "This way."

They enter together, their steps wary yet determined. Every cell inside Gabby vibrates with tension as she glances around. She won't let Colt get hurt just because she somehow thought this was a good idea.

They pass through a dark space and then through the open door on the other side. The moment Gabby's shoes press into soft grass the lights of the stadium come on, one by one, illuminating the manicured expanse.

It's empty.

There's no one, not even the angel who led them here.

Uneasiness ripples down her spine. "We should go—"

A bubble of energy ripples through the air, progressively revealing a large army of angel clones. What must be a hundred cold, impassive faces stare at them, wings tightly held behind them. The regimented rows look like a squadron of lethal weapons, waiting for the trigger to be pulled.

"Seems we have company," mutters Colt, his body a coiled live-wire.

A familiar, maniacal laugh ripples through the stadium and two angels divide to reveal Samandriel stepping through. "This was easier than I expected, Gabby," he purrs. "You're quite keen to be the heroine, aren't you?"

"I'm here for my friends," she says, her voice like flint.

A chaotic giggle tumbles past Samandriel's curled lips. "Where's the fun in that?"

Gabby wants to punch that evil grin right off his face. "Where are Maya and Kalisha?" she grinds out.

"Alive. Terrified, but alive." Samandriel shakes his head, looking nonplussed. "Especially that Kalisha. Is she always that loud and neurotic?"

"Let them go!"

Samandriel's smile drops. "Do you really think you demand and I comply? " he taunts. "You think these angel clones are here just for show?"

"Let them go, Samandriel!" This time it's Colt who growls the order.

The angel peals into more laughter. "You think I'm more likely to listen to a demon?" He sobers, the changes in mood almost giving Gabby whiplash. "I don't actually want you dead. If I did, I would've done it by now. But I do need something, and I'm willing to trade your friends' lives for it."

"Something the great Samandriel can't get himself?" Colt asked.

The angel's eyes flare silver only for it to be quickly banked. "I could if I wanted to." He waves a hand dismissively. "But I'd rather you guys do the dirty work."

"Which is?" asks Gabby, wishing Samandriel would just get to the point.

"The demon weapons being stolen as they are transported from the Tear, of course," says Samandriel with a shrug. "We could do with some weapons from Hell. Heard the latest ones are upgrades."

Colt laughs humorlessly. "You want us to deliver the weapons you've stolen yourself?"

Indignation has Samandriel drawing in a sharp breath. "I am no thief," he shouts, as if he actually has morals. "You think I'd ask you to give me the weapons I already have in return for the two friends? I may be crazy, but I'm certainly no fool!"

Gabby and Colt don't answer. If it wasn't Samandriel who stole the weapons, then who?

Samandriel's face turns smug. "It was demons who stole the weapons. From their own kind."

"You lie," snarls Colt.

"Are you for real?" Samandriel asks, now looking incredulous. "You don't think your precious Belphegor has enemies of his own? That any of the other demon factions don't want those weapons, too?"

Colt doesn't answer, but Gabby notices his hands tighten into fists. It seems Samandriel's statement is plausible.

The angel waves his hand again. "But I don't like to gossip." His face hardens. "I want those weapons and you, Colt, will get them and give them to me. Only then shall I release your two friends." He then turned towards Gabby. "And we can, like, hang out with all my other friends." He giggles coyly, indicating toward the clone army they're surrounded by.

"Gabby comes with me," says Colt.

"You don't understand how this works, do you, demon?" Samandriel glances at the clone to his left. "They really aren't very bright, are they?" he mock whispers. He turns his gaze back to Colt. "I hold the leverage here. And right now, the prospect of getting my hands on a demon cache makes me happy. If not, then I'll be...unhappy. And Maya and Kalisha will be dead."

Gabby reaches out to press her hand to his arm even as she keeps her gaze on Samandriel and his army of soulless pseudo-angels. "Go get this idiot the weapons."

Colt tenses. "No," he says unequivocally. "I won't leave you alone with this bastard."

"I can take care of myself, Colt. Maya and Kalisha need us."

Colt drags his gaze away from Samandriel, the fact that he's taking his eyes off the enemy showing exactly how unimpressed he is with her suggestion. Gabby stares back, wanting him to understand how important this is. She can't let Maya and Kalisha down. They're innocent in all of this.

"Skata," mutters Colt.

He turns back to Samandriel. "We don't even know if they're alive."

Samandriel clicks his fingers, now almost looking bored. Screams echo through the stadium.

"Help us!" Kalisha's desperate voice is unmistakable. "Please!"

A shiver skips down Gabby's spine. The cries sounded like they came from the center of the stadium. Maya and Kalisha are here. And terrified.

Gabby turns to Colt and she watches hard determination settle on his face. He nods once and shoots into the sky.

She senses a subtle shift in the clone army the moment he does. Her gaze returns to Samandriel, finding him smirking. She narrows her eyes, realizing this is all some big chess game for him. "You were behind the hellfires all along," she accuses. "You armed the cult we framed for the murders. You and your minions stole the hellfire stash from Belphegor."

His smirk grows. "Quite the bright spark, huh? It'll only make snuffing you out all the more rewarding."

Samandriel's top lip curls, the movement subtle but significant. The clone army jolts alive and surges forward. A wave of death is coming toward her.

Gabby smiles. She cups her hands in front of her and a lotus appears, unfurling as if life just graced it. Golden light spears from the center and divides into countless fingers of fire. They arc out like an umbrella of brilliant gold, landing on the perimeter of the oval. Then, they burst into flames.

The fire quickly forms a circle and contracts around the clone army. It engulfs them, scorches through them as it races for the center. The angels arch their spines as they throw their heads back, arms and wings splayed. But they don't scream. They either don't get a chance, or they can't, because they combust, leaving little more than a shower of white ash behind.

Gabby leaps into the air and unfurls her wings, not surprised to find Colt beside her. She knew he'd never leave.

But then again, they knew Samandriel would never keep his word.

Gabby slows down the fire as it constricts around the army. She and Colt power through the remaining angels, eliminating the few that remain. Progressively, they make their way to the center. The angels thin.

Until Gabby dispatches the final one. Samandriel is nowhere to be seen, the coward.

They find Kalisha and Maya tied to chairs, eyes wide and faces impossibly pale. Gabby's shoulders slump with relief. They're fine. They saved them in time.

But the moment she steps closer to undo their ties, both her friends shrink back. Their saucer-sized eyes are roaming over Gabby's white wings, then Colt's black ones. Gabby straightens.

Crap.

Maya and Kalisha know their true identities.

Colt glances at Gabby meaningfully. He intends on wiping their memories.

The night air fills with sirens then tires screeching over gravel. There's no time to do anything apart from tuck their wings back in.

The police are here.

15
COLT

olt watches as Maya and Kalisha are wrapped in blankets by the ambulance officers tending to them while police swarm the stadium, looking for evidence. But that's not the reason Gabby's hands are twisted together into a knot as she watches, too.

Detective Espinosa—Riley—has already questioned them and she had no choice but to believe that Gabby traced Kalisha's phone here and found her two friends tied to chairs, the remainder of the stadium empty. Riley had stared at them, especially at Colt, for a little too long before walking away to talk to Kalisha and Maya.

Gabby's friends talking is also not the reason Gabby's so wired with worry. Kalisha and Maya repeated the same story— they didn't see the guy who abducted them, and then he must've drugged them because they had no idea how they got here.

Riley had noted the white ash that sprinkled the grass like confetti, but she hadn't commented on it. How could she? The detective wouldn't be able to conceive what really happened here.

Gabby had annihilated an entire army of army clones in one, blazing circle of fire. Colt's still trying to wipe the awe from his face, and that's one emotion he hasn't felt very often. Then again, the same goes with attraction, the fierce need to protect, and desire.

Gabby sighs, leaning back so she's pressed more firmly against him. Colt grips her shoulder and squeezes, wishing he could make the worry he can feel weaving through her muscles go away. The authorities probing for answers she's taken in her stride.

But the fact her two friends won't even look at her is clearly upsetting. After Gabby and Colt had freed them, Maya had acted as if Gabby didn't exist, while Kalisha wouldn't stop shaking, yet flinched if Gabby came too close.

"They aren't going to talk to me anytime soon," mumbles Gabby.

"They just need time to process," he murmurs back, kneading her tense muscles. "You discovered yourself it's a lot to take in."

"A little part of me was hoping that the truth would clear the air. That they'd understand a little more."

"They may," Colt assures. "They didn't out you to the police, which is a good start. Give them time, then try to talk to them again."

She looks over her shoulder, her blue eyes heavy with sadness. "Kalisha might, but Maya... She's been so angry with me. This could push her over the edge." Gabby crosses her arms. "She could hate me for a very long time."

Colt doesn't have an answer for that. Maya's anger is powered by grief. Who knows how long that will take to resolve? Some humans never let that go...

"I'm going to kill Samandriel for this," says Gabby, her voice just as low, but now hard and fierce.

Colt turns her around, his hands still on her shoulders. "We will find him," he says just as resolutely. Hurting Gabby has ensured those words are a promise.

To his surprise, Gabby smiles, the sweet upturning of her lips taking his breath away. "Damn straight we will."

Warmth unfurls in Colt's chest, the sensation deeply foreign but one so beautiful, he doesn't want to live without it. The desire to kiss this amazing angel is overwhelming, but Colt steps back. There are too many people around, including Kalisha and Maya.

Although as Colt looks around and registers that the horizon is tinged with the faint glow of dawn, he acknowledges that's not the real reason he's stopping. He's spent centuries not caring what people think of him. And if Gabby were his, nothing would stop him from showing how he feels.

But Gabby isn't his. She may never be.

Because he's tasked with betraying her.

"Come," he says gruffly. "We need to get back to the academy."

Gabby sighs. "Yeah, we really do." She pulls out her phone, sighing even deeper. "And this time, we'll have to Uber it."

DAWN HAS TAKEN hold of the day as Colt and Gabby climb out of the car that's stopped at the academy gates to drop them off. It means the soft light that fills the air illuminates the throngs of students on the sprawling lawns.

"What is going on?" asks Gabby as they both break into a jog.

As they get closer, Colt can see most of the students are all still in their pajamas. Some of the teachers walk from one group to the other, their faces creased with concern as they touch an arm or offer a smile. A quick scan of the academy itself shows nothing. Not scorch marks from hellfire, or even earthly fire. Yet, for some reason, Colt doubts this is something as mundane as a burst water main.

He spots the dean standing a little to the side, talking to another teacher. "This way," he says to Gabby, changing direction.

Belphegor notices their approach and he says a few words to the teacher. The woman nods then scurries away, shouting to a nearby colleague that the cafeteria will be opened shortly. Apparently it's fine to return inside.

"What happened?" asks Colt the moment they're close enough.

The dean lifts his square jaw as his gaze flicks to Gabby. "Well, if you were here, you would know."

"I was dealing with another hellfire," says Colt evenly. "And then two Mercy Academy students were abducted by Samandriel."

Belphegor straightens. "What? When did this happen?"

Colt glances at Gabby, then quickly explains about the abduction, then following an angel to the stadium. He glosses over Gabby's decimation of the angel clones, focusing on the fact Kalisha and Maya were rescued and are now at the hospital for assessment.

Belphegor curls his lip. "A coordinated attack. Samandriel is getting clever."

"A coordinated attack?" asks Colt, not liking the sound of that. "What do you mean?"

"The scum angel has played us," spits Belphegor. "Samandriel must've known of the rift between Gabby and her friends, so he drew her to the stadium after having kidnapped them, forcing her to expose herself. That is, if she survived the clones.

If she hadn't, she'd be dead, which is exactly what the Grigori want. And if Gabby had agreed to his demands, he could've gotten his hands on the demon weapons."

And who knows what Samandriel would do with those.

"And while we were busy, Samandriel attacks this place," muses Gabby.

Belphegor glances at the pale-faced students. "I doubt they saw anything. We stopped them before they got close to the dorms. Then we raised the alarm, saying there had been a bomb threat. One that turned out to be nothing more than a prank."

Icy cold fury crackles through Colt's veins. The crazed angel thought of everything. "He was here for the hellfires," he growls.

Belphegor shakes his head. "He would never have found them. I've changed the location of my stash. Nobody knows where it is this time."

Gabby's eyes widen. "Samandriel was behind everything."

"Yes, he was," says Belphegor. "I received more news last night. Turns out there was a witness at both scenes of the crime. I suspect someone used a powerful spell to cloak evidence from the supernatural, but they didn't account for humans. There's a homeless person who lives beneath a nearby bridge. He saw everything."

Colt digests what the archdemon is saying, along with everything he's not. First, he didn't instantly summon Colt to tell him this, meaning Belphegor doesn't trust him. Second, he's relaying this information in front of Gabby. He's realized how powerful she is.

"The witness described a man who stood back and watched both weapon thefts," continues Belphegor. "I did some digging around. The man's name is Malcolm Hunsecker."

"And?" asks Colt. Belphegor would have access to countless databases he shouldn't.

The archdemon's lips thin. "A model citizen. No prior criminal record."

Gabby angles her head. "But you found out more."

Surprised at her perceptiveness, Colt's further shocked to see Belphegor nod.

"He runs a smuggling operation. I, ah, interviewed one of his men. He swore they didn't have any hellfires, but that they were looking to get their hands on some after Malcom spoke to a guy called Samandriel."

Colt and Gabby glance at each other. Samandriel is indeed behind all this.

"Samandriel made a deal with Malcolm to get hellfires for him." Belphegor waves a hand at the academy and the remaining students clustered on the lawns. "All this, and probably the hellfires in the city, were a distraction."

Colt rubs his chin. "The question is why Samandriel would steal hellfires for someone else."

Gabby nods, also looking thoughtful. "Malcolm has something he wants. Samandriel's ingratiating himself."

"Yes," hisses Belphegor, looking between the two of them, something glinting in his eyes.

Whatever it is, it has Colt taking a small step away from Gabby. Belphegor doesn't need to see how well they work together. He'll use it to his advantage.

"After our little chat, I dealt with Malcolm's man," says Belphegor. His eyes harden as they fall on Colt. "I've never liked traitors. And I'm sure the rest of the men were much the same." He shrugs. "They met the same end."

Gabby narrows her eyes. "You're a cold-hearted bastard, aren't you?" she asks.

Belphegor smiles. "Almost as cold-hearted as angels."

"Fair call," she quips right back.

The dean grunts but before he can say anything, someone

calls out his name. He waves to show he's coming, then turns back to Gabby and Colt. "With the thieves taken care of, there probably won't be any more robberies for a little while. Unfortunately, Malcolm is still at large."

With that, he strides away, puffing out his chest as if that can make up for his lack of height. Colt watches quietly, curious at the way his leader responded to Gabby. She was unafraid of him. And Belphegor liked that. His lack of anger for her impertinent response is proof of that. Is it possible that the archdemon might see the value in allying with Gabby?

She turns to Colt. "Well, now we know where to focus our attention." Her eyes harden. "Samandriel."

"Agreed. He's becoming dangerous."

He has ties to the Grigori.

A rival angel faction.

And now some mysterious, powerful man called Malcolm.

16

GABBY

The need to make Samandriel pay throbs through Gabby. But as she looks up at the cold, hard determination on Colt's handsome features, she wonders how much of her resolve comes from working with this calm, fearless demon.

She has to admit, anything seems possible with him by her side. She opens her mouth to say something to that effect when a hushed voice reaches her thanks to her angelic hearing.

"Surely they're not..." someone titters.

"Can you blame her? Look at him," says another. "And he's only a few years older."

Gabby and Colt step back automatically, Colt obviously hearing it, too. Their relationship isn't okay, no matter where they are.

"There's nothing to be worried about, Ms. Heartley," Colt says loud enough for his voice to carry. "The evacuation was the product of nothing more than a prank call."

"Thank you," says Gabby, nodding. "Obviously it was someone's idea of a joke."

"We take any threats seriously. Student safety is our first

priority." Colt steps around her. "Meet me at the back lawns," he says under his breath before striding away.

Gabby makes a conscious effort not to watch, no matter how amazing his butt is. Instead, she glances over at the group of girls. They quickly turn away, cheeks flushing as they hurry toward the east wing where the dorms are. Frustration has Gabby's hands clenching. She doesn't care what the universe tries to throw at her, she's not turning away from the way she feels about Colt.

As if the universe hears her issue the challenge, a police car pulls out outside of Mercy academy and Kalisha and Maya step out. They thank the officers, insisting they're fine to get to their rooms without further escort. They watch it pull away, and the moment the car's out of sight they pull each other into a hug.

Gabby's chest constricts at the vulnerability she's witnessing. She crosses the lawn, wanting to make this okay, somehow. Responsibility and guilt crowd around her heart, making her ribs ache.

Kalisha pulls back, her makeup mussed and hair awry in a way Gabby's never seen before. She registers Gabby walking toward them and her eyes widen. Maya spins around, her face hardening when she sees what caught her friend's attention.

"Have you come to lie to us again, Gabby? " she demands, anger vibrating through her body.

"Maya, I wanted to tell you. I really did..." Gabby's shoulders slump, knowing there are no words to make this okay. Her two closest friends' worlds have been turned upside down and inside out.

"But you didn't," spits Maya. "That's not what friends do. I want nothing to do with you. And neither does Kalisha." Gabby looks toward her friend, conscious that Kalisha doesn't let anyone speak on her behalf. But Kalisha's gaze slides away as she remains silent.

Maya's lips twist into a smile. "You dragged us into this mess. Now we're both in danger." She takes a step forward, and despite everything, Gabby's taken aback by the fury flashing in Maya's eyes. She never expected her to be so...nasty. "And Colt. Your boyfriend. He's a demon, isn't he?"

She nods, not wanting to hide anything from them anymore.

"Is that even allowed?" asks Maya, disgust tainting her voice. "Come on, Kalisha. We have better things to do."

Maya takes Kalisha's arm and leads her toward the dorms, neither of them looking back. Gabby stands on the gravel driveway, hurting for her friends, yet knowing she's the cause of it. All she can do is hope Colt's assurances that they just need some time will come true.

Turning in the opposite direction, Gabby makes her way around the sprawling academy building. Colt wanted to meet her on the back lawns, and right now she wants nothing more than to see him, even though it was only a few minutes ago that he left. It's so much harder to be confident about winning, about them, when all she can see are the hurdles the size of mountains.

She finds him standing at the edge of the lawns that the dean's office overlooks. A quick glance reveals Belphegor's office is empty, although it's still an odd place to meet. Gabby was hoping for somewhere a little more private, to be honest.

Colt turns around, ready to speak when his eyes narrow. "Something's happened."

Touched by his ability to sense her emotions so easily, she wishes she could hold him. Instead, she stops beside him, sighing. "Kalisha and Maya returned. They're fine physically, not so much mentally. Maya, in particular, is super angry with me."

Colt frowns. "Her anger runs deep." He holds Gabby with

his sure gaze. "This is about more than just discovering the supernatural."

"Losing all your living relatives will do that, I suspect."

"We have to hide the truth from humans, Gabby. It's dangerous for them, and for us."

"I know," she says, finding herself leaning a little closer to his warmth. "Although I'm not sure Maya will ever see it like that."

"Then they are not true friends," he says simply.

Gabby tilts her head to look at him, the morning light bathing his wine-colored hair. "That sort of loyalty is hard to find, huh?"

"I have discovered it is the true measure of someone's feelings." Colt blinks as if he's surprised those words came out. He clears his throat, turning back toward the lawn. "I think I have an idea what Samandriel might have been up to."

For a long second, Gabby considers pinning him down and asking what he means by that, but she realizes they have a crazed angel to find, sooner rather than later. "You think he wanted to ruin Belphegor's lawn?"

Colt smiles. "No, but I do think he knew how special this patch of grass is to the archdemon." He indicates toward the green expanse. "I've noticed Belphegor spends a lot of time watching over this from his window. I suspect he's hidden something here."

Gabby squats down, running her fingers through the prickly blades. She narrows her eyes as she registers it's not a flat expanse like the rest of the lawns around the academy. In fact, when she looks closely, she can see small bumps, even gentle undulations. Colt's right. "It looks like it's been uprooted."

He nods. "Maybe Samandriel realized it too, and tried to get the weapons."

Gabby pushes to her feet. "The question is, did they get their hands on whatever it is they were looking for?"

"There's no way to tell." His lips thin. "And I doubt Belphegor will tell me."

She'd noticed the way the wily archdemon holds his cards close to his chest. The thought makes Gabby's heart clench. Colt really has been alone for a very long time. Not even his leader has his back.

She slips a little closer, brushing her hand as she winds her pinky around his. "And I suspect his stash contains more than just hellfires."

"Agreed," says Colt, his little finger tightening around hers. Somehow, just that small touch has her heart soaring.

"Gabrielle," comes a voice behind her, and the soaring abruptly turns into a nosedive. Her father's here.

She turns, maintaining the sweet hold on Colt as she watches Mr. Davenport, the academy's head of security, walking toward them. With each step, the illusion of the wiry man fades as her father's true form appears. Tall, broad-shouldered and powerful, the archangel he really is appears. Although Gabby knows that no one else would be able to see it. To others, it's Mr. Davenport pinning them with a steely glare.

"Samandriel must be stopped," her father growls.

"So you heard?" asks Gabby, noting the way Colt stiffens. He's probably wondering where her father was when the academy was being attacked, leaving the demons to protect it.

Her father draws in a deep breath, his nostrils flaring. "That traitorous scum ravaged the clubhouse."

"The clubhouse?" asks Gabby, frowning. "What did he want there?"

"Lotus fire," spits her father. "Powerful celestial magic."

Gabby glances at Colt. "The same thing I used at the stadium." And it had certainly been powerful. She hadn't expected to be quite so...effective.

Her father's chest inflates. "Well done, daughter. What happened at this stadium?"

Gabby gives her father a quick summary of Maya and Kalisha's abduction by Samandriel and using the fire lotus to take care of the angel clones. "And Colt was there, by my side, through it all."

Her father's gaze flickers to Colt, then their entwined fingers, and his lips thin. "It seems Samandriel has been working to get the fire lotus' for some time," he says, clearly ignoring Gabby's last statement. "We believe he was here during your initiation celebration, trying to steal them, but was caught by one of my angels whom he then killed. And now the attack on the academy."

"That's most definitely a well thought out plan," says Colt. "He attacked from multiple angles, with multiple goals. It's almost admirable."

"That's because he's an angel," snaps Gabriel.

Gabby rolls her eyes. Her father would prefer to side with a loony angel rather than a demon. "All the more reason to stop the sphincter face," she says tartly. Her father and Colt are currently connected by one degree of separation, whether her father likes it or not.

Colt's lips twitch. "Well said."

Before they can figure out how to do that exactly, another person appears, walking swiftly toward them. Gabby recognizes Moroni, her father's first in command, and she tenses. She doubts he's here to report on whether there are waffles at the cafeteria.

"Sir," says Moroni, nodding at Gabby's father differentially. "There has been an explosion outside the mayor's offices. Only a handful of staff injured, but reports are that a cult member has been apprehended."

Colt straightens and Gabby knows what he's thinking. She turns to him, pressing her hand on his chest. "You go see what you can find out. I'll stay here and check out the clubhouse."

He stares at her for long moments and she wonders if he realizes she's doing this just as much for her father's benefit as his. She's showing her father she trusts Colt. That they work as a team.

"I'll let you know what I learn as soon as I can," he says, his brown gaze heavy with promise.

"Looking forward to it," she murmurs huskily.

Colt turns and walks away, not acknowledging Gabby's father or Moroni. She's not surprised when her father spins on his heel and stalks in the opposite direction, shaking his head in disgust, although it doesn't bother her. Her father needed to be around for longer than a few months of her life to have his opinion count. Oh, and he has to lose the demon bias.

Gabby glances at Moroni, expecting him to do the same. Colt mentioned to her that the angel had a word with him. It's clear he carries the same hatred for demons that her father does. He won't approve of Gabby dating Colt any more than his commander does.

Except, he doesn't move, instead leveling her with an intense gaze. "Is there something you wanted to talk about?" she asks, bracing herself. If Moroni starts lecturing, she's outta here. She won't hear him talking trash about Colt.

"I'd like to have a word, Gabrielle," he says. "I believe I have an offer that might interest you."

Gabby doubts that, and she raises a brow to communicate the sentiment.

"We have a common interest in ending Samandriel," says

Moroni. "He must pay for what he's done. If we work together, you will have the force of your father's angels behind you."

Gabby blinks as her mind quickly shifts gears. The idea certainly has merit. The more people out there hunting that psycho, the better chance they have of catching him, something she hasn't been able to do yet. She studies Moroni as she mulls it over, noting the way his shoulders are bunched and his jaw is tight. "I get the sense this is personal, Moroni," she observes.

He inclines his head. "Yes, I want to make him pay for what he did to me."

Gabby waits. Did Samandriel kill someone Moroni loved, assuming angels cared enough about anyone but themselves? Or is this ego related? Did Samandriel show Moroni up?

"I do not tell many of this," says Moroni on a sigh, "but it may help if you understand. What do you know of the Latter-Day Saints?"

"Not much," says Gabby, wondering what it has to do with anything. "They were founded by a guy called Joseph Smith, right?"

"Yes, he founded it in the 1820s. 1823 to be exact. I know. I was there."

"Wow," she says, surprised.

"Yes, that was the year Joseph found a set of golden plates buried deep in a hill inscribed with an ancient language. I appeared to him then and told him that the language is reformed Egyptian. Smith translated the material and made an entire book out of it. That book has come to be known as the Book of Mormon."

"Oh," says Gabby, conscious she's being reduced to single words, but learning Moroni was so central in forming the religion is a lot to take in.

"He gathered testimonials from eleven men, later came to be known as the Eleven Witnesses."

Gabby resists the urge to rub her forehead. "But how is this connected to us?"

"I'm getting to that. You see, after Smith created the Book of Mormon, he returned the plates to me. And I ascended to Heaven with them. But on the way, I was attacked. Guess by whom?"

"Samandriel," she spits, conscious that the word is starting to leave a bitter stain on her tongue.

"Yes, Samandriel. I fought him, but he fled. By the time I realized he'd stolen the plates, he was nowhere to be found. Your father, Gabriel, joined the search. By the time we tracked him down, he no longer had the plates, nor would he divulge where they are. We imprisoned him and I've never given up the search. When the Tear appeared, Samandriel broke out of Heaven's prison and descended to Earth. We tracked him here, but he's always one step ahead of us."

"I'm sorry to hear that, but I'm not sure how this helps me." Gabby doesn't have time for more ancient artifacts.

"These plates contained additional information, written in an obscure form of Egyptian, which wasn't translated and transcribed by Smith." Moroni's eyes light up as if the punchline has been worth waiting for. "Information that documents a way to end the Grigori once and for all."

Gabby gasps. "The plates have a way to kill off the Grigori?"

"Yes. We find the plates, and we're one step closer to ending the Grigori permanently."

She chews her lip. In some ways, she understands Moroni's personal grudge against Samandriel. The crazed angel destroyed her friendship with Kalisha and Maya, and almost exposed her to the world. What's more, he's a murderer.

Moroni must sense that she's tempted, because he takes a step forward. "There are angels and demons who want to bring on an apocalypse. Every move they make is a threat to humans." Gabby almost finds herself nodding. "I want the same thing your father wants," he continues. "Peace on earth and demons back in Hell."

The final words are like a slap. Demons back in Hell. Sure, Moroni wants Samandriel captured, but he also wants demons out of the picture. And that would include Colt.

"What do you say?" says Moroni, actually smiling. "Shall we work together?"

Seems he's not as astute as she thought he was. Moroni is clueless that she's no longer deliberating on her decision. Instead, she's made it.

Gabby takes a step back. "I'll take everything you've said into consideration, Moroni," she says, holding his gaze. "Once I've spoken to Colt, I'll let you know *our* decision."

The satisfaction of seeing Moroni's double take doesn't last long. He straightens and lifts his chin. "You will regret trusting a demon," he promises before stalking away.

Gabby sticks her tongue out at his retreating back, knowing it's childish, but not caring. She won't let them undermine her trust in Colt. Not when she has every intention of proving her father and Moroni wrong.

Colt can be trusted. They'll see.

17

COLT

olt enters the precinct, a two-story building on Eleventh Street, not far from the Mercy City shopping district. A squat, concrete building, its only aesthetic is that is overlooks a large lake. A proportion of lucky detectives would have an office with a view.

He pauses inside, noting the business of the foyer. Beyond the front desk is a glass wall, revealing cubicles created by low dividers, messy desks at each one. Uniformed and plain clothed officers mill around, a few carrying cups of black coffee. To his left sit a couple on hard plastic chairs that are bolted to the ground, looking pale. Possibly witnesses to the latest attack by the cult.

Colt walks up to the front desk, tension making his muscles feel like taut rubber bands. When he framed Leopold for the murders the Grigori had committed, he hadn't known the cult members would resort to violence, let alone use of hellfires to torment the city. And now they had attacked the parking lot beside City Hall. Their violence wasn't stopping.

The officer behind the desk eyes Colt up and down as he

approaches, probably trying to figure out on which side of the law he spends most of his time. "Can I help you?"

"I'd like to speak to Detective Riley Espinosa, please."

"Sorry, she's busy," says the officer, seeming to decide that Colt isn't the most savory of characters. Colt admires him for his astuteness.

He shrugs. "I'll wait, then."

Without waiting for an answer, he takes the seat furthest away from the couple. Now isn't the time to use his demon magic to get what he wants. Too many people are watching his every move. He sighs as he wipes his hand down his face. Or maybe he just wants to prove to Gabby that her trust isn't misplaced.

Even though it is.

Turns out, he doesn't have to wait long, which is a relief. Dwelling on problems that have no immediate solutions is unpleasant. Riley steps through the glass doors, her eyebrows raised. "Colt, what are you doing here?"

He stands. "I'd like to have a word, if that's okay."

She studies him, then nods. "Sure. I'll see if there's a room empty."

Colt follows as she steps back through the glass doors. Riley weaves her way through the desks piled with files and empty coffee cups. "Sorry," she says over her shoulder. "We'll probably have to use one of the interrogation rooms."

Colt notes the handful of doors to their right and he wonders which one the cult member is in. It's him he really wants to talk to.

"The Eleventh Precinct hasn't got a lot of love with all the budget cuts in the past few years," explains Riley as she continues toward the first door. She pushes it open and waits for Colt to pass through. "Although that's about to change."

Colt takes in the small, square room. A table sits in the

middle with two metal-framed chairs, but apart from that, it's bare. The cramped cement room is downright suffocating. "Moving on from the bomb shelter decor?"

Riley snorts. "Hell yes. The mayor has made a significant funding promise. An upgrade for not just the building, but our technology and the creation of a cyber division."

Colt raises his brows. "That's very generous of her."

"A thank you for solving the ritualistic murders," says Riley, her gaze steady on him. "Putting Leopold behind bars put us firmly on the map. For which we have you to thank."

At least something good came of framing Leopold, thinks Colt. Discovering a cult that worshiped the devil had seemed like a good idea at the time. And yet, they were far darker than even he realized.

At least Riley's gratitude may be helpful as he tries to fix the complication. "I know you have a cult member here, Detective. I'd like a word with him."

She's already shaking her head before he's finished. "No can do, Colt, and you know that. You're not a cop."

"I only need ten minutes," says Colt, not willing to back down so easily. "I can make him talk."

Riley cocks a hip as she crosses her arms. "Really? What makes you think you've got something I don't?"

So she hasn't got the cult member to talk, yet. That works in Colt's favor. Riley wants answers as much as he does.

"I have certain...ways to persuade people," he says, his face hardening with determination. "And no red tape to hamper me."

Riley looks at him for long seconds, obviously weighing up her options, which he takes as a good sign. She didn't shut him down straight away again.

But then she shakes her head again. "I'm afraid it's against every rule and regulation."

Colt huffs out a frustrated breath as Riley makes her way to the door. She's about to open it when she stops. "Of course, if you managed to get into the interrogation room adjacent to this one without my knowledge, then that's out of my control."

With that, she exits, leaving Colt alone in the room. Knowing exactly where he's going next.

He counts to twenty, then peeks out the door. There's no one in the immediate vicinity, so he straightens and steps outside. Without looking at anyone, he steps to the next door, opens it, and enters it like he's supposed to be here.

Inside, the decor is identical to the room he just left, but there's one significant difference. A man with long hair and a well-kept beard is glaring at him.

Colt takes the seat across from him, taking his measure. The man's hands are cuffed to the table, his clothes rumpled but clean. He leans back a little, openly staring back. Anger ripples through Colt. This man is part of a cult that sacrifices innocent humans in order to please the devil.

And yet Lucifer has never liked sacrifices. Never wanted them.

This is about the human need for dark power.

The prisoner curls his lip. "Colt Grayson," he sneers. "The humans couldn't get anything out of me so they sent a filthy demon to do their bidding? Are you their dog now?"

So, the man knows of the supernatural. Colt angles his head, watching him even more closely. "You insult demons, and yet you claim to worship them."

"How little you know of our cult," spits the man.

"Then tell me," invites Colt, wondering exactly how much he's willing to spill.

"What you do know is that Leopold, our High Priest, had nothing to do with the murders you framed him for. Everything that's happened is your fault, Colt Grayson!"

"Then why target the mayor?"

The man leans forward, looking like he's enjoying this. "Samandriel wants her to pay."

Colt stills. Samandriel's behind the Satanic cults?

The prisoner guffaws, slapping the table. "Demons really are stupid. The cult were nothing but a harmless group of people worshiping nature in the woods. Wiccan, in fact. It was Samandriel who turned them into venerating Lucifer as their God, then had them making sacrifices so they get the energy necessary to perform a spell."

Colt leans forward. He'll figure out why this man is so forthcoming later. Right now, he's going to find out everything he can. "What spell?"

The prisoner smiles. "I'll tell you since I've nothing to hide, and because you won't be able to do anything about it," he says, as if reading Colt's mind. "Samandriel had a few angels possess these humans and made them make sacrifices so they had access to darker energy forms. They channeled this energy into performing a spell that's been keeping the Tear from closing."

Colt sits back, trying not to look as stunned as he feels.

The man smirks, enjoying being the one with all the information. "That's the reason demons and their weapons are pouring out of Hell. *We* are the reason. Very soon the spell will be complete and the Tear permanently open."

"Why are you doing this?" asks Colt, his mind going from shocked stillness to confused whirling.

The man's eyes blaze as if he has yet to get to the best part. "Demons pour out, more angels arrive, and then full-on chaos. Michael and Lucifer will finally settle their score." The man sucks in an excited breath through his smiling teeth. "Armageddon, that's what it's going to be. And we will then rule the earth because Michael will surely win the battle, like he did the last time round."

"We?" asks Colt, realizing there was indeed another revelation waiting to detonate. He leans forward, staring into the man's eyes.

And there it is.

White light glimmering deep in the blood-thirsty depths.

"Angel," breathes Colt. "Do you not care how many will die?"

"Humans have harmed the world Father created for them. They never appreciated the gift, nor do they deserve it," the angel spits. "Their faith in us has lessened as they've embraced Lucifer's free will. We can't let it happen." He slams his fist down on the table, making the chains clatter. "We will not!"

"You'll cause a war!" roars Colt, shock and fury whipping through him.

The angel simply chuckles. "You'd be surprised, Colt Grayson, to know how many angels and demons alike want war to come on this earth." He leans back, extending his hands apart as far the cuffs will let him. "Now it's time for me to ascend into Heaven. I'll return here once again as part of the armies that will come out of the Pearly Gates."

Colt leaps to his feet even though there's nothing he can do. The man tips his head back and white, shimmering smoke pours out of his mouth. It shoots for the small vent in the ceiling and the man slumps.

Colt steps around, checking the pulse on his wrist, as if he's hoping for a miracle. Nothing.

The prisoner is dead.

"Skata," mutters Colt.

He spins on his heel, knowing he needs to be as far from this dead body as possible, yanking open the door.

Riley is standing on the other side, her arms crossed over her chest. "I heard everything."

18

GABBY

There are three things Gabby keeps in mind as she glares at the man tied to the chair before her.

One, the angel Colt spoke to at the police station ascended before they could learn too much more.

Two, Detective Riley now knows of the paranormal because of that. These slimeballs will run, no matter what, leaving them to clean up the mess.

That means that, three, she needs to get this angel to talk.

Sitting in the bare, concrete room in the underground rooms below the academy, he yanks on the ropes holding him in place, blood trickling from his split lip. She almost feels sorry for him. Almost. But Colt told her what Samandriel's faction is planning—war. One that will be of epic proportions. No human will be safe.

Gabby leans forward. "If you don't talk, you'll start to think Moroni was the good cop," she growls. Fury at the threat these angels are creating, all in the name of power, infuriates her.

The man looks up, flicking his tongue to moisten his damaged lips. Spite and scorn have the silver flashing bright in his eyes. He yanks on the ropes again, even though he's been doing that for hours. He'd know the ropes were fashioned in the Pearl City. The faint iridescence pulsing from the strands is unmistakable, hinting at the celestial strength of the fibers. But the angle fights it, anyway. He wants her to know that if he was free, he'd take great satisfaction in trying to kill her.

"Where. Is. Samandriel," Gabby bites out.

She'll find that asswipe. Then she'll find the Grigori.

Not that she expects Samandriel to blab. He'll be like this guy, his very own minion. But Gabby's willing to do what it takes to make Samandriel talk. Just like this angel.

His jaw remains clenched tightly closed. He even raises his chin in disdain.

"I'll only ask nicely one more time," she warns, stepping closer. "Where is he?"

"We both know I have no intention of telling you," spits the angel. "Save yourself the breath and sore knuckles."

Gabby cracks her hand across his face, letting her fury power the strike. If anyone had asked her six months ago whether she had it in her to do this, she would've vehemently denied it. But she knows too much. Seen too much. Is terrified of what it could mean if Samandriel wins. What's more, her own angel within her is pissed. It's giving Gabby a taste of what every other angel is powered by.

Knowledge she has power.

The need to restore order.

And the willingness to wreak retribution on those who threaten it.

The angel sneers at her as another trickle of blood crawls down his chin. Resolve hardens within Gabby. She lifts her hand to hit him again, prepared to give him a taste of what she's really capable of, only to find someone gripping it.

She turns to find Moroni beside her. "I think we need to try a different angle."

Gabby frowns ferociously. "But I *really* want to be bad cop."

"We need him well enough to talk," he says, not letting go of her hand.

She drops it, the anger roaming through her veins like a caged predator. "Except he's not talking. And the moment he can, he'll exorcize himself just like all the others."

This scumbag isn't the first angel Moroni has caught. Two others have been in this room in the past two days. Both of them ascended before they could learn anything. They're no closer to knowing where Samandriel is, why he's making deals with some guy called Malcolm Hunsecker, or whether there are more hellfires out there.

Moroni smiles at that. "He's not going anywhere. I cast a spell to ensure exorcism isn't possible." He slides a satisfied look at the bound angel. "If he does try, it'll hurt like nothing he's ever experienced before."

That has the angel roaring in frustration. And hopefully a good dose of fear. "I will not talk!"

Moroni curls his lip at him. "There is more than one way to change your mind," he snarls, the expression on his face showing Gabby exactly how he became her father's lieutenant. She's never seen a face be so sharply carved from cold, hard determination.

He turns to Gabby. "You take a break. We have time to get the information we need."

She rolls her shoulders, grimacing at the tightness she finds. A break does sound good. And now that she's not going all full-angel on Samandriel's minion, the thought of beating him to a pulp isn't as tempting. Vacillating between her human and angelic parts can be exhausting some days.

Gabby pulls her cell phone out of her pocket and startles when she sees what time it is. She has training with Colt in five minutes! She's obviously spent longer down here than she realized. Without windows, it's easy to do.

"I'll go do a workout," she tells Moroni. "Then check in to see if he's caved yet."

Moroni nods, his icy glare settling on the prisoner again. "It's only a matter of time."

Jogging up the stairs to the ground floor, Gabby quickly makes her way out of the courtyard and to the gym. Her human side is definitely getting more and more excited. Ever since Colt resigned as an instructor at the academy and started one-on-one tuition, training in martial arts has elevated to a whole new level of awesomeness.

With all the darkness and uncertainty swirling around them, and some days feeling like it's closing in, it's probably the highlight of her week. It's not only fun, but physically challenging, giving all the pent-up tension an outlet.

She slows as she nears the doors, a female voice reaching her. As far as she knew, Colt didn't have anyone scheduled in the session before her.

"I want to learn how to fight."

Gabby's brow creases as she realizes the voice is familiar. She stops at the open door, recognizing Sabrina, the werewolf she met at the welcome party.

"I want to be Alpha someday," she says, looking up at Colt. "And to do that, I need to defeat Denzel."

"Why would you want to do that?" Colt asks. "Denzel has been the Alpha for some time now."

Sabrina's face tightens. "Because he killed my parents in cold blood." Her hands clench into fists. "He has no right to lead any pack."

Gabby enters, sympathy rushing through her. Sabrina looks up, not seeming to be disturbed by her appearance. "I will have my revenge."

Gabby stops beside her, taking in the tension vibrating through the young woman. It reminds her of the vengeance that has taken hold of Maya. "I'm so sorry to hear that, Sabrina."

Colt nods. "I can teach you to fight, but as with any powers, you must know when to use them just as much as how."

Sabrina's hands only tighten more. "Oh, I'll know when to use them, all right."

A tattoo on the inside of the young werewolf's wrist catches Gabby's attention. "Nice tat," she says with a smile, trying to lighten the mood.

Sabrina lifts her arm and turns it, revealing a septagram with three interconnected crosses in the center stamped on the inside of her wrist.

"Does it have a special meaning?" asks Colt, also seeming to want to change the subject.

"Nah," says Sabrina, dropping her arm. "I just saw it in some book in the library, liked it, and had it drawn."

"Cool," says Gabby, even though a trickle of unease is winding around her spine. Something about the image felt dark. Even evil.

"We can start tomorrow, if you like," Colt offers. "At this time."

"That would be great," beams Sabrina. "I appreciate it. See you then."

Sabrina leaves, throwing a quick smile over her shoulder. Gabby waits until she's gone before turning back to Colt. "How many of your clients are female?" she asks curiously.

Colt glances at her. "I've never compared."

Yet Gabby notices he didn't ask why. She sidles a little closer. "I'm just guessing that's where the demographic of most of your clientele come from."

"So they should. It's important for women to be able to defend themselves."

She's not sure if he's being deliberately obtuse or not, so Gabby takes another step, leaving only an inch between them. "If I were them, that's not why I'd be enrolling."

A flush creeps up her demon's cheeks, making Gabby smile. "Then I'm not interested in teaching them."

Colt's words warm her, as does the surety in his voice. What's more, he's not even trying to make her jealous. She pouts, still enjoying teasing him. "So I should cancel today's class? Because I'll be honest, the instructor is the main reason I'm here."

"I've learned the rules don't apply to you, Gabrielle," he says huskily. "Or to us."

This time, his words are a song through her veins. Gabby grins so hard it hurts. "I like hearing that," she purrs.

Right before she drops and tries to sweep him.

Colt leaps up and back, his chocolate eyes flashing with challenge as he raises his fists. Her own body coming alive, Gabby does the same. They come at each other simultaneously, punches flying and arms blocking. Their movements are fast. Sure. Perfectly synchronized even though they've never coordinated these steps.

Each strike, block, thrust, parry, is a product of trust. Of an instinctual awareness of the other's body. Of the desire to take part in this duel.

They move around each other, coming closer and breaking apart, the fight almost a dance. Although Gabby realizes pretty quickly this is one fight she doesn't want to win. In fact, she surrendered to Colt long ago. He has her heart.

It means their orbit toward each other is inevitable. Smiles flash instead of focused glances. Gabby giggles when she slips under Colt's arm when he strikes. She slips around him, her fingers brushing over the ridges of his back, before returning to the front. He chuckles when he pulls her to him, pretending to try and hook her ankle with one of his.

To Colt's surprise though, Gabby's legs give out. She falls back, clutching his shirt and bringing him with her. Colt moves fast, just like she knew he would. She doesn't try to break her fall, nor does she worry she's about to be crushed by this muscle-bound demon. Colt would never hurt her.

Just as she expected, he braces their fall with one hand while holding her with his other. Gabby lands on the mat, quickly entwining her arms around Colt's neck, just in case he doesn't realize this is exactly where he's supposed to be. But he doesn't pull away, instead slowly lowering the rest of his weight as he props himself on his elbows. "Gabby," he groans, as if he doesn't have the ability to fight this.

"Colt," she breathes right back, her pulse spiking as she finds their lips inches apart.

Sweet heavens, his body is so hot and heavy. It compresses her curves in the most delicious of ways. Gabby doesn't know if she wants to hold still for the rest of her life and just savor how this feels, or start moving and see what other delectable parts there are to rub.

Who's she kidding? There's no way she can have Colt so close and not move.

Her arms curve over his shoulders, loving the way the muscles tremble beneath her touch. His breath is hot and moist, his eyes darkening with each flutter of her out-of-control pulse. Just like their bodies can't fight the magnetism that brought them to this point, their mouths seek the others.

The sound of a throat clearing is like a dousing of ice water. Colt leaps to his feet, bringing Gabby with him. Even though he no longer works at Mercy Academy, they still shouldn't be melting into the training mats like that.

Gabby's aunt, Sierra, arches an amused brow. "Sorry. Did we interrupt something?"

Relief surges through Gabby as she registers Sierra and Blaise, who's standing beside her. "We were just training," she says, grinning.

Blaise snorts. "If that's how you plan on taking down angels and demons, we could have a problem."

Colt rubs the back of his head, one of the most human gestures Gabby's ever seen him do. "You were looking for Gabby?"

"Actually, we were wanting to talk to both of you," says Sierra. "But if this is a bad time..."

Gabby rolls her eyes. Poor Colt wouldn't be used to this kind of teasing. "It didn't stop you from coming in and interrupting, so you may as well tell us."

"It has to do with the parchments," Sierra says, falling serious again. "We think we've narrowed down the location of seven black stones the Grigori are seeking."

"You've solved the riddles from the parchments?" Gabby asks, excited. Although she could read them, all they got were lines of puzzling words that hurt her head when she tried to understand.

Blaise holds her hand up. "Only parts. But we think the stones might be in the Middle East."

"The Middle East?" Colt repeats, the shadow of a frown pulling down his eyebrows.

Gabby can't blame him. Although that narrows it down, the Middle East is still a large region. Who knows where the stones could be.

Sierra nods. "Yes, we don't know exactly, but we believe there's a symbol that may mark their locations." She rummages through her purse and pulls out a slip of paper, passing it to Gabby.

Gabby gasps as she registers the pentagram with the three interlinked crosses within. She looks up at Colt, seeing the same recognition on his face. "It's the same symbol as Sabrina's tattoo."

"Sabrina?" Blaise asks. "Who's Sabrina?"

"A werewolf," Colt answers. "She has this tattoo on her wrist. Claims she found it in a book and liked the design."

Gabby looks back down at the piece of paper. "And this symbol is related to the obsidian?"

Sierra nods. "Yes. It's the symbol for the obsidian. We believe it may also have clues to the locations of the seven pieces. We need to decipher it before the Grigori do."

"We're going to the Middle East for a short visit," adds Blaise. "To see what we can find."

"Just a short visit?" Colt asks.

"Yes, we have some Archivist business to address."

"Oh?" says Gabby. The commissions that come through are always interesting. "Some rich historian wants you to find the lost city of Atlantis?"

Blaise laughs. "Of course not. Only an Arthurian can find a way to Atlantis."

"But Atlantis is Greek," Gabby points out.

"Many folklores have Atlantis as a pivotal city in their mythologies," Blaise explains. "Mermaids, for example, are said to inhabit Atlantis, and they're folklore comes from around the world. Anyway," says Blaise, probably realizing she's off topic, "This commission is finding some ancient treasure on an island off the west coast. According to my client, an old Chinese seafarer left a treasure chest in one of the caves on that island."

Yep. Their job is a cool one.

"But the Middle East first," says Sierra. "We just wanted to let you know." She clasps Gabby in a quick hug. "We'll be in touch soon."

They say their goodbyes, but her aunt stops at the door. "You should probably finish your training," she says, the teasing glint in her eye returning.

She's gone before Gabby can say anything, but even if she did, it would've been a token response. It's actually nice not to have to sneak around for once and pretend there's nothing going on between her and Colt. Not when passion like that is always a hairbreadth from detonating.

Colt sighs. "We need to learn whatever we can about this symbol."

Gabby nods, hiding her disappointment that their training session has been cut short. She's been hoping for a lead, and they just got one.

Colt walks over and picks up his training bag. He seems to hesitate for a second. "Maybe we should research back in my cottage?"

The realization he doesn't want their time to be over, either, has Gabby sashaying over to him. "I'll see you in an hour," she promises.

She can feel Colt's gaze on her the whole time she walks out. It makes her feel beautiful. Sexy. And far more powerful than any Grace ever has.

Gabby smiles as she practically skips toward the dorms. The obsidian, the Grigori, whatever else the universe wants to throw at them, will never stand a chance.

Not as long as they're up against the two of them.

19

GABBY

G abby's flash of euphoria fizzles out the moment she reaches her dorm room. Maya or Kalisha, or both of them, are possibly on the other side of the door. And they haven't spoken a word to her since the morning out on the lawn several days ago.

To say things are tense and uncomfortable in their room is an understatement.

But that's where Gabby's clothes are, along with the shower she needs to take before meeting with Colt. Deciding just the promise of time with him is enough for her to face the rejection of her two close friends is even more evidence of the strength their relationship gives her, she opens the door and steps in.

And is instantly relieved when she finds only Kalisha is here. She's sitting on her bed, papers scattered around her, frowning. She looks up at the sound of someone entering and the frown instantly deepens. What's more, she shrinks back a little.

Gabby hides her wince. "I'm just taking a quick shower and heading back out," she says quietly.

She keeps the shower quick, and even spends half the time she normally would on picking out an outfit. She decides on a denim miniskirt along with a white top with a scoop neckline. Gabby hesitates as she stands beside the communal dresser, scanning the makeup in her designated drawer. She knows Kalisha's is overflowing. In fact, she has a whole little suitcase for all the stuff that doesn't fit. She'd be able to give Gabby some tips on what makeup will have her looking amazeballs.

But Kalisha's scared of her. And she's probably terrified of Colt, so knowing Gabby wants to look her best for him is even worse. Giving her hair a quick brush, Gabby stops when she reaches the door. She looks back at Kalisha, but the girl who was once her friend doesn't look up. After several long seconds Gabby lets out a heavy sigh, hitches her satchel higher up her shoulder, and exits. As she makes her way through the corridors to the rear of the academy, the strained interaction only reinforces Gabby's determination to find Samandriel and end him. He's hurt too many people.

On the other side of the door, Gabby smoothes her hair one more time, even though the thick curls fully intend on doing what they want. Then, she walks down the corridor in long strides. She's going to arrive early at Colt's, but maybe she can help him throw some crisps in a bowl or something. Although she'll be lucky if his demon bachelor pad even has those.

Thinking of Colt allows her to push away the uncomfortable feelings that being around Kaisha sparked, and Gabby adjusts her shoulders as she leaves the academy building. Colt's cottage is only a few yards away, tucked beneath a large old oak, somehow feeling private even though it's so close.

She raises her arm to knock and her top slips off one shoulder. There's no time to adjust it because Colt answers almost immediately, and then his gaze is capturing her. Roaming over her face. Registering her exposed shoulder. And she has no desire to cover it up. She's too busy reveling in the heat that sparks in his earthy eyes.

"Sorry I'm early," she says with a smile. "Things are still tense in the dorm room."

Colt steps back and opens the door wider. "It's fine. I have everything ready."

Gabby enters, registering the plate of cheeses and crackers sitting on the coffee table. Right beside a rose in a small vase and two flickering candles. "Ooh, I like," she breathes.

Colt's gone to some effort, and in double-time considering she's here early. He's obviously looking forward to this as much as she is.

He smiles. "I wasn't sure which cheese you liked, so I bought several."

More than several, in fact. At least a dozen have been artfully arranged amongst an assortment of crackers, little bowls of olives and cute bunches of grapes.

Gabby enters and stops beside him. She presses her hand to his chest, noting the way his breath catches. She smiles up at him. "This is very thoughtful. Thank you."

"That smile makes it all worth it," he says quietly. Honestly.

So achingly tenderly.

How could she not fall for him, demon or no demon?

Colt's lashes flutter and he takes a small step backward. "I've collected what books I could find in the library to see if there's anything on the symbol in them," he says, indicating the stack beside the platter.

He shuts the door and Gabby enters the living room, reminding herself she's here to research and hopefully get some answers. Even if this is precious alone time with Colt, and he looks especially hot in snug jeans and well-fitting t-shirt...

She sits down on the couch and pulls a notebook out of her bag. "I've started journaling everything we've found so far." She grins. "Our task tonight is to fill as many pages as possible."

Colt's lips edge upward. "I do like a challenge."

Gabby shuffles back as she makes herself comfortable. "You read while I write up what we have so far?"

Just as she finishes, her stomach rumbles and Colt arches a brow. He sits next to her on the cozy couch, his arm brushing hers as he reaches for the cheese platter. "Maybe we also eat."

Gabby nods, although as her eyes roam over the way his shirt sculpts his chest, she muses it's not food she's hungry for. She shakes her head, telling herself to focus. "What little we know of the Grigori—the angels who were tasked with protecting Eden and were then trapped in seven trees until my aunt accidentally released them—is all here," she says, flipping through the pages full of handwritten notes. "The same with the obsidian. A dark energy that was trapped in a stone that was divided into seven pieces."

"Very thorough." Colt reaches over and slices off a piece of a pale, firm cheese and places it on a cracker. "Here, try this. It's called Vacherin, from Switzerland."

Gabby takes it and pops it in her mouth. One crunch and she rolls her eyes in delight, realizing maybe she needs more than just Colt to survive. "Delicious!" Her stomach rumbles again in agreement.

Colt grins. "That's two votes for the Vacherin."

Gabby beams then quickly scrawls a few lines as she chews. "I've just made a note that Aunt Sierra and Blaise believe the seven pieces may be in the Middle East."

He grunts. "And they're hoping the symbol may lead them to it." He reaches over and places a piece of already sliced mellow colored cheese. "Manchego," he says, passing it to her. "Spain."

Gabby takes a bite. "Mm, they do know how to make good cheese in Spain," she says appreciatively.

This time, Colt's gaze drops to her lips, heat kindling in its earthy depths.

She swallows, already forgetting the taste of whatever it is she just ate. Gabby clears her throat. "So we have the Grigori, super evil and at large. A dark stone waiting to wreak death and destruction. Then Samandriel, elusive psycho angel. And now Malcolm, unknown-but-probably dangerous dude."

It's Colt's turn to clear his throat. "I keep wondering if they're all linked, somehow. Or are we dealing with a battle on multiple fronts."

She taps the end of her pen against her bottom lip, conscious of the way it draws Colt's gaze back there. "All the more reason to take Samandriel out. It'll either be the domino that topples the others, or mean one less fight coming our way."

Colt yanks his gaze away, frowning a little as he reaches for more cheese. "Feta," he says, holding it out. "From Greece."

Something strikes Gabby as he mentions yet another location. "Did you actually go to any of these countries?"

He shrugs. "The supermarket had most of the ones I was seeking, but not all." His mouth twists. "Feta isn't the same unless it's from Greece."

Gabby blinks. Seems her boyfriend is a cheese snob. But not only that, he's gone to far more effort than she realized. The realization takes her breath away. It has her sliding her journal to the side, forgotten. She leans forward, coming onto her knees as she opens her mouth and encloses it around the feta and Colt's fingers.

He stills. His own mouth parts as he inhales sharply. His skin flushes.

Feeling every part the seductress and loving it, Gabby sucks, relishing the salty cheese and warm flesh. She flicks her tongue over his thumb, restless desire pooling in her stomach.

"Gabby," groans Colt.

It's all the invitation she needs. She practically pounces over the short distance between them, straddling his hips as her mouth crashes down on his. Colt meets her, his own lips hot and demanding. They kiss hungrily, flaming the inferno that's exploded between them.

Gabby scoots closer, needing to feel as much of her pressed against him as possible. Colt's hands spear up her back, moving up and down, left and right, as if he's determined to mold every inch of her to him. And then his hands are beneath her shirt, scorching and searing as they roam her bare skin. She groans, willingly losing herself to the sultry sensations their contact is creating.

With an impatient mutter she tugs at his shirt. She wants more skin. More contact. More Colt.

But he pulls back, panting. "We need to stop."

At first, she's not sure she heard him right. Stop had left her vocabulary. But his hands slide down, coming to rest on her hips. "What?" she asks, trying to think past the haze of passion she was lost in. "Why?"

He doesn't answer straight away, which has Gabby leaning back, studying his face. "Why, Colt?"

Their feelings for each other are strong, and reciprocated. Plus, Colt's centuries old. She's sure he knows the mechanics of what comes next.

"We can't rush this, Gabby," he says on a huff.

"We're surrounded by those who want to stop us, i.e. kill us, and you think we shouldn't grab the moment with both hands?" she asks incredulously. He opens his mouth, but she continues. "And if you're going to try some 'I'm protecting your virtue' line, then I'll stop you right there. It's my virtue and I decide what I do with it."

Not going all the way with past boyfriends was a choice. Turns out, she was waiting for Colt. And what she was hoping might be this moment.

"Gabby..." His voice fades away, as if he doesn't know what to say. Or can't.

Gabby's back curls as she realizes that despite everything, something's still holding Colt back.

And she doesn't know what that is or why.

Before any of them can speak, there's a knock on his door. They still, but the knock comes again a few seconds later. Whoever it is, they're not going away. Colt frowns, obviously not expecting anyone. Gabby climbs off with a sigh and readjusts her skirt as he walks to the door.

She stands as she steps to the side to see who might be here, expecting to see Belphegor, maybe even her father. He would definitely want to put a stop to what's happening here. But it's neither of them. "Nim?" Gabby asks in surprise.

Blaise's partner rolls her wheelchair in with a smile. "Hey." She glances between Colt and Gabby, seeing they're both surprised. "I texted you to tell you I was coming."

A fire alarm could've sounded and Gabby doubts she would've heard it. "Sorry, I must've missed it."

"It's kinda urgent," Nim says apologetically, indicating toward a wooden box sitting in her lap. "There's something I need to show you."

Colt closes the door, following behind Nim as she wheels her way into the living room. He glances at Gabby, clearly clueless about what's going on.

"Sure thing," says Gabby. Seems Fate isn't keen on her and Colt spending too much time alone. Even when they escape to his place. Gabby sits back down on the couch. "How did you find me?" She's not in her dorm room, which is where Nim would've looked for her.

"I was just heading to your dorm when..." She grins. "When the spirits sensed an, ah, energy surge and directed me here."

That's one way to describe it. Gabby resists the need to

glance at Colt. Nim didn't actually interrupt anything, in the end. It seems there's more than just their physical connection that's unresolved between them.

Nim lifts the lid off the box. "I've been actively searching for this for a long time. There are very few in existence."

Gabby shuffles so she's sitting on the edge of the couch, now curious. Colt sits beside her, looking cautious.

Nim reaches in and pulls out what looks exactly what she'd expect a crystal ball to look like.

"Each person can only use it once in their lifetime," she says reverently. "I was going to use it to try and scry what's coming, but the spirits spoke to me. They want you to see, Gabby."

"Me?" asks Gabby, wondering when the spirits started thinking so highly of her.

"Your destiny is foretold by the prophecy," Nim says simply.

Gabby glances at Colt, knowing the same words are whispering through his mind.

The seventh daughter of an archangel shall be the Grigori's doom.

No pressure, huh?

Nim extends the crystal ball. "The spirits want you to see this."

Gabby takes it, even though she's not sure whether she wants to. The ball is heavy and cool, the clear crystal almost translucent. Nim wheels closer, placing her own hands besides Gabby's. Instantly, a white mist unfurls in the center. Gabby peers closer, wondering what she'll see in there.

Suddenly, she finds herself surrounded by darkness. Before her is a stone table, seven pieces of black gem sitting on it in a circle.

The obsidian!

The seven pieces fly into the center and fuse together, black energy detonating outward. Gabby runs toward it, instinctively trying to stop whatever's coming, but the scene changes.

She stops, finding herself standing in the center of a large hall, seven doorways surrounding her. They soar higher than any door she's ever seen, the stone carved with ancient symbols. Seven white figures appear, each standing sentinel in front of each door. Before Gabby can try to understand what she's seeing, seven wisps of smoke, each a different color, spear down and divide, each one wrapping around one of the figures. The tendrils contract around their throats, cutting off the screams that had just erupted. Behind them, cracks fracture through the stone monoliths.

"No!"

But the scene changes again. She's in a bedroom she doesn't recognize, a manicured garden visible from the window. But it's the pale girl lying on the bed that has Gabby's attention. There's a man standing over her, full of dark magic, chanting in a language she's never heard. Gabby takes a step forward, realizing there's something familiar about the girl. She just needs to get a better look—

She gasps when she finds herself floating on a rainbow, blue sky her new backdrop. She glances up, seeing two mammoth gates shining like pearly arches. Behind them is a pillar shaped like a fractured shard. Looking down, Gabby sees a city, and another shard, this one of stone, sits in the center like a monument. Even deeper still she sees a crimson doorway, and beyond it is another pillar, this one made of molten lava.

Confused, Gabby looks between the three, clueless as to what she's looking at. Except the spirits don't give her a chance to understand, because with the next blink, she's standing in front of a large stone. Within it is impaled a majestic sword.

Excalibur? But what—

White mist billows around her and when it dissipates,

Gabby's once more somewhere else. In an instant, she recognizes it as Hell. Nowhere else could be as desolate. There's a cage in front of her, rocking and rattling. Gabby takes a step back, somehow knowing what will happen next.

The gates of the cage fly open with such force that they're flung into the air, disappearing into the ether around her. The ground beneath her feet rumbles as if something just irrevocably changed. A white figure appears in the opening, blazing so bright Gabby covers her face with her arm.

When she lowers it, she discovers she's surrounded by people. A woman is a few feet away, holding a wooden stake in her hand. A tall monster-like creature with blood-filled eyes stands across from her, a crown on his head. It's clear they're about to fight.

Gabby wants to leap in and help, knowing the woman is facing a deadly opponent. Something about it isn't alive. But of course, she doesn't get to move. The scene fades and Gabby finds herself back in Colt's living room. She yanks her hands back from the crystal ball, blinking.

What the hell did she just see?

"There were seven visions," she whispers. "I don't know what any of them mean."

"You will when the time comes," Nim says with conviction. "There's a reason the spirits wanted you to see what you just did."

Colt leans forward, a hand reaching up to gently knead Gabby's shoulder. "What did you see?"

She swallows, knowing she's going to have to try and explain the strange scenes she just witnessed, although she's glad she saw them. "We need to be prepared. Some pretty scary shit is coming our way."

20

COLT

C olt strolls through the grounds of the academy, enjoying the cloak of night. Gabby had looked exhausted after recounting her visions, so once Nim had left, he'd walked her back to the dorms. She needs sleep.

And he needs to think.

He hadn't expected their passion to be a force to be reckoned with. He knew it was consuming. But tonight, it almost combusted every intention he had of taking it slow with Gabby. The deeper their relationship develops, the more complicated this becomes. Especially when he doesn't have a solution for the debt he owes Belphegor.

Colt winds his way down the driveway and toward the gates. The two security guards are tucked in their little office off to the left, a cigarette glowing red in one of the men's hands. All Colt can hear is crickets chirping. Not even a breeze disturbs the dark scene. Beyond the gates is the road leading to Mercy City. All that separates it and the academy is a small woodland.

And it's that woodland that Colt likes to cast an eye over each night. He leans against a tree, his demon sight scanning between trunks, through the underbrush, and even scouring the canopy, looking for any sign of demons or angels. Even though Belphegor created a ward around the academy after the attack from Samandriel's angels, ensuring only those with an invite from entering, Colt still feels restless. Samandriel is crafty.

And he could turn up at any moment.

The crunching of gravel behind him has Colt spinning around, two lines of fire running down his back as his wings prepare to unfurl. But it's not Samandriel. It's not even a super-natural.

Maya crosses her arms, her gaze flashing. "Planning another murder?"

Colt resists the urge to cross his own arms. This girl is getting annoying. It's clear her grief means she's unwilling to entertain any other explanation for her family's death apart from him killing them in cold blood. "It's past curfew, Maya. You need to return to your room."

"You don't work here anymore," she spits. "Although I'd never follow instructions from a demon."

Remembering that Maya now knows his true nature after Samandriel kidnapped them—obviously ignoring any part he had in saving her—Colt wonders if maybe now she'll listen to the truth. He didn't kill her aunt and uncle or any of the others, the Grigori did. Maybe learning of the supernatural now means Maya will be open to listening to what really happened.

"I tried to save them, Maya. Both Gabby and I did. But we were too late, and for that I'm sorry."

But Maya only scowls deeper. "And then you framed an innocent life."

"Leopold was far from innocent," he growls, wondering why he even bothered.

"Stop lying," cries Maya. "He led a Wiccan community, nothing more." She steps closer, conviction blazing from her face. "I know you're hiding something, Colt Grayson. Samandriel told me. And the moment I find out, everyone will know. Everyone."

The emphasis on the last word tells Colt exactly who she means. Gabby.

Maya spins around and stalks away, and he bites back a curse. And then another. In fact, there aren't enough languages for the frustration needing an outlet.

What does Samandriel know?

And what has he told the human girl festering with the need for vengeance...

COLT SPENDS the following day buried within the pages of any book he can get his hands on, only to find no mention of the obsidian symbol. It doesn't help the frustration that is now his constant companion. It's progressively feeling like the ceiling and walls are pressing in on him. Like maybe even Fate and Time themselves are on a collision course, with him as their target.

It means when it's time for Sabrina's training session, he's looking forward to working off some tension. Maybe he'll go for a run afterward, too.

Sabrina's already waiting for him outside the gym, leaning against the wall, staring at the floor as if it's personally insulted her. Colt wonders for a moment why she's so determined to overthrow Denzel, even if that means a fight to the death. Although he doesn't involve himself with the business of werewolves, or any other supernatural until Gabby came into his life, he's still curious. From what he's heard, Denzel is a strong, fair Alpha. He looks after his wolves.

But Sabrina obviously believes Denzel killed her parents, and she's here to learn to fight because of it.

"Hello," he says as he draws closer.

She startles enough that she almost drops her phone, and Colt instantly knows that's unusual. It's almost impossible to sneak up on a werewolf, their hearing is exceptional. Some of the best in the supernatural world. It seems her wolf needs training as much as she does.

"Oh, hey, Colt." Sabrina pushes away from the wall, adjusting her shoulders as if she's preparing for a fight rather than training. "I've been doing some reading on martial arts to give me a head start."

He nods but doesn't comment that martial arts cannot be learned through books. At least she's keen.

He leads her inside, placing his gym bag beside the wall and then walking toward the mats in the center. Sabrina follows, dropping into a stiff looking fighting stance the moment he turns to face her.

"Drop your shoulders," he says, and she instantly complies. "Legs shoulder width apart, keep your knees soft."

Sabrina nods, doing as she's told. "I was reading about a strike called the crane's beak. I've been practicing it." She molds her hands into the shape of a beak then her arm as if it's a swan's head, bouncing a little on her toes.

He wonders if she also read that the way of the crane is through stillness. Sabrina is far from still. Every cell in her body is wired and pulsing with energy.

Colt isn't sure whether to be amused or insulted on behalf of all kung fu masters. Instead, he mirrors her action, showing her what it should look like. "The beak is often used in circular movements to deflect an attack."

He snaps out a punch and Sabrina's arm swipes to block it a second too late. He pulls the punch in before it can make contact, indicating it's her turn. With her face set in hard lines, Sabrina attacks, strikes flying out with speed but little accuracy.

Colt blocks each and every one of them with smooth arcs of his own crane beak. "As you can see, the technique can also be used as a block." The moment her arms fly wide after an erratic strike, he moves in closer. "And even a counter-strike, aiming for any areas of vulnerability."

This time, he allows his hand to make contact just under her chin. Sabrina's teeth click and she yanks her head back, knocking herself off balance. He quickly grabs her by the shoulders. "Steady, there. If that was Denzel, you'd now be at a significant disadvantage."

Her eyes flash. "If Denzel had his hands on me, I'd do this."

She shoves her hand into Colts chest, and he releases her, a little impressed. Sabrina yanks her hand back, looking pleased with herself, and he sees a glimpse of the tattoo on her wrist just as he brushes his arm.

In an instant, pain flashes across his skin as if she just branded him. But not with heat. With ice.

Colt drops to his knees as the cold feels like it's freezing his veins, his breath echoing loudly through his confused mind. His body is somehow suffused with pain and strangely numb. It means he's unable to stop himself falling onto his side, his head thudding against the mat.

Blackness swallows him.

He finds himself standing before a stone table, seven pieces of onyx gem laid in a circle, each as black as the next. A figure approaches him and he instantly recognizes her.

"Gabby," he calls, both relieved and worried. Something is very wrong.

But she doesn't respond. She walks to the table and touches each of the seven stones. Her caress seems to bring them to life, because once she's finished, they arc to the center, fusing together into one.

The obsidian.

It pulses with a black aura, one he recognizes. It's the dark power of Hell.

"No, Gabby!"

But she can't hear him. She picks it up and places it atop a silver spear, one he's never seen before. Colt struggles against the icy paralysis, wanting to stop whatever's unfolding. The need to go to Gabby is overwhelming.

But he's helpless, bound by pain, forced to watch what he hopes will never come to pass.

Gabby's hair flies out as the power of the obsidian fuses with that of the spear. She slices it through the air, executing several graceful maneuvers. The spear moves as if it's one with her, each arc and slash elegant and deadly. She straightens, bringing the spear back to her side. Her eyes are an eggshell white, and yet a dark aura is wrapped around her like armor.

Waves of power pour off her.

Hands grip his shoulders. "Colt? Colt! Wake up!"

He blinks groggily, finding Sabrina looking at him, clearly concerned. Suddenly embarrassed that he's lying prone in a training session he's supposed to be running, Colt leaps to his feet. The room spins nauseatingly, but he grits his teeth.

"What the hell just happened?" Sabrina asks, sounding a little panicked.

"It was nothing."

"I'm pretty sure it was something. I hit you and you blacked out."

"I haven't eaten much today," he says, knowing how implausible this sounds. "And you obviously are still learning to control your wolf. That was quite a hit."

Sabrina looks down at her hands and then back up. "I did?"

"Yes." Colt raises his fists. "You need to learn control."

He leaps in with a quick strike, stopping it an inch before Sabrina's nose, then pulling back. She startles, then goes on the offensive with a scowl. As they spar, Colt ensures he never comes in contact with the tattoo.

The one connected to the obsidian.

The one that triggered the vision the moment he touched it.

Revealing to him exactly how far-reaching the power of the obsidian can be.

And that Gabby is destined to be a part of it.

21

GABBY

Gabby walks back from breakfast at the cafeteria, mulling over last night. She's not sure what was more unsettling, the visions, or the revelation that Colt has drawn a line when it comes to their relationship. When what she feels for him is so boundless, the thought disturbs her. A lot. Being sure about their relationship was the only certainty in all the madness going on right now.

And she doesn't even have that anymore.

A hand brushes her arm. "Everything okay, Gabby?"

She looks up at the unfamiliar voice and it takes a couple of seconds to place the friendly face smiling at her. Donald. The guy who ran the tour of the academy on orientation day. Also the guy who seemed to stare just a little too much for her liking.

He shifts his books from one hand to the other, angling his head. "Sorry, you just seem a little preoccupied."

Where the hell does she start? Even if she knew, she can't tell this guy who's looking at her with friendly curiosity, yet she's not sure if he's a bit of a creep. "Oh, you know, exams and all that," she says vaguely.

He nods, his face folding into lines of understanding. "It can be really overwhelming." To her surprise, he steps a little closer. "Especially if there are other...issues happening in your life."

Gabby smiles politely, adjusting her center of gravity to reinstate the distance between them. "Oh, there's nothing like that going on."

"Sure thing," he says easily. "That's good to hear, because if there's any relationship stuff going on, that can really make concentrating hard."

Her smile freezes. What does Donald know? Have his overly-long stares noticed what's happening between her and Colt? "Or maybe it's just the sheer amount of information I have to memorize. Did you know that the history of theater goes back as far as ancient Greece?"

"If you were having a few reservations," Donald continues as if they're actually having this conversation, "then just remember, learning to trust your heart is the key."

"Even if they're keeping secrets?" Gabby finds herself asking before she can stop herself.

"Isn't that what trust is all about?" asks Donald with a kind smile. "Believing in the other person, against the odds? Even when it's hard?"

Before Gabby can answer, he pulls out his phone—the one that's not ringing or vibrating—and taps the blank screen. "Sorry, I have to take this."

He strides away, leaving her a little open-mouthed. What was that all about? And since when did Donald start dispensing relationship advice, especially when it wasn't asked for?

Still, as she begins walking again, his words echo through her mind.

Learning to trust your heart is key.

Somehow, hearing that just melted away her concerns. She

does need to trust Colt. He went to Greece to get her feta, for crap's sake! If that's not commitment, she doesn't know what is.

Feeling buoyed once more, Gabby enters her room. She's just closing the door when she discovers Maya and Kalisha are both here, huddled on Maya's bed and deep in discussion. A discussion that stopped the moment Gabby entered.

Maya shoots to her feet, glaring at Gabby as if she'd deliberately interrupted them. With a huff, she storms past and out the door, closing it with a sharp thud. Gabby finds herself sighing again. What else can she do to tell Maya she's sorry? That she never wanted to hurt her or Kalisha.

Kalisha sniffs then daintily wipes at her eyes with a tissue, her artful makeup looking none the worse for wear even though it's clear she's been crying.

Gabby takes a tentative step forward. "Is everything okay?"

Kalisha looks away, her lips pressing into a firm line. Gabby contains another sigh. This is getting frustrating, but she also doesn't want to scare Kalisha any more than she already is. Deciding to get her books and go hang out in the library, she makes her way to her desk.

"I broke up with Guy," says Kalisha in a small voice.

Gabby's heart does a triple backflip—Kalisha just spoke to her!—but she turns around casually. "Ah, who's Guy?"

Kalisha sniffs. "No one, it turns out. I met him a few days ago but he..." She trails off, staring at her tissue.

"Joined the Douche Brigade?" asks Gabby, lowering herself into a chair. She wants to go and wrap an arm around her friend, but she remembers how scared Kalisha was of her.

Kalisha looks up, her dark eyes twinkling. "He most certainly has. He was all over me but when I told him first week, first base, the dick ghosted me."

"His loss," says Gabby tartly. "Second base with you would've blown his mind."

A wave of pleasure washes through her when Kalisha bursts into giggles. She sighs as the laughter dies. "We missed you, you know." She bites her lip. "But we were scared of you. Well, I was. And angry because you hid the truth from us. I don't know if Maya can bring herself to forgive you for that."

"I know," Gabby says with a sigh, wondering how many she's going to utter. "I don't know how I can fix that."

"She's convinced Colt, and you by extension, had something to do with the murders of her aunt and uncle. Even after we learned the truth about what you are."

"I'm so sorry you were kidnapped by that lunatic of an angel," says Gabby. "You were never meant to get involved."

"I don't think it could've been avoided, to be honest." Gabby glances at Kalisha, wondering what she means by that. "Maya already knew Samandriel."

"She what?"

"When we were kidnapped, it was clear Maya and Samandriel not only knew each other, but had some kind of...relationship. She told me that all of this was just a ruse because Samandriel wanted her to learn the truth of what you and Colt really are. Maya's feelings only worsened after that."

Shock has left Gabby immobile. Samandriel had been speaking to Maya? That bastard had been exploiting her vulnerabilities and feeding her lies! The shock is quickly melted away by anger. No, fury. The asshat's manipulations are becoming too much. Stopping him just became her one and only goal.

And to do that, she needs to find him.

"You said they became friends?" she asks Kalisha.

"Yeah, at first I thought it was more than that, but I think they were more like partners in crime."

But they had a connection. Maybe one Gabby could exploit.

Looking around, she notices a stack of freshly laundered clothes. On top sits a handkerchief. Maya's the only person their age she knows who uses them, but right now, she's glad. She picks it up, rubbing the soft cotton between her fingertips as she thinks.

"What are you going to do?" Kalisha asks, her hands clutched in her lap. A wisp of the fear Gabby saw flickers across her face. No doubt she's remembering how deadly and dangerous Gabby can be.

And yet, Gabby can't hide from that. Not anymore. "I want to find Samandriel and end him," she says simply.

Kalisha's back to chewing her lip. "You know..." Her thumbs rub over her hands and she clears her throat. "When I learned you're an angel, it terrified me. I'm still pretty scared, to be honest. But I decided I needed to know what I was up against. I started doing some research into that Leopold guy."

"What kind of research?" Gabby asks, frowning.

"At first it was all about the Wiccan cult he led. Maya encouraged it, even taking me to one of their sessions. The whole thing weirded me out, though. They had these weirdass weapons, shaped like a reaper's scythe, with strange runes on them that sometimes freaking glowed. I could feel the power they exuded." Kalisha rubs her upper arms as if she just got goosebumps, and this time, Gabby goes to her, pressing a reassuring hand to her shoulder. "There were photos in one of the rooms of dead men."

"Wow, that sounds intense." And probably dangerous.

Kalisha nods. "It got me thinking. Maybe Leopold getting arrested was a good thing. And maybe Maya was wrong. She was hurting so much from the loss of her aunt and uncle that she just wasn't being objective about anything. She wanted someone to blame."

"Wow, Kal," says Gabby. "I don't think you should go there again. Not alone, anyway."

Kalisha glances at her. "But I could show you where it is."

Gabby acts before thinking. She throws her arms around Kalisha, hugging her tightly. Her friend freezes for a second, and she worries she's moved too fast. Gabby's about to pull back when Kalisha's arms wrap around her, too.

"I missed you," whispers Gabby.

"Me, too," says Kalisha, giving her a squeeze.

Gabby pulls back. "I say we go get some ice cream."

"For second breakfast? You're a genius!" says Kalisha, leaping to her feet. She sashays to the door, looking more animated than Gabby has seen since Samandriel forced her to reveal herself. Kalisha turns around, her hand on the door. "Your wings are pretty cool, by the way."

Gabby giggles. "The ultimate accessory."

Laughter bubbles up through Kalisha and they exit the room and Gabby finds her smile doesn't fade.

At least she has one of her friends back.

Gabby hurries to her secret cache, her taste buds are still in a happy state of torpor after gorging on a buttload of ice cream so early in the day. As she flicks on the light, she muses that it feels like a lifetime ago that she led her father, Sierra, Blaise, and Colt down here to show them what she learned about the Grigori. So much has happened since.

Including learning that Samandriel is working for them.

She pulls Maya's handkerchief out of her pocket, rubbing her thumb over the monogrammed initials. It's time to find the crazy-assed prick.

Picking up a piece of chalk from the table, she squats down in the center of the room and draws a large pentagram, then drops the handkerchief in the center. Next, she sits five candles at each point. A quick flick of her fingers and they come alive with small, golden flames. Sitting at the base of the symbol, Gabby crosses her legs and closes her eyes.

"I'm coming for you, Samandriel," she murmurs.

Pulling up an image of the handkerchief, Gabby then imagines Maya holding it. Although their friendship is so fractured right now, she still has to believe their connection is strong. No matter what's happened, they'd forged a strong bond.

Once Maya's alive in her mind, Gabby dives deeper, searching for any traces an angel would leave on the human psyche. Her father had told her that whenever an angel visited a human, they cast an illusion spell to prevent the human from seeing the angel's true form. This spell would leave deep imprints on the human psyche. Samandriel would have surely done the same.

She searches for Samandriel's signature, the whisper his magic would've left behind. And finds it. Drawing power on the connection Maya would have shared with him, Gabby begins to chant a spell, calling on the ancient language of Adamic.

Images flash as Gabby progressively peels back every layer of Samandriel's connection to Maya. Waves of power try to block her, but she manages to push through each of the barriers Samandriel has erected. Any normal locator spell wouldn't have been able to find him. But using Maya's memories and connection to him has created a back door. By the time the wards realize what's happening, it's too late.

Gabby's able to learn exactly where Samandriel is hiding.

She opens her eyes, her lips curling with satisfaction. In front of her, Maya's handkerchief is nothing more than ashes. One more thing to apologize for.

Once Gabby takes care of Samandriel.

Exiting the secret cache, she takes out her phone, deciding there are two people who are best accompanying her on this little visit. Two others who have a personal vendetta with Samandriel.

Colt.

And Moroni.

22

GABBY

Gabby stands outside the ranch, Colt on her right, Moroni on her left, ignoring the uneasy glares the two are sending each other. They'd both wanted to be here, even if it meant being in close proximity to their mortal enemy, so they need to deal with it.

They have a job to do.

The music pumping from the ranch is apparent even at this distance. Samandriel's throwing a party. Despite everything he's done, or probably *because* of everything he's done, he's having a good time. He fractured her friendship with Maya, possibly forever. He murdered an angel in the clubhouse and pinned them to the wall as an example. He stole the hellfires from Belphegor and gave them to a Satanic cult so they could terrorize innocent people. Oh, and he sided with the Grigori so he could help them find the obsidian. Samandriel is the king of the douche club. She's pretty sure he founded it.

"Seems he's celebrating," mutters Colt.

"Not for long," says Gabby, anger heating her blood. She shoots into the air, her wings exploding out, then spears for the ranch, Colt and Moroni quickly catching up. There will be no attempt at a surprise attack.

Samandriel is about to discover exactly how pissed she is.

Gabby smashes through the double front door, slams into the first angel she comes across, and powers him into the floor. The marble tiles crack and shards scatter. She brings her wings to the front and impales the tips of her feathers into his chest. He dissolves into a cloud of dust.

"Clones," she shouts.

Leaping up, she grabs the neck of the next one and throws him. He collides with the wall and bursts into another cloud of dust. Colt appears beside her, his own ebony wings extended as he plows through more clones. On the other side, Moroni is a blaze of movement, striking and kicking without mercy.

A flash has Gabby's attention and she turns to find another angel coming at her carrying a blade that ripples with light. She ducks as it slices toward her, narrowly missing her head. The angel sneers, seeming to believe she already has Gabby on the defensive. But rather than step back, Gabby leaps forward. She grabs the angel's hand and twists sharply. The blade drops to the ground and Gabby kicks the angel, making her stagger backward.

She picks up the weapon and slices it into the angel's chest. She screams and her Grace ejects from her mouth, angling to the nearest window where it disappears, no doubt off to Heaven. Seems not all the angels are clones.

A sharp pain pierces Gabby's back and she spins as she cries out. Another angel is glaring at her triumphantly, her blood staining the sword he's holding. Beyond him Gabby sees Colt, rage now hardening his features. But she doesn't need saving.

Not when she's this angry.

Gabby waves her free hand in a circular motion, channeling all the fury that's only growing with each minute. The blood on the edge of the sword bursts into golden fire. Hungry flames eat the steel, devouring it and then the hilt. The angel leaps backward, releasing the last remnants of the molten blade. But then he's running at her, releasing a battle cry.

Gabby slashes and swipes with her own blade, but the angel's fast. Really fast. He ducks and weaves, quickly regaining any distance between them. He even gets a punch or two in, his movements like lightning.

It means she never sees the kick coming. It powers into her chest and sends her flying. Her back collides with a wall, knocking every drop of breath from her body. Telling herself oxygen is overrated, she clambers to her feet, but she's not quick enough. The angel delivers a vicious uppercut to her chin, stunning her. Her head snaps back, hitting the wall again, and the blade drops from her numb hands.

The world spins for dangerous seconds. She sees Colt, running, everything about him far more terrifying than any avenging angel could be. But then she sees Samandriel up on the second floor, his hands on the banister as he watches, grinning triumphantly. He's relishing watching this.

Gabby stays on her feet through sheer force of will. She looks past the angel to Colt, trying to communicate to him she still doesn't need saving.

She has a maniacal grin to wipe off an angel's face.

Turning her attention back to her opponent, Gabby flinches as he throws another punch. She blocks it, even crying out for good measure, then turns and runs.

"Coward," screams the angel, chasing her.

Feeling a little like she's playing the terrified blond girl in a horror movie running from the big baddie, she darts up the stairs.

"The great fighter is on the run!" cackles Samandriel over

the grunts and shouts of the fight below him. "If only the great Gabriel could see her now!"

The angel chasing her laughs, too. "Stop and fight, girl!"

Two more angels meet her on the stairs, but Gabby grabs them and hurls their bodies at the angel behind her. He side-steps them, but it slows him down.

Below, Colt is fighting beside Moroni, stopping any angel who might try to come up the stairs. His show of trust touches her deeply, even amongst all this violence. All the more reason to trust him, back.

Gabby reaches the second floor and spins around to face her opponent.

"Realized there's nowhere to run, huh?" he snarls, beating his wings as he spears toward her.

"Something like that," says Gabby, lifting her hands palm out. A golden ball of flames hovers just above it.

The angel registers what she's holding, instantly trying to change directory as he attempts to flee the celestial fire, becoming the coward he accused her of. But it's too late. With a powerful swipe of her arm, Gabby hurls the fireball at him. It hits him between his shoulder blades, the flames instantly exploding out. Across his wings. Down his torso. Swallowing his screams.

His Grace hasn't finished pouring out before Gabby turns around, a hard smile spreading across her lips. Colt appears and together, they dispatch any other angels coming at them, working seamlessly together. Gabby ducks an angel and Colt slams a fist into his face as he's off balance. Colt kicks one and shoves another toward Gabby. She flicks out her own kick, sending the angel flying back down the stairs. He explodes into dust as he hits the bottom step. They flash a smile at each other, finding a brief moment of appreciation amongst the carnage. God, he looks hot. To her left, Gabby hears Moroni snort in disgust. He doesn't approve of their flawless chemistry.

Gabby turns back toward the second floor, scanning it with alert eyes and pleased at what she finds.

There are no more angels or clones between her and her target.

Samandriel realizes it at the same time she does. He pushes away from the banister at the other end of the second-floor landing, making a run for it.

"Like hell you are," growls Gabby. Two massive beats of her wings and she bowls into him, grabbing him by the neck and shoving him into the wall. Samandriel grunts, but pushes back, using his own wings to shove away. But Gabby was expecting it. She allows herself to be propelled backward, keeping her hands on his neck. The moment their momentum slows, she changes trajectory. All it takes is one beat of her wings this time and Samandriel spears into the ground. The floor gives way under the force and they crash through wood and plaster. There's a brief moment of free falling and then Samandriel lands on the marble tiles. The stone fractures like eggshell, cracks exploding out like lightning.

Samandriel groans, the billows of dust sticking to the blood trickling from his nose. Gabby hauls him up and props him against the nearby wall. "Where are the plates?" she demands.

He pushes her hands off him and she lets him, noting that Colt and Moroni are coming up behind her. Samandriel won't be going anywhere.

He wipes his hand across his face, the blood already drying up as his healing kicks in. "What stupid plates?"

"The ones you stole from me," says Moroni, stepping in closer.

"Oh, those plates," says Samandriel, his cockiness returning. He uses both hands to style his hair back into a point on his forehead. "You don't actually think I'm going to tell you, do you?"

Gabby takes an ominous step forward. She's had enough of this dirtbag. His reign of chaos is over. "Tell me where they are," she bites out.

Samandriel glares at her. "Or what? You'll kill me?" He taps his temple. "You need this too much."

Fury explodes like a volcano. Gabby grabs him and throws him across the room. Samandriel hits the opposite wall with a grunt and slides to the floor. She strides over but Colt reaches out before she can get to Samandriel.

"We need information from him," he says somberly.

She smiles, but the action feels cold. "I'm just giving him incentive to talk." She turns back to Samandriel. "It's up to him how long this takes."

The angel's lip curls as he staggers to his feet. "Stupid girl. No amount of torture will get me to talk."

Colt lifts his wings, casting dark shadows over the angel. "Tell her where the plates are or you'll also have the wrath of Hell to deal with."

Samandriel throws back his head, a dry cackle climbing up his throat. "Now things are actually sounding fun!"

Colt strikes him across the cheek with his onyx wing, snapping Samandriel's head to the side and sending blood splattering across the wall. "Tell her."

Samandriel turns back, his eyes hard and cold. "I can do this all day."

This time, Moroni crowds in. "So can we."

"You'll have to kill me first," he snarls back, spitting a globule of blood at their feet. Then, he smiles widely, exposing red-stained teeth.

Realization detonates through Gabby.

Samandriel's enjoying this. He likes the power his knowledge gives him.

And he has no intention of talking.

The understanding triggers another explosive mountain of fury. This demented angel needs to be stopped. She's going to make sure he never hurts anyone ever again.

Gabby extends her arms to the side, calling forth the fire inside her. A ball of golden fire explodes around her right hand. An emerald green one encases her left. There's a gasp from Moroni. Colt goes very still.

She just conjured both celestial fire and hellfire together.

Samandriel's eyes widen as the smile wipes from his face. He takes an involuntary step back and crashes into the wall. His fear shoots hot satisfaction through Gabby. He just learned he doesn't hold all the cards.

Bringing her hands close together, Gabby shoots out streams of green and gold, the dual flames hitting Samandriel in the center of his chest. He spasm, his arms thrown out wide as if he's just been crucified. A scream pours out his wide open mouth, high-pitched and agonized as green-gold flames devour him.

He falls onto all fours, looking up at her. "A great...power...is coming—"

Samandriel collapses, his body ashen and charred.

Wisps of white smoke escape his mouth but a quick glance around reveals a mason jar lying on its side a few feet away. Gabby extends her hand and the jar flies into it. She traps Samandriel's Grace and then conjures a lid, trapping it.

Turning around, she finds Moroni and Colt immobile. Moroni looks gobsmacked. Colt looks...thoughtful.

"Why did you do that?" Moroni demands. "He would've told us the location of the plates eventually."

Gabby shakes her head. "He had no intention of telling us."

Samandriel was looking forward to the torture, because each hour and day he kept his mouth shut, they would've been getting more and more frustrated. "We'll find the plates another way."

"Unless nobody knows where they are," snaps Moroni. "You just incinerated our one chance to learn how to end the Grigori for good."

"He was dying one way or the other," says Gabby, her voice hard. "And doing it now achieved something far more important."

"Which is?"

Gabby turns to Colt, sure she did the right thing, no matter what Moroni says. But will Colt think the same? Will he understand why she did this?

He regards her with steady, inscrutable eyes. "You sent the Grigori a message."

Damn straight she did.

Now they know what they're up against.

And that she's coming for them.

23

COLT

Colt watches as Moroni storms off angrily, his own mind reeling. Samandriel's dead.

It was an outcome he wanted. Was looking forward to it.

And yet he can't chase away the uneasiness that's crawling through his veins.

Witnessing Gabby kill the deranged angel, and her unwavering conviction that she did the right thing, reminds him far too much of his vision he witnessed when he touched the obsidian tattoo. Gabby just wielded both celestial and hell fires. She was pulsing with power, both dark and light.

Could the vision come true? Will Gabby ultimately wield both the power of good and evil?

Gabby huffs then takes his hand. "Come on, we need to get out of here."

Colt lets her lead him to his car, assuming they're heading back to the academy. They certainly need to be away from this ranch, in case more of Samandriel's angels, clone or not, arrive.

But when they reach the intersection that would take them

there, Gabby directs him to Mercy City. He looks at her in question.

"There's something we need to check out," she says. "Sooner rather than later."

Colt does as he's asked, wondering where they're heading. A quick glance at Gabby reveals her face scrunched in thought.

"Do you think I shouldn't have killed Samandriel?"

Colt knows that's a loaded question. All he can do is be honest with her. "I'll admit, I'm confused. Moroni's right. Samandriel held a lot of knowledge, and not just about the plates and the way to end the Grigori. We don't know what his connection to Malcom Hunsecker was or whether he knew the location of the demon caches that were stolen."

She clasps her hands in her lap, the same hands that have done what no supernatural has done—held the fires of Heaven and Hell. "He wasn't going to talk, Colt. I could sense it. And now the Grigori no longer have a gopher boy. They're far more likely to show their faceless faces."

He nods, seeing the truth in that. Without Samandriel, the Grigori are going to have to do their own dirty work.

"I need you to trust me on this," she says, watching him carefully.

Colt takes a corner as Gabby points left, suddenly focused on driving as if he's just learned how to do it...rather than being second nature because he's been driving since the invention of the car. Does he trust Gabby? He knows she trusts him, when she shouldn't. He knows she's more powerful than any being he's ever come across.

And he knows that they'll never be able to defeat everything they're up against without trust.

"I do," he says, feeling the truth of those words in his marrow.

He's trusted her with his heart. There is no greater faith than that.

Gabby lets out a breath as she leans back into the seat. "Good. Because I suspect there are a lot more tough choices coming up."

Colt resists the desire to reach over and clasp her hand, maybe even give it a squeeze. He wants nothing more than for Gabby to believe they're a united front. But in the same way he won't let them get any closer physically, he won't give her false promises.

It's the only way he can protect her from his demon nature and his debt to Belphegor.

Gabby directs them to the gates of a large woodland on the other side of the city. The afternoon light filters in between thick trunks, but doesn't get very far. Dappled shadows and darkened shades of green and brown are all that's visible after a few feet. Colt looks at Gabby as they climb out of his car, wondering what they're doing here.

"Kalisha and I spoke today," she says, leading him to the edge of the forest and flashing him a smile. "We've sorted things out. Then she told me she'd been researching the cult and even visited them. Just like the angel told you, the cult was originally Wiccan and purely about nature-worshiping. But then Samandriel infiltrated and had angels possess some of the leaders."

"And they became a cult that worshiped Lucifer."

"Exactly. And the ones responsible for the spell that's keeping the Tear open."

Colt drags his gaze away to study the trunks standing sentinel. Gabby hasn't mentioned the Tear up until now. "And Kalisha's information brought you here?" he asks, subtly adjusting the focus of the conversation.

"Yep. One of Samandriel's lairs might be in here."

That perks him up. "Do you think the plates might be here, too?"

Gabby shrugs. "There's only one way to find out."

"We'll have to be quick. Samandriel's death wouldn't have gone unnoticed by both angels and demons."

"Agreed. And although the dirtbag is kaput, I can still use his residual energy to track where the lair might be."

Gabby closes her eyes, her lips working as she chants a spell. The Grace she collected from Samandriel would also have forged a magical connection to him. Colt suspects she'll find it easy to trace Samandriel's movements through the forest.

Just as he expected, Gabby flashes him a smile and breaks into a run. He follows as they weave their way through the trees, her blonde curls flashing gold in the dying light. It's only a handful of minutes later that they're standing in front of a cave.

Gabby takes his hand. "Come on. Let's see what we can find."

The cave is a shallow one, and despite the gloom, the mess inside it is apparent. Colt creates a flame with his spare hand, molds it into a ball, then leaves it hanging in the air. It illuminates the disarray even further. And a quick rummage through the overturned furniture and smashed torches. Even a thorough scan of the cave walls doesn't reveal any hints of secret doors or hidden compartments.

"Shitsticks," mutters Gabby.

The owners either left in a hurry, or the place had been ransacked.. Colt presses his lips together, refraining from throwing out a few curses of his own. Even if there was something to be found here, they're too late.

As they turn to walk back through the woodland, Colt feels his phone vibrate in his pocket. He pulls it out and glances at the screen, suppressing a frown.

Belphegor wants to see him.

And it can only be about one thing.

Samandriel.

BELPHEGOR IS PACING HIS OFFICE, his square face set in deeply etched lines when Colt enters. He stands in the doorway, waiting to be acknowledged, pretending not to chafe at the need to wait.

The archdemon either senses that, or likes to remind Colt of his superiority in the demon hierarchy, because he paces for several more laps before speaking. "You've been busy, I hear."

Colt nods. "Not by choice."

Belphegor stops and pins him with a hard glare. "You're really inserting yourself amongst the angels, aren't you? First Gabby, now Moroni."

Colt doesn't ask how Belphegor knows. The archdemon has eyes and ears everywhere. "You want results, Belphegor. I'm doing what's necessary."

"Angels are our enemies," Belphegor snarls. "You seem to have forgotten we don't work with them unless absolutely necessary. You've spent too much time with humans, Colt. It's warped your mind." The archdemon stalks forward, the fires of Hell kindling in his eyes. "But I haven't forgotten that you asked a favor of me when you last fought the Grigori. You owe me."

Colt nods, acknowledging that the last part is true. He does owe Belphegor. The knowledge is never far from his mind.

"And speaking of that, what have you learned?" Belphegor resumes pacing. "How close is Gabby to closing the Tear?"

"No progress as far as I know. She's been focused on Samandriel."

That has Belphegor stopping again and spinning around to face Colt. "Whom she killed!" he snaps angrily. "How could you let that happen?"

"There was no warning," says Colt, omitting that Gabby used both celestial and hell fire to kill Samandriel. "She acted fast."

Colt is still trying to understand what that means.

Belphegor huffs. "Have you considered what will happen next? Your girlfriend has sent the Grigori a challenge. They'll be furious. Not only that, now they'll return! And those ancient angels are no friends to demons. This doesn't bode well for us." His jaw works for a few seconds. "And hadn't Samandriel's angels taken over that cult? The one that's connected to the stolen demon cache?"

"Yes, that is our understanding. They may be able to lead us to it."

Belphegor's eyes gleam as if another thought has struck him. For some reason, it makes Colt even more uneasy than he's already feeling. "The demon cache can wait. Those remaining cult members are far more useful to us in other ways. They're working a spell that keeps the Tear open?"

Colt nods, unhappy that the conversation has returned to the Tear again.

"As long as that spell exists, Gabby cannot close the Tear."

"That's true." Essentially, doing Colt's work for him.

"Which means that you, Colt Grayson, need to ensure that Gabby doesn't close it. Especially considering another shipment is coming in."

Colt's gaze sharpens. Another shipment of demonic weapons.

"I'll be sending a contingent of my own demons," Belphegor continues. "You will concentrate on finding the cult members and making sure they are free to work on the spell that will keep the Tear open. Keep Gabby away from them and make sure she doesn't get in the way."

And there it is. A direct order from Belphegor to undermine Gabby.

To betray her.

Colt nods, saying the only thing he can. "It will be done."

Belphegor flicks his fingers, signaling it's time for Colt to leave. He does exactly that, too relieved to be out of there to object to being treated like an annoying insect, and only stops once he's back inside his cottage.

He needs peace and quiet. Time to think. He has to find a loophole so he doesn't have to do this.

His phone rings before the thought is even finished. Colt picks it up, having to unlock his jaw to answer. "Yes?"

"Colt, it's Riley, Detective Espinosa. A contact of mine just reached out. Looks like the cult's going to target the mayor's rally that's going to be held in a few days."

He rubs his forehead, muttering under his breath. "Skata."

There will be no time to think. Even in death, the events that Samandriel had put in motion won't leave him alone.

24

GABBY

When Gabby opens her eyes the following morning, it feels like she's lifting weights. Her eyelids weigh a ton! The knowledge that although Samandriel's dead, there's still so much to do has her raising them in incremental winces. They hadn't found the demoniac cult, the demon weapons they stole, or anything that could point them in the right direction. The lair they found in the park turned out to be a dead end.

What now?

Gabby pushes her hair out of her face and stares at the ceiling. Maybe Colt and Moroni were right. Maybe she should've kept Samandriel alive. Had she let her anger get the better of her? Did her human emotions have her acting before thinking?

Yet, she told Colt the truth. Samandriel wasn't going to talk. She could sense it. And she wanted to send the Grigori a message. They can't hide forever, and this ensured it.

Which comes back to the issue of the cult. She may not be able to hunt them down, but she can definitely stop them from getting their hands on any more demon weapons. Colt told her they're the ones keeping the Tear open.

Their next job seems obvious. They need to close the Tear so they can't get their hands on any more deadly armaments.

Her decision made, even if she has no idea *how* she and Colt are going to do that, Gabby climbs down from her bunk. She notes that Kalisha's still asleep in the bed below, while Maya's already left, no doubt avoiding Gabby. Ignoring the sting that thought causes, Gabby slips into the bathroom. A quick shower and a hot pink miniskirt later, and she's feeling better. What's more, she has a new focus.

Find the Tear. Close it.

The cafeteria is pretty empty this early in the morning, but Gabby's fine with that. She grabs a muffin and is about to head back out, idly wondering if Colt might be up yet, when she sees Klae sitting at her usual table.

Gabby heads over, wondering if anyone makes the effort to talk to this girl. "Hey, Klae."

She looks up, her wide grin exposing the metal of her braces. "Gabby, I was just going to call you."

"You were," she asks, slipping into the seat across from her. "About what?"

"Just to let you know the script's coming along beautifully."

The one that has a whole bunch of parallels to the obsidian. "Oh?" asks Gabby, then takes a bite of her muffin.

"I found a new book in the library, actually. It really fleshed it out and now I'm all done!"

"That's great," Gabby says warmly. Klae's enthusiasm for her plays is always adorable to watch. "Did you say another book?"

"Yeah, I just returned it to the library yesterday. Lots of interesting stuff in there."

Gabby leans forward. "I'd love to read it. It'll help me get into character for the protagonist."

Klae beams. "Sure thing." She collects the papers she'd had spread out and stands. "I'll show you."

Gabby quickly wolfs down the rest of her muffin as she follows. The library has only just opened and is even more empty than the cafeteria. Klae leads her through the rows of shelves, obviously familiar with the layout. She walks confidently down an aisle, skims over a row of leather-bound spines, and pulls out a book.

"Here it is."

Gabby takes it, smiling. "Thanks, Klae, you really are the best."

The shorter girl ducks her head. "Anytime, Gabby. You know that."

She impulsively gives Klae a hug. "Thanks, I'm hoping this information can really help me."

Klae's bright red when Gabby pulls away. "Why do you think I chose this topic for my play?" She grins. "Apart from it making a great play."

"You're the best."

Klae leaves and Gabby sits at a nearby desk to read. She's only flipped a few pages when a symbol catches her attention. The pentagram with three crosses at its center. The symbol of the obsidian.

Gabby hunches over the book as she focuses on the typed words, blinking as she learns more about the story Klae's basing her script on. It outlines a secret faction that's been seeking the obsidian for centuries but has been unable to find it. Gabby wonders if this faction is significant, but as she flips through more and more pages, there's no more information on it. Although it's rumored to exist, no one knows much about it. Maybe it's nothing more than legend.

The two people who may be able to tell her are Sierra and Blaise. The archivists would be the only ones with information on this, but Gabby's aunt and her friend are in the Middle East. This is starting to feel suspiciously like another dud end.

Gabby's cell rings and she winces as she discovers she didn't put it on silent. She quickly picks up. "Hello?" she says in a hushed voice.

"Gabby, we're back."

"Sierra? I was just thinking about you!"

"Great timing then. I was hoping we could talk. We learned a few things in the Middle East that you should know."

Not quite believing her luck, Gabby agrees to meet Sierra at Veritas Library. Maybe this wasn't a dud end, after all!

VERITAS LIBRARY IS one of those places that take your breath away, no matter how many times a girl has been here. Stepping through the unobtrusive doors that look like they lead into an abandoned shop to anyone else, Gabby breathes in the scent of wood and enchantment. The expanse that stretches before her shouldn't fit in the physical space that's visible from the street behind her, but someone has done some serious Tardis magic. The ceiling soars high above, a floating chandelier sending down a soft glow on the rows and rows of bookshelves that seem to extend back in an optical illusion. To be honest, she shouldn't expect anything less from a library dedicated to the supernatural.

Gabby enters, absentmindedly running her fingers over a nearby shelf. Thick, leather-bound tomes sit on it, their spines level and orderly as only Nim, the head librarian here, likes them to be. Gabby's about to walk on to see if Sierra and Blaise are already here, when the book at the end catches her attention. Reaching into her bag, she pulls out the book she was reading at the academy library. Just as she suspected, they look extremely similar.

The same publishing logo sits at the bottom of both spines. What's more, so does the name of the author. *E. A. Latimer.* If the book Klae was reading contained information about the obsidian, Gabby wonders what kind of information this book would have. A quick flick reveals information on legends and folklore from all over the world...in great detail. Gabby's about to read more carefully when a familiar voice calls out to her.

Turning around, she sees Sierra and Blaise approaching her, both with their serious pants on.

"What did you find?" asks Gabby, unsure of what to expect.

"We didn't find any stones, but we did come across a couple of people with the obsidian tattoo," says Sierra, glancing at Blaise. "What's more, they were artifact hunting."

"What sort of artifacts?"

Blaise sighs. "I performed a mind meld on one." She shudders. "Such a dark and violent mind, too. For the most part, they pay others to find artifacts for them, then massacre the mercenaries. Although it's only one thing they're looking for, something that's deeply warded in their minds. I did learn they pray to a dark power, one they believe will bring chaos into the world."

If that's not the obsidian, Gabby will eat every book in Veritas. "Anything else?"

"The name of their faction was also deeply warded, but I did learn the name of their leader," says Blaise. "A man called Malcolm Hunsecker."

Gabby's spine stiffens with surprise. "Malcolm?"

Sierra frowns. "You know the name?"

"Yeah, we recently found out he's been stealing the demonic weapons coming out of the Tear. He also made a deal with

Samandriel for the stash of hellfires. Whatever this faction is, it's dangerous."

Blaise glances between the two of them. "I don't like that they now have demonic weapons in their possession."

Sierra's frown deepens even more. "And if this faction wants the obsidian, it's probably searching for the parchments, too."

"Maybe they tried allying with Samandriel?" Blaise suggests. "Although we thought Samandriel was working with the Grigori..."

Gabby's lips twist. "Who knows with that loony toon. He could've been playing both sides, for all we know."

Blaise's features pull down in a frown to match Sierra's. "This is most definitely getting dangerous. There's more than just the Grigori hunting the obsidian. And they have demonic weapons."

Determination cements in Gabby's veins. "We have to find a way to close the Tear." She made that promise when they defeated the Grigori. "We can't afford for this faction to get their hands on more demonic weapons."

"But how?" asks Sierra.

"Samandriel had angels possess cult members and they're using a spell to keep the Tear open," says Gabby. "All I have to do is put a stop to that spell."

Sierra and Blaise glance at each other, the furrows on their foreheads smoothing out a little. They can both see the merit in that plan.

Before Gabby can say anything else, her phone rings. She looks at the screen, registering Colt's name. "Hey," she says, stepping aside and ignoring the second glance Sierra and Blaise exchange, this one far more knowing.

"Hey, can you meet me?" Colt asks. "The cult has threatened to attack the mayor."

Gabby resists the urge to rub her forehead. She supposes at

least the cult is still rearing its ugly-assed head. "Sure thing. I'll be there shortly."

"Great, I'll text you the address."

Gabby hangs up and turns to the two women. "I gotta go. Looks like the cult's made its move."

25

COLT

Finding the cult members hadn't been easy. Once Colt had realized the cult members had a few witches among them and they were using strong warding spells, he'd had to dig deep. A part of him welcomed the challenge. Not only did he have to get past the wards, but he had to do it in a way that didn't alert the cult members that he had breached their protective spell.

Some serious demon magic had achieved it, though. And the moment Colt learned of their location, he'd reported it to Riley. The detective had immediately applied for a special task force. Colt hadn't been sure whether he should be surprised or not when the mayor granted it without hesitation. After all, it's the mayor herself who the cult seems to have their targets on.

Which is what's brought him to be standing at the edge of an estate only five miles from the academy, police officers in black uniforms and bulletproof vests milling around. Turns out the cult was holed up right under their noses.

The sound of a car in the distance has Colt walking further up the road and past all the black vehicles lined down the verge. His heart pumps double time as he sees it's Gabby. It goes to triple time as she climbs out. She's so lithe and graceful. So downright sexy. His mouth goes dry and his hands itch. But he stays where he is.

He has no right to touch Gabby in the way he wants. As if she's his.

She saunters up to him, stopping several inches closer than he would like. It always makes it hard to think. "Hey," she says, that breathy tone in her voice that always feels just for him.

"Hey," he says, his own voice gruffer than it should be. Why did he have to go and fall for an angel? Does Fate hate him?

Gabby glances over his shoulder at the mansion in the distance. "What's up?"

"We've found the location of the cult."

Her beaming smile steals what little breath he has left. "We can close the Tear."

The words are ice water down his spine. Fate does, indeed, hate him. "Hopefully."

"Is everything alright?" she asks, a faint furrow appearing across her brow.

Damn her perceptiveness. "It's fine."

"It's just that you're usually all 'thy will be done just because I said so.'"

Colt's saved from answering as Riley approaches them. "I wanted to talk to the two of you."

He turns to the detective, the motion creating a little distance between himself and Gabby. "Yes?"

"Now, I know you two can handle yourselves." She throws them an ironic glance. "But to this task force, you're just civilian consultants who helped us close in on the cult. You can't enter the mansion."

Colt feels Gabby bristle as he nods. "Of course, Riley. Whatever we can do to help this go smoothly."

Gabby crosses her arms, muttering something that very much sounds like a parroting of what he just said.

Riley looks at her strangely. "We also did a little digging. The house is owned by a guy called—"

"Samandriel?" Colt asks bitterly.

"No, Malcolm Hunsecker."

Gabby curses. "This cult really is tied to everything."

"What do you mean?" Riley asks, her gaze sharpening.

Gabby's lips press together and she looks like she's debating something.

"It's okay," Colt assures her. "You can speak freely in front of her."

Her brows shoot up and for some reason, she looks like she doesn't like hearing that. "The cult may be linked to a larger organization that's been searching for the obsidian for a very long time." She glances at Riley, who's nodding. Gabby turns back to Colt. "How much have you told her?"

"Enough for her to understand the dangers."

Gabby's eyes narrow, the movement barely perceptible. "You two got chummy fast, didn't you?"

Colt blinks, surprised by the turn in the conversation. "I thought I was supposed to protect humans?"

Riley leans in closer to him. "She's jealous, you fool."

Jealous? Jealous of what?

With a chuckle, Riley turns back to the tactical squad. "Just stay out of the way, okay?"

She makes a motion in the air for them to move out, and the convoy of vehicles roar away. Colt mulls over what Riley said as the dust settles, watching them disappear down a valley then reappear on the hill beyond it. Beside him, Gabby's arms are twisted tightly across her chest.

"Gabby..." He huffs a breath through his nose, struggling to find the words. She needs to understand. At the same time, he can't say too much. "I'm here because of you. I've spent centuries floating, never staying too long in any location. I had to, but I also didn't want to do anything else. Meeting you changed everything."

She gazes up at him from beneath her lashes, her blue eyes warm and captivating. "I've never felt anything like this, either."

They shift a little closer and their shoulders brush. Ahead, the convoy has reached the palatial mansion. The black-clad squad pours out of the cars and storms in, several dividing up and running around the back of the house.

Colt can't help himself as he takes a step closer, glancing over when he registers Gabby does the same thing at exactly the same time. They grin at each other.

"It's hard to stand back and watch," Gabby says.

He chuckles. "It most certainly is."

They both strain to use their supernatural hearing, but all he hears is a faint breeze and the call of a frightened bird as it flaps away from the mansion.

It's only a few minutes later that the first cult member is escorted out, her hands cuffed behind her back. She's pushed into the back of a black van and the door slammed shut.

Gabby clutches his hand. "They've got them."

It would appear so. They watch as two more cult members are led out, out with long dark hair and no shirt, another guy lurching and limping as if he may have put up a fight. Over the next twenty minutes, Colt counts five members being escorted into the black vans.

And then there's no more.

Gabby frowns. "Surely there's more than that."

"There must be," he says, wishing he could go down there and search the place himself.

Colt's cell rings and he answers it without glancing at the screen. "Yes?"

"Colt," says Riley. "We got five, but that's it."

"She has your number?" mutters Gabby.

"They could be hiding. There are likely all sorts of hidden rooms or spaces in that building," he says.

"Thanks Captain Obvious," says Riley, her eye roll apparent. "Even if we find a few more, my sense is we haven't got them all. There are lots of papers strewn around, though, so I'll get those brought into the station."

"I'll be there when I can."

He hangs up, pinning Gabby with a look. "I've never used the word 'hey' in my life. What does that tell you?"

Her frown dissolves as she beams at him. "That you're expanding your vocabulary for me."

"Not something that was a priority," he says wryly, considering how many languages he speaks. In fact, nothing was a priority apart from staying alive until Gabby came into his life.

Her lips twist ruefully. "The jealousy thing might not go away any time soon." She takes a step closer. "Unless you wanted to make things official, somehow?"

She's looking for reassurance. The one thing he can't give her.

Colt does the only thing he can, even though he shouldn't even do that. He steps forward, clasps her face, and kisses her. He shows her what he feels, even if he can't say it. The press of their lips, the dance of their mouths is hot and hungry. Yet tender and filled with longing.

A small moan filters up Gabby's throat and the sound sends hot shivers gliding over Colt's skin. He pulls back before any shred of common sense is burned away by their chemistry. He stares at her, wishing he could give her more, but this is all he has.

Not until he can make sure she's not collateral damage thanks to his binding agreement with Belphegor.

Gabby smiles softly. "If I wasn't so Colt-bedazzled, I'd think you're trying to distract me."

He chuckles, trying to make the sound as warm as he can. "If I were going to do that, I'd mention that it's obvious Malcolm now has control of the cult."

Gabby's brow puckers as she pulls back, his hands instantly missing the warmth of her skin. "I'd say you're right."

Hating himself a little, Colt nods. "It's a good thing the Grigori haven't taken your bait and returned to the city. We have enough to deal with right now."

She throws him a dry look. "Let's focus on the cult and their connection to the faction. We need to close the Tear before either of them gets their hands on more demonic weapons."

Colt nods, the mention of the Tear clenching his jaw so tight he wonders how his teeth don't crack.

Gabby taps her chin in thought. "And the cult has threatened the mayor," she says thoughtfully. A second later, her face lights up. "Can I borrow your cell?"

"Of course." Colt unlocks it and passes it to her, curious— and a little apprehensive—at the light that just appeared in this powerful yet unpredictable angel's eyes.

With a quick smile of thanks, Gabby taps on the screen then brings it to her ear. "Hi Riley, it's me Gabby. I have an idea. Our one link to the cult now is their threats toward the mayor. We need an insider there. I think it's time I started an internship."

Colt stills. Gabby wants to intern with the mayor? That's a downright dangerous idea!

"Yeah, I think it's a great idea, too," says Gabby. "Can you set something up?" Colt can hear Riley agreeing, then promising to get back to her. "Thanks. You're the best."

Gabby hangs up and holds the cell phone back out.

Colt takes it, trying to reign in his emotions. "You can't intern for the mayor. She's a target!"

"I know. That's exactly why it makes sense."

"I don't like this," he growls as he takes the phone, a part of him wanting to crush it in his hand like a can.

Gabby steps back in and places her hand on her chest. "We have to stop this, Colt. And I can take care of myself. I've proven that."

His teeth work against each other. "But—"

"No buts," she says, softening her words with a smile. "I'll be fine. We find the cult, we close the Tear, the faction gets no more demonic weapons. We have one less threat on our hands so we can deal with the Grigori." She presses a kiss to his chin and steps back. "Now, do you want a lift back to the academy?"

Colt's not sure his body is going to fold into a car without snapping, but he follows her regardless. He can't ask her to keep herself safe when he won't allow their relationship to progress beyond where it is now.

And she's right, she can take care of herself.

It's just that Colt's sole reason for existing now is to keep her safe.

He rubs his hand down his face. The cult. The faction. The Grigori.

His debt to Belphegor.

There are so many variables at work here, and yet he can't see what his next move is. If this was a chessboard, he'd be one step away from a checkmate

And he has no idea which direction the next threat will come from.

26

GABBY

It's evening as Gabby says goodbye to Colt at the academy doors, wishing she could kiss him one more time. It's in those moments that everything seems so sure. She can *feel* how real this is between her and Colt. It's in those moments that the uncertainty that Colt's in this as deep as she is doesn't exist.

She can trust that what they have is unbreakable. That it will be the foundation for her to deal with everything that keeps being thrown at them.

Sighing, she slips through the front doors, locking them behind her again with a wave of her hand. She's looking forward to a good night's sleep. Colt's determined to find the remaining cult members, suggesting she focus on her studies. As tempting as that sounds—memorizing a thousand facts feels far more achievable right now—she has other things on her mind.

While she waits to see whether she can score an internship with the mayor, she has to think about the Grigori. Killing Samandriel was about bringing them out of the shadows, except so far it hasn't worked. Does she up the ante or focus on the cult and the faction?

Gabby brushes her fingers over her lips. Would she be this confident without Colt? She's not so sure...

"Is it the physical attraction that's the problem?"

Gabby stops in her tracks as Maya morphs from the shadows of an alcove.

"Is that what has you so blinded?" she demands.

"Look, Maya, I don't see any point arguing about this anymore." Gabby goes to step around but Maya mirrors her, blocking her way.

"Because you don't want to hear what I have to say? Or because you feel guilty for framing Leopold?

"Leopold killed innocents," Gabby says, conscious that she's starting to lose patience with this. "But you won't believe me."

"No, you won't believe *me*!" says Maya, her eyes glowing with fierce conviction. "Because Colt has you wrapped around his little demon finger."

"I know you're still grieving, Maya, which is why I'm going to let this conversation go. But it has to stop. You obviously need someone to blame, but Colt isn't the bad guy here."

"Really?" Maya sneers. "If you'd overheard the conversation he had with the dean you wouldn't be saying that."

Gabby tenses. "You're spying on him?"

"What other choice do I have?" Maya snaps back. "You're so determined that he's got your back. And it's a good thing I did, too. Did you know that the dean, who's his boss by the way, has ordered Colt to sabotage your promise to close the Tear? Which makes sense, really. Of course demons would want the Tear to remain open. And Colt is a demon."

Gabby's stunned into silence. But before the lancing pain reaches her heart, she shakes her head. Maya believes Leopold is innocent. That he leads a harmless Wiccan cult. And she'd say anything to discredit Colt. What's more, she knows Gabby well enough to go for the jugular. Colt betraying Gabby would shred her.

"He wouldn't do that to me," she says through gritted teeth. "So take your lies somewhere else."

"Then you're even more of a lovestruck idiot than I suspected," Maya spits. She narrows her eyes and steps closer. "And I won't be there to pick up the pieces when you find out how wrong you are."

Maya looks Gabby up and down, disgust, no pity, twisting her features before she turns and stalks away. Gabby watches her leave, conscious that she's barely moving, as if doing so will break something.

Possibly the armor she rapidly threw up the moment Maya started flinging all those bitter words. Or is she worried her faith in Colt will be fractured?

Gabby shakes her head, refusing to think like that. When did Maya become so hateful? Has the loss of her adoptive parents twisted her that much? Or had Gabby missed the signs that Maya wasn't the sweet, nice girl she'd seemed to be?

She crosses her arms, frowning in the dark. Colt would never betray her. Not like that. He knows how important it is to close the Tear. He wants their relationship as much as she does.

Feeling a little more secure, Gabby heads to her dorm room, hoping she can get back and be asleep before Maya creeps in late like she has every other night. She's only taken two hurried steps when her phone vibrates in her pocket. She frowns a little when she sees the name on the screen.

Riley Espinosa.

"Hello?" says Gabby. If she wants to talk to Colt, Gabby's going to—

"Gabby, I have good news," says Riley, sounding far too

chirpy considering how late it is. "You start your internship at City Hall tomorrow."

"Wow. You work quick."

"It was easier than I thought. The mayor's happy to work closely with the police while all this is going on."

"Ah, thanks. I'll report first thing in the morning," says Gabby. They hang up and she stares at the screen.

The Grigori may have to wait.

Seems she's focusing on the cult and the Tear.

CITY HALL IS ALREADY busy when Gabby arrives there first thing in the morning. She tugs on the sides of her black pencil-line skirt, then adjusts the shoulders of her dark red knitted top. She has no idea what to expect from today, but at least she's dressed for it.

She enters the foyer, her low heels clacking on the marble floor as she surveys the place closely. There are guards at the front doors but also at the doors further in. Riley had sent Gabby an email stating that security had been ramped up here. While the mayor's popularity is the highest it's ever been after putting Leopold away and ending the ritualistic killings, a rally had been organized for a few days' time. It's suspected that's when the cult would strike. The mayor welcomed anyone who wants to be part of the fight against the dark forces that seemed to have targeted her specifically, which is why she agreed for Gabby to come on board.

Not for the first time, Gabby wonders if the cult have decided to focus on the mayor because she made a public show of locking Leopold up. Unless the cult was really connected to Malcolm and his secret faction. Or have the Grigori been pulling strings the whole time... She shakes her head, deciding not to get on that dizzying merry-go-round again.

A blonde woman walks up to Gabby, her hair in a neat chignon and wearing an equally neat pantsuit. "You must be Gabrielle?"

"Please, call me Gabby."

The woman nods efficiently. "I'm Elena Dober, Chief of Staff for Mayor Virginia Goodstone." She passes Gabby a thick envelope. "Inside you'll find your pass, a floor plan, the contract that outlines this is not a paid position, and the evacuation plan if there's an emergency. Please familiarize yourself with all the documentation.

Gabby takes it. "Sure, thing," she says, blinking at the way the information was just rapid-fired at her.

"Excellent." Elena flashes a half-second smile. "The Mayor is waiting for you in her office. Come, follow me."

She leads Gabby past the second set of guards and into a large ballroom. Never glancing right or left, or giving Gabby time to take in the grandeur of the place, Elena briskly walks up a curved flight of stairs on the opposite side of the room. Then she power walks down a wide corridor lined with photos of what's probably past mayors. It's not until she reaches a large set of double doors that she turns, checking that Gabby's still with her. When she confirms Gabby hasn't lagged or tripped or impacted the no-doubt three minutes Elena allocated to escorting her, she flashes another brief smile. "The mayor's office."

Gabby steps through, suppressing the small jolt when she hears Elena close the doors behind her. She finds herself in a large office, her cleaned-this-morning pumps edging a thick, oval rug. The room is well lit with pretty watercolors on the wall in ornate frames. A large desk stretches on the other side, the dark timber gleaming and heavy-looking. A woman stands from behind, her brown hair framing her face in stylish waves. She smiles, this time for longer than a blink. "Hello, you must be Gabrielle Heartley."

Gabby walks over to shake the mayor's extended hand. "Please, call me Gabby, Mayor Goodstone."

"If that's the case, you must call me Virginia."

Gabby finds herself smiling right back. Power and confidence envelop the Mayor—Virginia—which Gabby expected. The woman's been in this position for three years, and after a landslide win. But she hadn't expected the friendliness. A warm intelligence glitters in the imposing woman's eyes.

The determination to stop whoever has their sights on Virginia only hardens within Gabby.

The mayor sits, indicating for Gabby to do the same in one of the plush leather chairs on her side of the desk. "So, you're interested in an internship, Gabby."

"Yes. One of my majors is political science. I'd love to learn more." Which is actually the truth. The more Gabby's immersed in the machinations of everything that's happening, the more she's learning she has a knack for strategy.

"So it has nothing to do with your boyfriend putting Leopold behind bars?"

Gabby blinks. The mayor certainly knows what's going on in her city. "In part," she says carefully. "Now there are the green fires—"

"Hellfires, Gabby. Let's call them what they are."

This time Gabby blinks twice. How much did Virginia actually know?

Amusement dances in the mayor's eyes. "Green has always been the color of Hell, after all."

Gabby frowns, trying to process this unexpected turn in conversation.

"Not that most people know that," Virginia continues. "Hell

was actually green when it was first created, before it was... ah...corrupted."

"By Lucifer?" asks Gabby, now curious.

"Presumably so, although popular folklore often vilifies Lucifer as the Devil." Virginia waves a dismissive hand. "But folklore isn't the reason I brought this topic up. Hellfires have been seen on Earth. We can't afford to thin the line between the known and the unknown."

"So," Gabby clears her throat, "you know about the supernatural?"

Virginia's face hardens. "Ancient enemies walk the earth again. If this isn't handled efficiently and thoroughly, chaos and destruction are inevitable. My personal issue is the Tear being open all these years, letting out who knows how many demons."

"Yes, it's definitely an issue," says Gabby. She's conscious she's sounding a little flaky, but even though she didn't know what this interview would look like, discussing hellfires and the Tear was definitely not the 'this could happen' list.

The rest of Virginia's body hardens, and she now looks like a war-hardened general. "A way must be found to close it. We don't want more demons let into this world. Because demons bring angels. And they would rather battle it out. I won't have the humans become collateral damage in what would surely mark the beginnings of an apocalypse."

Gabby shuffles forward to the edge of her seat, deciding if Virginia's going to be so open with her, she owes her the same. "The cult means to attack you, Virginia. Your life is in danger."

A tense smile tightens Virginia's lips. "I know. Detective Espinosa has informed me. I also understand that's why you're here." She angles her head, her gaze turning assessing. "Although why she sent *you* to protect me, I have no idea. But I know Riley is a strong operator. You must be here for a reason."

"Yes, I am," says Gabby, her own thread of steel lacing through the words.

"Excellent," says the mayor, her entire demeanor softening. "While you're here, you'll work with Elena, who is also close by. You might even learn a thing or two about city administration. She'll introduce you to my head of security, Sergei. He's ex-KGB, defected here just before the Soviet Union collapsed. He's extremely capable. Anything you need in relation to security, he's your man."

"Thank you."

Virginia pushes to her feet. "It's lovely to have you on board, Gabby. I'm sure we're going to work well together."

Gabby smiles as she also stands. "I'm looking forward to it." She turns and walks to the doors and discovers Elena is already opening them for her. The Chief of Staff had to have been listening in.

But Gabby thanks her and continues on, tucking the information away.

She's in.

And that's all that matters for now.

As GABBY WALKS to her car the following morning, she makes a mental note to buy more skirts. She's wearing the same one from her interview yesterday seeing as it's the only one she has that reaches her knees. But all thoughts of her attire flee when she sees who's leaning against her car.

Colt's ankles are crossed and his hands are shoved in his pockets, his broad shoulders hunched. The early morning light is running its fingers through his wine-colored hair, then caressing the hard length of his body. Lucky bitch.

But once Gabby's gaze connects with his, even that thought fades away. He's watching her. Branding her with just a look. It's the most intoxicating thing she's ever experienced.

"Hey," she breathes as she comes to a stop in front of him.

He smiles, the warmth starting somewhere deep in his chocolate eyes. "Hey. First day, huh?"

They'd texted last night, but there hadn't been any chance to catch up. "Yeah. Do I look okay?"

Colt's hot gaze sweeps over her, making her feel all tingly and kinda restless. "You always look amazing." He grins, suddenly looking every part the dark demon. "Although I prefer the shorter skirts."

"Me, too," she says, wrinkling her nose in an attempt to focus so she doesn't spontaneously combust. "How am I supposed to kick ass in this?"

He chuckles, and the sound seems to be directly connected to something deep in her abdomen. But then his face falls serious. "The threat to the mayor is still very real. You have to be careful and on guard."

Gabby's tempted to roll her eyes but she knows Colt's coming from a place of caring, and a part of her needs to hear that right now. "I know. And I can look after myself."

"This is a significant risk, Gabby. One I'm not sure we need to take." He pushes away from the car. "Maybe I should come to City Hall and help too."

But Gabby shakes her head. "Mayor Goodstone knows about the supernatural. And demons aren't exactly her favorite."

Colt frowns. "I see."

"And she knows of the Tear. She stressed it has to be closed."

Is it Gabby's imagination, or did Colt just stiffen?

"Haven't we got enough problems to worry about than to worry about the Tear right now?" he asks.

Against Gabby's will, Maya's words filter through her mind.

The dean has ordered Colt to sabotage your promise to close the Tear.

But Gabby shoves the insidious thought aside, annoyed that Maya's got to her after all. Now isn't the time for doubts.

"We have a buttload of problems, yes, but what if everything is related to this open Tear?" she says. "And I think all of this is related."

"You do?" asks Colt, watching her closely.

Gabby pulls in a deep breath, hoping she's about to make sense. "What if Samandriel and the cult brokered a deal with this secret faction? Hellfires in exchange for demonic weapons to cause more chaos in the world. That means the cult comes up with a spell to keep the Tear open."

He nods, looking thoughtful, although a little...guarded. "Definitely plausible."

"What if Samandriel's angels are now also working for the secret faction, who aren't happy with the mayor's involvement? Now that they've had a taste of demonic weapons, they would want to keep the Tear open, right? And the Mayor may have been working on closing the Tear. What if she's a far greater threat to the faction than we realize?"

Colt's mouth twists in thought. "But what evidence do we have to suggest the mayor has been trying to close the Tear?" he asks. "And even if she has been, she hasn't had much success. The Tear's still open."

Gabby acknowledges that with an incline of her head. "Yeah, that's the one sticking point. But the way she talked about the Tear got me thinking. She might be working to close it."

"We can only speculate at the moment."

He's being cagey again. And we're talking about the Tear.

Gabby shakes her head, trying to rid herself of the mutinous thought. Of course her Grace would default to that. "Well, I'm going to find out. She could help us with this."

"Be careful, Gabby," he says with a quiet intensity. "This is becoming more and more dangerous."

See! He does care!

She smiles, trying to pretend this crazy-assed conversation isn't happening in her head. "I know. I'll be on extra high alert."

He lets out a long sigh. "I'd better get going. I want to find those cult members. The sooner they're no longer a threat, the sooner you don't need to go to City Hall anymore." He glances over his shoulder at the imposing building that is the academy, although Gabby's not sure if he's reminding himself or her that they're possibly being watched. "I'll see you later," he says, quickly walking away.

No kiss. No reassurance.

Just when Gabby needs it the most.

27

COLT

Colt's never experienced feeling torn before. Despite his centuries on Earth, he always had one goal. Survive. That meant the life of a wanderer, always staying one step ahead of Belphegor's drive for vengeance. Life had been simple.

But now, he's being tugged at from every direction. Viciously. Relentlessly.

With no solution in sight.

Not only does he not know what to do about his promise to close the Tear, but he can't look for the cult members and keep Gabby safe while she walks straight into the new focal point of this entire mess. Images of Gabby trapped in one of the long corridors of City Hall, surrounded by angels with weapons, constantly haunt him. What if the faction has armed the cult with demonic weapons? A shudder ripples down his back, agitating the acid churning in his stomach.

Yet, finding and ending the cult members neutralizes the danger hanging over City Hall. There will be no one to threaten the angel who means more and more to him each day.

"Skata," mutters Colt as he strides back to the academy.

He's about to continue through to his cottage so he can prepare for a day of hunting when he pauses.

There's someone else who's invested in Gabby's safety.

Colt quickly changes direction, his instinctive actions telling him he's not too proud to do this. He almost jogs to the courtyard that houses the celestial hound, quickly murmuring the word that will allow him entrance. This time, he does jog as he makes his way down the stairs that will take him to the club-house. The one Gabriel established to bring the supernatural community together. Colt's about to find out exactly how inclusive it is.

Colt stalks through the corridors, ignoring any glances thrown his way. He only stops when he reaches the great hall. Was it only a few days ago that he was here with Gabby? Memories of their dance warm his mind. Everything is so simple when he's holding her. All he can do is feel.

The memory of the murdered angel has Colt straightening. It had been a taste of Samandriel's crazed thirst for death and mayhem.

"What do you want?" growls a voice behind him.

Colt turns to find Gabby's father standing just inside the room, his arms crossed over his chest. He even snaps out his wings for good measure.

"Gabby's accepted an internship at City Hall," Colt says by way of greeting. He wants to have this conversation as much as Gabriel does. "And the City Hall is where the cult will strike next."

Gabriel retracts his wings and unwinds his arms. "Gabby's an angel, Colt," he says condescendingly, "and she can take care of herself just fine."

"You're not invincible," Colts snaps. "Someone needs to watch her back. I would if I could, but I'm hunting down the cult members so I can stop this before it starts."

"Even if I thought she needed the help, I have Samandriel's legacy to deal with. Angels are going rogue. They've been found with demonic weapons."

Every muscle in Colt's body locks. "What?"

"We found a few of Samandriel's remaining angels with a couple of weapons. They had Hell's signature upon it. Must be some of the ones that were stolen when they came out of the Tear."

Colt takes a step forward, snapping himself out of the dual grip of fear and fury. "If they have any more, they've probably distributed them to the cult members."

It's the archangel's turn to go still. "Why would the angels arm human cult worshipers?"

"Some of the cult members were possessed by angels," Colt grinds out. "Samandriel's angels."

"Angels cannot possess humans, demon," Gabriel snaps. "We are not like you."

"And yet I saw it with my own eyes. They must've found a spell or something."

"Impossible," dismisses Gabriel.

Colt arches a brow. "See for yourself."

He allows the archangel to see the memory of Colt questioning the cult member. Once Gabriel's done, Colt arches a brow. "You haven't learned from underestimating Samandriel?

Gabriel glances away, staring at the wall. "Samandriel often invented his own spells," he says after a moment. "But even then, a way to possess humans... That's one complicated spell."

"Well, he obviously did."

"Then he's created an abomination. Angels are not to possess human beings. It weakens their link to their Grace."

Colt waves a hand dismissively. Samandriel's dead. They have more urgent issues at hand. "We have to stop the cult. As if hellfires weren't enough, those demonic weapons could wreak havoc on Mercy City."

Gabriel's lips thin. "You're right."

The grudging words almost make Colt smile. Gabriel's willingness to admit that is a testament to how important his daughter is to him. "I'm going to find the cult members like I said, but Gabby..." She's in even more danger.

"I'll watch over her," Gabriel promises, his words carved in stone

Colt nods then walks past, relief loosening the hard knot in his chest a little. If someone's looking out for Gabby, he can focus on the cult members. Hopefully, they won't be in existence much longer. In fact, he'll go see if that paperwork that was found in the mansion has any names worth following up.

Colt's just reached the top step when an angel he doesn't recognize lands in the courtyard. He braces himself, but the angel shoves past him with barely a glance. Colt shakes his head. "Just when I was thinking they might not be that bad," he mutters.

His foot joins the first as he's back at ground level. He's just decided to fly when he finds himself hesitating. An angel would've done more than barely acknowledge his presence. There was no sneer. No eyes spitting hatred.

That angel was on a mission.

Colt's wings snap out, but he doesn't launch for the sky. Instead, he skims back down the steps and powers through the corridors. He bursts into the Hall, a crimson ball of fire appearing in his hand when he sees he needs to act fast.

The angel has Gabriel pinned to the ground, a curved blade arcing down toward his chest.

Colt launches the fireball and it incinerates the blade. A second fireball knocks the angel off Gabriel. One thud of his wings and he's across the room, slamming his fist into the angel's face. He crumples to the ground, unconscious.

Colt raises an eyebrow at the stunned Gabriel still lying on the floor. "Now do you understand why I wanted someone to watch over Gabby?"

THE MURDEROUS ANGEL returns to consciousness to find himself tied to a chair. He blinks groggily, his body tensing when he finds Colt standing in front of him.

Colt smiles with all the cold fury he's feeling. He recognizes this traitor. This angel was there when Samandriel caught him and interrogated him. There's no doubt where his allegiance lies.

"Why are you here?" Colt demands. "Why did you attack Archangel Gabriel?"

The angel's mouth twists into a mockery of a smile. "You think torture is going to work on me, demon?"

"We're about to find out," he growls. Nothing will stop him from finding out what threat exists for Gabby.

"Hell's ways won't work on me," the angel scoffs. "How many lifetimes are you willing to give up for this?"

Colt's about to snarl that he's willing for this to take a thousand lifetimes, even though he doesn't have that sort of time, when Gabriel returns.

"If Hell's ways won't work, Raguel, then perhaps I could remind you of Heaven's." He slams the end of the scythe he's holding onto the marble floor with a crack. The angel, Raguel, shifts a little as if he's testing the strength of his bonds.

"I'll ask you again," says Colt, stepping back to give Gabriel more room. "Why are you here?"

Raguel throws a hateful glare but keeps quiet.

"The scythe is a beautiful weapon, you know," Gabriel says, running a finger down the glinting steel. "It is a reaper's blade. Most know that it collects people's souls. But it is also known to torturously collect an angel's grace."

Raguel openly struggles against his ties this time, his horrified eyes focused on the crescent blade.

"Last chance, Raguel," Gabriel warns. "You cannot imagine how painful this will be."

"I won't tell—"

Gabriel moves swiftly. He brings the blade down in the center of Raguel's chest and presses down. The deadly scythe slices through skin as if it were cake. Raguel throws his head back, agonized screams pouring out of his throat as he writhes, unable to escape.

Gabriel steps back, removing the scythe, his face as emotionless as the cold tiles they're standing on. Blood smears the blade, dripping onto the floor as the gaping wound in Raguel's chest opens and closes with each of his panting breaths. "I'll ask again. Who wants me dead?" roars Gabriel.

Blood bursts from Raquel's mouth, running down his chin and over his wound. It's not healing like any other angel wound would.

Gabriel steps in again, wielding the bloody scythe. "Tell me or I destroy you."

"Samandriel!" Raguel screams, crimson droplets spraying from his lips. "He tasked me with killing you, and I was going to see it through whether he was dead or alive."

Colt clenches his teeth.

Samandriel. He's the gift that kept on giving.

28

GABBY

Gabby's only on the second day of her internship when she discovers she's lost in the maze-like corridors of City Hall. She looks one way up the hallway then the other, huffing when they both look identical. How was it that only a few moments ago she was in one of the rooms full of volunteers preparing for the rally? It was heartwarming to see how much support the mayor has. It was a credit to the woman.

But Gabby must've taken a left instead of a right. Or maybe a right instead of a left. Either way, she isn't in Kansas anymore. She plants her hands on her hips. Not even the ever-present security is in the vicinity. Between City Hall's usual security, police officers both uniformed and plain-clothed, and the mayor's personal guard headed by Sergei, the place is crawling with dudes with guns. Yet right now, they all seem to have gone on a lunch break.

Deciding to go left, Gabby breaks into a brisk walk. She'll either find someone who can direct her or get even more lost, but she'd rather know what the outcome is going to be sooner rather than later. Walking with determination, she wonders whether the rich lord who designed this place made it hard to navigate on purpose. Built before the American War of Independence, the building was taken over by American fighters in the fight against the British. It was even rumored George Washington had visited the mansion. Gabby's pumps sink into the carpet, no doubt part of the renovations since the building was gifted to the city administration to become City Hall, wishing the place could've been a little smaller. Who needs this many corridors and rooms?

She reaches the end of the corridor, finding it's not the T-intersection she expected it to be. To her right, another corridor stretches out. But to her left is nothing more than an alcove.

With the symbol of the obsidian etched on it.

Gabby studies it, surprised, yet somehow unsurprised. The pentagram keeps coming up in the oddest of places. On Sabrina's wrist, then the Latimer book. But even in City Hall?

"I see you've found it," Virginia says from behind Gabby.

She spins around, keeping the surprise molded to her face while she figures out whether being caught is a good thing or not.

Virginia smiles, her hands tucked behind her back. "Most people with an understanding of the fine balance in this world usually do." She glances over Gabby's shoulder, her gaze flicking over the symbol. "A secret chamber lies behind this wall, home to cursed objects, I am told. There's another door on the other side, its entrance marked by this same symbol. Just as dark and evil as what the room contains, as the story goes."

"Darkness?" Gabby asks, maintaining the guise of ignorance.

Virginia arches a brow full of disbelief, but must decide to explain anyway. "The symbol first originated in darkness. In a cave actually. Its actual history is now vague, but has always been known to represent a dark object that can wreak untold havoc upon the world, corrupting everyone who lives in it." Her brow compresses as she glares at the symbol. "Every time someone has found it and brought it to earth, it's done nothing but cause wars and wanton destruction. And even when it now lies in its hiding place, it still influences the world. Considering the instability of the current world climate, I hope for everyone's sake that the object is never found."

Gabby nods, her own gaze drawn to the symbol. Although she already knows most of this, it's still ominous. Terrifying, actually.

The jangling of metal has her turning back toward the mayor, this time genuinely surprised as she discovers Virginia's hands are overflowing with a metal chain. The links are thick and silver, but with a strange coppery hue. The colors seem to shift from steel to gold depending on the light.

Tension steadily knots through Gabby's muscles. What is the chain for? Or more accurately, who? "And that is?"

"Chains that can bind even the most powerful supernatural," Virginia says, hefting their weight. "They are completely indestructible, and once rumored to have imprisoned the Titan Prometheus as Zeus punished him for bringing the gift of fire to man."

"Impressive," Gabby says noncommittally, a part of her ready to run.

"I believe you're going to need these when the time comes. These chains will bind even the Grigori, Gabby."

"You know about the Grigori," Gabby says, the words more a statement than a question. Seems the mayor knows pretty much everything.

"Yes. After being released from their prisons, they've rested, gathered their power, and researched. Almost two decades later, they've revealed themselves. They are a force to be reckoned with, and there's no weapon we know of that can end them."

Gabby sighs. She knows of one, but Samandriel took that secret with him to his death. The one she enacted. "No, we have no way to kill them at this stage."

Virginia extends the chain to Gabby. "Binding them is the best option. You'll need this when the time comes."

"Thank you," says Gabby as she takes them. Turns out the mayor is even a greater ally than she hoped.

"Anything to save this city," Virginia says fiercely before turning and walking away.

Gabby watches for long moments, noting that the mayor turns right at the end of the corridor, which is clearly where she went wrong.

Unless she was supposed to find this symbol. And have the talk with Virginia.

Gabby glances down at the chain she's now holding. It's sturdy, but not heavy. She tests it with a quick, hard yank. The metal jangles softly, the sound almost muted, but the links stay strong.

She has a Plan B.

Walking away, Gabby follows the path Virginia took, but leaves several minutes between them. The talk they just had was private for a reason. At the end of the corridor Gabby's acute hearing picks up the faint sound of voices. She follows them, finding herself back in familiar territory. A quick right and she's at the cluster of offices that hold both Virginia's and Elena's. Gabby slips into Elena's, relieved to find it empty, then quickly tucks the chain in the cupboard she was allocated for her things.

Straightening, she seats herself at the small desk she was also allocated in the corner of the room. Elena must be with Virginia, possibly talking about Gabby's gift, but at least she has a chance to hide it away in case the ever-efficient Elena isn't in on this.

Gabby smiles to herself. She can't wait to tell Colt the good news. They have the mayor of Mercy City on their side.

The files stacked on her desk catch Gabby's attention. Elena had said something about reviewing the previous mayoral policies, asking her to write a summary of her findings once she was done. Although Gabby's pretty sure they're just trying to make her role here look legit, she opens the top folder, a little excited at what she might find. These documents outline how her city has been run. They've molded policy and growth.

Realizing she's nerding out a little, she shakes her head as she starts reading, her angelic heritage letting her do it far faster than any human. Hours pass, and she even reads through her lunch break, perusing some policies twice. Especially when she discovers there are some discrepancies.

Gabby frowns as she cross checks something with the law enforcement policies. Her suspicions are correct. The wording is subtle, but there's a loophole. One a clever criminal could exploit. Another double check and she finds that an organization that doesn't actually exist was granted a large tract of land outside the city in exchange for a considerable sum donated to the city's treasury. She sniffs with distaste. The whole thing reeks of corruption.

Virginia needed to see this.

A quick check reveals the mayor's office is as empty as Elena's has been, but voices can clearly be heard not far away. Gabby navigates her way through the hallways, making sure to memorize her route, discovering herself outside a conference room packed with people. Whiteboards line the walls, full of columns, calendars and lists. The tables spread out in a long U-shape are covered in stacks of different colored paper. Gabby spots Elena on the other side of the room, a clipboard in hand, no doubt the maestro of this well-oiled machine. Then she spots Virginia.

Except she's slipping through a door.

Gabby quickly darts after her, stepping around a guy juggling two boxes of photocopy paper and a woman talking rapid-fire into her cell. By the time she reaches the door, Virginia's gone, but Gabby slips through, wanting to pay back the favor to the woman who gave her the chains.

She pauses when she finds herself in an alley. Virginia must've ducked out for a bit of a break. Maybe even a cigarette. Gabby's information on possible corruption can probably wait. She's about to turn back in when hushed voices reach her. She glances around, wondering at the tension she picks up.

Two steps and she peeks past a dumpster a few feet away. A car is parked at the end of the alley, facing toward the street. And Virginia's standing beside it, talking to him, her whole body vibrating with intensity. All that's visible of the man is his spiked hair above his headrest and the edge of his dark sunglasses as he turns his head to reply. Virginia says something Gabby can't hear and the man nods. He reaches up to adjust his rearview mirror and Gabby sucks in a sharp breath as she ducks behind the dumpster.

The man had a tattoo on his wrist. The symbol of the obsidian.

Reeling, she quickly slips back inside. Was the guy associated with the faction? Or was he like Sabrina, oblivious as to what the tattoo actually means? And why the flock is the mayor meeting with him in a dark alleyway?

As the questions pile up, each lacking an answer, Gabby walks back to her desk, one question rising to the top.

Is the mayor an ally? Or is she playing them?

Gabby's phone buzzes and a small jolt of joy pierces her when she sees Colt's name on the screen. But then his words have her frowning.

I've found the location of the remaining cult members.

29
COLT

Colt has often felt sorry for mortals, but as he watches Gabby descend from the sky, his pity multiplies a hundredfold. The breathtaking angel gracefully landing on one foot then sashaying toward him would be cloaked to humans.

But he gets to marvel at every second of it.

The evening light catches on Gabby's alabaster wings, making each feather look like it's been dipped in pearl. They're magnificent. Pure white, yet when the slightest change of angle, they hint at every color in the rainbow. They glow with the power she carries within her. The expanse shadows her sweet curves, but Colt's memorized them by now. The silky skin. The tempting swell of her hips.

"Hey," she murmurs, brushing a blonde curl from her mesmerizing face.

Colt swallows. Then swallows again. Right now, no one would know he's been alive for hundreds of years. He's been reduced to an affliction he's often seen in humans. He's speechless.

He clears his throat. "Hey."

She sighs. "I saw the mayor talking to a guy with an obsidian tattoo. In an alleyway with no one else around."

That has him frowning. "You need to be cautious as to who you trust." As soon as the words are out, his chest tightens. Is he giving Gabby an unconscious warning?

"Here's hoping I'm a good judge of character," she quips. There's a teasing glint in her eyes, but does he also detect a thread of uncertainty in those blue depths?

"Trust your instincts, Gabby. That is where the truth is most likely to lie."

Her lashes flutter. "My instincts tell me to trust you," she says softly.

"That's because I would never choose to hurt you," he responds roughly.

"Well then, let's hope the mayor is as trustworthy as you." She turns to face the abandoned tenement building they're standing before. "So, this is where you traced the remainder of the cult to?"

He nods, glad for the change of topic. "Yes. I haven't seen any movement, but I'd expect them to be hiding."

"Only one way to find out," Gabby says, her voice now steely with determination.

They cross the road but the moment they try to step onto the cracked pavement leading to the door, they're both repelled. Gabby curses. "There's a barrier spell."

"Then we'll have to break it."

She glances at him, her eyes glinting with challenge. "We can try Aramaic?"

Colt inclines his head. Aramaic is an ancient language they're both familiar with. They step forward and place their hands on the invisible barrier. He instantly feels the energy encasing the multi-story building. It's powerful, but is it as powerful as their combined magic?

Gabby begins chanting and recognizing the spell, Colt joins in. Their voices blend, lending the other strength. And then the same happens with their magic. It melds. Then explodes.

It's the same connection he felt when they danced in the Hall of Dreams. There's the same ripple of power, as if their auras just blended. The same hot and cold shivers skittering over his skin. The explosion of power is undeniable

The barrier spell fractures, splinters, then fragments like a giant piece of glass. The invisible pieces fade into nothing.

They glance at each other, a sweet sense of victory that feels so much larger than removing a barrier spell swelling between them. They step forward simultaneously, ready to face whatever it is that's within the building.

The interior is decrepit and musty. They survey the entire first floor, finding bare apartments with mold stains and peeling paint. The second floor is much the same, although with the odd bed leaning on a dejected angle or wardrobe lacking doors. The third floor has a little more decaying furniture, even a couple of dirty, saggy mattresses as those who had to leave didn't have the energy to drag them down flights of stairs, but once more, little else.

They pause on the stairwell to the top floor. "There's no sign of anyone," Gabby observes.

"Not recently," Colt agrees, now wondering if his research was wrong. Maybe the cult or Samandriel's angels were never here.

"Which means no sign of the spell that's keeping the Tear open," she adds, sounding both disappointed and frustrated.

"Let's keep going," says Colt, gritting his teeth. Finding the cult is a double-edged sword for him. He protects Gabby, but he also is one step closer to having to decide.

Honor his debt to Belphegor and betray Gabby.

Or turn his back on the archdemon, putting himself and Gabby in danger.

They reach the top floor and find a door not only intact, but also closed. Gabby glances at Colt, then pushes it open. She gasps.

Ready to defend her, no matter the cost, Colt is by her inside before his next heartbeat. But the studio apartment that seems to encompass the entirety of the top floor is empty.

"The Grigori have been here," Gabby says.

She's right. Colt can feel their aura—a strange mix of angelic essence and icy vengeance.

But the large expanse holds nothing but sparse furniture. Their presence is no longer here.

"They're gone," mutters Colt. And some time ago from the feel of things. He curses. Another dead end.

Gabby enters, her footsteps rapping on the timber floor. In the center of the room is a large oval table, seven seats around it. She brushes her hand over the pale, glossy surface as she slowly scans the place.

"What are you doing?" Colt asks.

"This may have been the cult headquarters," she says, walking over to a chest of drawers made from the same light wood. "Maybe they've left something on the spell keeping the Tear open."

His teeth back on edge, Colt walks to the other side of the room where a small kitchenette is. He opens each cupboard and drawer, unsure whether he wants to find anything. The relief he experiences when blank shelves and empty spaces greet him tells him the answer. He's not ready to be backed into a corner. He hasn't come up with a solution yet.

He curses Belphegor as he moves onto the bathroom. One solution is to be rid of the archdemon. No Belphegor, no debt. If Colt could think of a way to end the cunning bastard, he would.

As it is, if Colt's forced to hurt Gabby, he swears to every level of Hell, he will make the archdemon pay. Belphegor may remain alive, but he'll come to regret it.

"It's here," says Gabby in a half-whisper.

Colt spins around as she takes a few steps back from the back wall, a large painting hanging in her hand.

The mark of the obsidian has been etched onto the wall. It's faint. But there.

"It might not be anything," he points out as he joins her. "It's not surprising considering the Grigori are hunting for it."

Gabby glances at him with her eyes narrowed. "You're really a naysayer when it comes to the Tear. Why is that?"

He yanks his gaze to focus back on the symbol. "I just know we've been disappointed before. I don't want to see you get your hopes up."

In the same way he's held back with their relationship. He doesn't want Gabby getting her hopes up.

She rolls her eyes. "If I'm sobbing on the floor, you can pick me up."

Stepping forward, she presses her hand against the wall. "I can feel something," she gasps.

Colt watches, unable to breathe, as she leans forward a little, putting more pressure on her palms. To his dismay, the symbol flares bright white and turns on its axis. Then the bricks are moving, separating from each other, each alternate one moving in an opposite direction. A soft grating sound scrapes over his nerves as a new space opens up.

A small chamber is revealed with a stand in the center. On it is a glowing red gem. It sends out crimson light, lighting the small space with a hellish glow.

They step inside simultaneously, but Colt doubts Gabby's entranced for the same reasons as he is. Dread is knotting his insides with such intensity it hurts.

He can feel the power radiating from the large gem. It has goosebumps dancing over his skin. Have they found the artifact that houses the spell keeping the Tear open?

Gabby steps around it, the red glow painting her skin. "If this is what we think it is, there's only one way to find out."

Break it.

Colt opens his mouth to tell her it would be too dangerous. That maybe they should take this back to her father. That they need to think this through. But he knows she won't listen. Danger doesn't stop Gabby. She resists her father's involvement. And she's a girl of action, not contemplation.

If he wanted the Tear closed, no matter what, he'd do the same.

The moment that's been hanging over him like a guillotine has finally arrived.

Gabby hovers her hand over either side of the floating gem. "My father suspected the spell may have been tied to an enchanted object. He had me learn a spell to break them. We're about to find out whether I was paying attention."

Colt is locked to the spot. His dislike of Gabriel just climbed one notch higher. He wants more time. He doesn't want to make this choice.

Gabby's eyes flutter closed as she draws in a deep breath. The air around her intensifies, even shivers as she calls on her power. White light crackles between her fingertips, flicking out toward the red gem as if testing it. The magic must find what it's looking for, because the crackling bolts converge on it hungrily. They assault the red gem, weaving around it like a cocoon of lightning, no doubt finding any weakness in the spell protecting it.

He needs to stop her. Break her concentration. Undermine the electric magic unfolding before him.

A gust of wind blows Gabby's curls back, revealing parted lips and flushed cheeks. Her mouth feathers with a smile.

She's breathtaking. Divine.

And he's irrevocably, undeniably in love with her.

Images seem to fill the trembling air. The first time he saw her, standing at the academy gates. Attraction had punched him in the gut even then. It's one of the reasons he'd been so determined to push her away.

But she hadn't let him. Not to mention he was helplessly drawn to her.

Her words after they'd defeated the Grigori. "I really like you, too."

Their first kiss.

Every touch after that.

And in that moment, Colt knows he can't stop her closing the Tear. He can't betray her. What's more, the Tear needs to be closed. The world doesn't need more demons and their hellish weapons. It will only mean war. Or worse, an apocalypse.

He straightens his spine, suddenly feeling lighter even as an ache settles in his chest. One he'll be carrying for the rest of his days. He's outmaneuvered Belphegor before. Gabriel will have to keep his daughter safe.

Once this is done, Colt will have to leave.

The white ball of energy contracts around the gemstone and the sound of glass fracturing pierces the air. Gabby's spell is working. She's doing it! Splotches of fiery red flare across the white ball like electric blood. The white flares brighter, stinging Colt's eyes. The ball constricts, tightening its hold. He braces himself. This is going to be one heck of an explosion.

In a rush of energy, the gemstone expands, shrinks, then implodes, sucking the white light with it. Then, there's nothing. The silence is almost anticlimactic.

Colt steps forward. "What happened?"

Gabby curses. "It didn't work!"

"What?" He looks around as if expecting to see someone else here, sabotaging her spell. "How?"

"Surely not..." Gabby's gaze meets his. "It was a fake."

"It can't be."

"It's the only answer," she says, her voice tight. "That's why it didn't explode."

"You're right," says a voice behind them. "It was a fake."

Colt spins around to find Maya in the doorway. The look of satisfaction on her face is undeniable.

"Maya!" gasps Gabby, coming to stand beside Colt. "What are you doing here?"

Maya's gaze never leaves Colt. "To show you the truth."

30

GABBY

"**M**aya, you need to get out of here," Gabby warns. "It's too dangerous." Surely her hatred of Colt hasn't blinded her to that.

"You need to listen to me, Gabby."

"No, I don't!" Gabby quickly modulates her tone as the words are almost a shout. "I've had enough. Colt isn't—"

"He's lying to you!" Maya screams. "He has been all along."

Colt is silent and still beside Gabby and the fact he hasn't thrown Maya out the window is a testament to his self-control, but also how much he respects Gabby. Despite the fact hatred is practically erupting from Maya, he knows she was once a close friend of Gabby's.

Now, she's not quite sure what they are.

Gabby focuses her gaze on Maya. "You need to leave and this has to stop. I trust Colt. He would never deliberately hurt me."

As she says the words, Gabby can feel their truth. Everything they've been through is evidence of their connection. It doesn't matter that she's an angel and he's a demon. That they're supposed to be mortal enemies.

She's fallen in love with him.

And she has to believe he feels the same for her.

Gabby raises her chin as she shifts closer to him. What they have transcends any rule Heaven or Hell have come up with. Maya's grief-driven hatred doesn't stand a chance.

"I have proof," says Maya, her hard gaze flicking to Colt then back to Gabby. "Proof I'm telling the truth."

"Enough," Colt snaps, the one word sounding like it was just forced through gritted teeth. "Gabby has asked you to leave."

"We've had enough of your lies," adds Gabby.

Maya angles her head, her eyes turning calculating. "Has he ever told you he loves you, Gabby?"

Gabby hates that her lashes flicker as she tenses. "That's none of your busin—"

"Or of his agreement with Belphegor?"

"Another of your lies—"

"Or that he sabotaged you?" Maya points an accusing finger at the stand behind them littered with broken shards of the fake gem.

"Leave!" roars Colt. "Your words are nothing but vile lies! I would never do something like that!"

Maya pulls her cell out of her pocket. "You're a good actor, Colt. I can see why Gabby's so deeply under your spell. Of course, if you have nothing to hide, then you won't mind me showing her this."

Colt is almost vibrating with fury but he doesn't move as Maya taps and swipes on her phone. Gabby grits her teeth. If Colt had something to hide he would try to stop this, but he hasn't. Maya can throw her little conspiracy theories around, but it's not going to break them up. Now, Gabby just wants this over and done with. Maya may be ignoring that it's dangerous to be here, but she hasn't forgotten.

"This place may be abandoned, but the cult has cameras everywhere," says Maya, still focused on her cell. "Samandriel insisted on it, in fact. He also let me access whatever I wanted in exchange for the whole kidnapping ruse."

"You've betrayed me far more than anyone else," Gabby says quietly, a shiver in her voice. She's not sure if it's her own fury, or the hurt slicing through her.

Maya glares at her. "You really have no idea what's coming, do you?" she says, clearly disgusted.

The hard, angry girl in front of Gabby is far removed from the sweet, caring one who became an instant friend. In fact, Gabby doesn't even like the lying, hateful person standing in front of her. The thought makes her sad as much as it makes her angry.

Maya taps the screen of her cell and holds it up to show that a video has started playing. "Take it."

Wanting this over and done with, Gabby does, noting the video isn't a long one. Whatever Maya is showing them, at least it will be quick.

An image of the room they're in appears, a handful of men and women there. Somehow, Gabby can sense they're angels.

"She killed Samandriel," one of them growls.

Another slams their hand into her fist. "We will retaliate!"

Gabby wonders if that's what sparked the angel attacking her father. Another time Colt demonstrated his loyalty, because he was the one who saved her father's life.

Another voice filters through the phone. A cold, raspy voice. One that sounds like it's a collective voice of several beings.

The Grigori.

"We've been found."

Seven white lights appear in the image, pulsing with agitation. They shoot for the open window and fly out, quickly disappearing. Proof they'd been here. Also proof that the cowards ran.

Gabby glances up, noting the window's now closed. The angels must've shut it before leaving. Did they know she and Colt were coming? Is Maya going to try and tell her that Colt alerted them somehow?

Now feeling her own disgust, Gabby's about to pass the phone back when a sound makes her stop. A cry. A pain riddled one.

Gabby focuses back on the screen, even pulling it a little closer as the images blur. More cries and shrieks tumble from the speakers. Something is in the room, but it's moving too fast for her to be able to tell what it is.

A spray of blood hits a wall. There's a flash of metal then the thud of flesh. More screams have Gabby's blood turning cold. Something is butchering the angels.

It feels like a lifetime rather than the brief span of half the video before there's silence. But she doesn't get a chance to blink before someone enters the blood-spattered frame. Not a something. But a someone.

He stands in the center of the room, letting the long, blood-stained blade drop from his hand and onto the floor.

"No," Gabby moans.

It can't be.

She's vaguely aware of movement beside her, but she isn't able to focus on the Colt in the room with her.

Not when Colt is on the screen.

She watches, stunned and silent, as he walks to the obsidian sign and opens it in the same way she had. He enters the hidden room, picks up the red gem and replaces it with another, identical gem.

"I told you," Maya sneers, the smugness in her voice salt on the gaping wound that just tore through Gabby's heart.

She looks up at Colt. "How could you?" she asks through numb lips.

Colt is shaking his head, pulling off dismayed like the actor she accused him of being. "That wasn't me, Gabby. I didn't do this. Someone must've taken my form. I've been framed."

Gabby shakes her head, wondering how the tendons of her neck don't snap. "They even walked like you." She should know. She's spent so long memorizing everything about him.

Because she stupidly fell in love with him.

Which makes her the foolish, naive human she wanted so desperately to prove she's not.

Gabby takes a stumbling step back. "I can't believe you did this to me."

Colt opens his mouth only to snap it shut. He glances around furiously, a vein standing out against his temple. "You!" he roars, spinning one way then the other.

But Maya's gone, not even bothering to take her phone. Maybe she wanted to leave Gabby with the opportunity to watch the awful treachery as many times as she wanted. She hurls the cell across the room and it smashes against the wall.

She's seen enough.

"Gabby," says Colt, starting to look desperate. "That wasn't me—"

"Belphegor asked you to keep the Tear open, didn't he?" So more demons can pour into this world. More demonic weapons. More chaos and death.

Colt doesn't answer, but the truth twists across his face. He was ordered to betray her.

So he did.

"You've been lying to me this whole time!"

Once again, Colt doesn't reply. He knows there's no point denying.

"You knew it would come to this."

"No," he says, taking a step forward but then stopping. "I didn't want to hurt you. And in the end, I chose you. I didn't stop you from breaking the gem and ending the spell."

"Because you knew it was fake!" Gabby isn't sure whether she screams or whispers the words. The roaring in her ears is muting and amplifying everything. Her strangled breaths. Her choked heartbeats.

The staggering pain of betrayal shredding her insides.

"Gabby," he says, almost sounding as broken as she feels.

"No!" She moves before she's even aware of it. She flings her arms out as if Colt's coming at her and he flies across the room. He slams into the wall, creating an instant crater before sliding down. He lands on his feet but doesn't move.

"Please, I—"

Gabby's hands are still outstretched and she flexes them, her fingers almost becoming claws. Tears blur her vision as she sees Colt look down in shock. He watches in silence as a hard, gray coating shoots up his legs, encasing them. Her lip trembles as she flexes her fingers again and the grayness stretches across his hips, his abdomen, then his chest.

Colt's gaze shoots to hers, shocked but strangely, not fighting this. He could pitch his magic against hers and use it to get away. But he simply lets the immobilizing casing progressively cover him.

A sob erupts from Gabby as the cement-like substance reaches his neck. His jaw. Then encases the lips she's kissed, the eyes she's lost herself in, the hair that she loved to run her fingers through.

And then, it's done. Colt is frozen, his hard statue eyes staring at her.

Gabby looks away, disgusted at what she's done, yet unwilling to reverse it. His heart is as cold as stone. The rest of him may as well match it.

She turns away and walks out of the apartment on legs that feel as frozen as Colt looks. She doesn't look over her shoulder. She doesn't acknowledge the statue she just molded from the demon she stupidly fell in love with. She's barely keeping herself together as it is.

She's only a handful of steps out the door when her cell buzzes. Gabby's tempted to ignore it—she's not even sure if her tear-clogged throat will allow her to talk—but she knows she can't.

The Grigori are out there. So are the cult. And the faction.

And what's more, the Tear is still open.

Swallowing hard, she answers the call. "Yes?" she croaks.

There's a pause. "Man, I hope you don't have the flu," Riley says on the other end. "Because we have a situation."

The tension in Riley's voice sounds taut enough to snap.

"What's happened?" Gabby asks, bracing herself. Each throb of her heart hurts, making it hard to think.

"You need to come to City Hall. It's been taken hostage."

31

GABBY

When she arrives, Gabby discovers City Hall is in as much chaos as her heart.

The building isn't just under siege. It's under *supernatural* siege.

The green flames of hellfires are devouring the gates, the gardens that surrounded them now nothing more than char and ash. The gates themselves hang crookedly, partially obstructing the entrance.

Not that anyone could get close, anyway.

Squadrons of police cars have the area cordoned off. Fire trucks are parked around City Hall itself. Dotted between them are ambulances, stretchers already unloaded. Everywhere is a disco of red and blue lights, the flashes glancing off the uniformed men and women's tense faces.

Gabby walks toward a group of people standing at the barriers directly across from the damaged gates. About half of them have their phones held high, the hellish image of blackened gates hanging at precarious angles, green fire dancing all around multiplied in miniature across all their screens.

"Sir," calls a woman as she extends her microphone as far as she can past the barrier. "Can you give us an update? Is there news of the Mayor?"

Gabby's heart jolts. Virginia is in there?

"What about the hostages?" shouts the woman when she doesn't get an answer.

This time, Gabby's heart leaps painfully. Innocent people are trapped in there?

A surreptitious wave of her hand along with a few murmured words and she cloaks herself to look like a carbon copy of the police officer stoically refusing to answer the reporter's questions. Gabby hurries away before anyone can start asking identical twin questions, slipping between the barricades and half-running toward City Hall.

The closer she gets, the more alarmed she is. The large entry to the imposing building is surrounded by hellfire. Although firefighters are rushing around, spraying powerful jets of water onto them, the flames aren't being doused. They're not growing, but they're also not going away. Gabby realizes they're guarding the entrance. No one will be going through the front doors.

Gabby continues around, having to stop herself from looking away as two ambulance officers push a stretcher to a nearby ambulance. The black body bag lying on it catches the eerie green light of the fires.

"Poor guy," says a female ambulance officer. "What do you reckon the guards of City Hall get paid?"

"Not enough," mutters her partner. "This guy looks like he was close to retirement, too."

Gabby nods to another police officer walking past as an excuse to drag her gaze away. It means she notices something else. Her gaze rakes the woman, then the officer beside her, then the group of four posted just a few feet away. Every police officer's hand hovers over their gun. Gabby's not sure if they're ready to attack or defend, but she knows one thing for certain.

City Hall is a powder keg waiting to blow.

And there are hostages inside, and probably the mayor.

"This wasn't what I had in mind," she says under her breath as she does a slow scan. She finds what she's looking for in the parking lot.

A large, dark blue tent has been pitched, the Mercy City police logo emblazoned on the side, and Gabby makes a beeline for it. As she steps through the entrance flap, she drops the glamor. It's served its purpose, although how she's going to explain her presence here, she has no idea.

She finds who she's looking for almost immediately. "Detective Espinosa."

Riley looks up from the table she's standing beside. "I'm sorry," she says briskly. "You can't be in here." Lightly gripping Gabby's arm, she leads her out. "I'm glad you came," she says under her breath, smiling briefly at the officer standing guard at the entrance flap.

Riley leads them down the side of the tent and a few feet away. They slip behind a black van.

"How many hostages?" Gabby asks the moment they're alone.

"At least thirty," Riley says, her lips a tight, thin line. "And yes, Mayor Goodstone is also in there."

"Skata," Gabby curses.

Riley glances around. "Speaking of Colt, where is he?"

The mention of his name is like a white-hot blade slicing straight through Gabby's chest. "He..." Lied. Betrayed. Never loved me. Gabby clears her throat. "He's a bit tied up right now after we lost the lead on closing the Tear."

Riley's brows twitch, either with disbelief or confusion.

"Right." She shakes her head. "Well, we have a Grigori situation here."

Gabby's spine stiffens. "Are you sure?"

"Seven robed figures killed the guards."

"That's them," spits Gabby. She hadn't expected them so soon.

"They had a small army with them, too. Samandriel's angels, I'd say. They're the pricks who sprinkled the hellfire around. Then they stormed the building and killed anyone who didn't like it."

Gabby suppresses the need to curse again. How could angels side with the Grigori? Even with Samandriel dead, they are blindly following the seven vengeful angels who are willing to kill to get what they want. The thought disgusts her. And angels say demons are selfish, cruel creatures.

Conscious that her thoughts are coming precariously close to Colt again, Gabby gives herself a mental slap. Seems demons are just as willing to hurt others as angels.

She pins her focus on Riley and the crisis at hand. "What do they want?" she asks. "Have they communicated?"

Riley shakes her head. "It's been an hour since they went inside. There's been zero communication from them, but our hostage negotiation team is ready and waiting."

Gabby almost rolls her eyes. No matter how hardened or experienced the negotiators will be, they won't stand a chance against the Grigori.

"I know, I know," sighs Riley. "We're not up against your regular psychos who want a helicopter and a million bucks. But we have to follow protocol or this will all descend into chaos."

Gabby nods, seeing the logic in it. The illusion of control is better than realizing there's no way humans can have a say in how this turns out.

"Detective Espinosa," calls out a voice. "We have contact."

Riley snaps to attention. "We're on," she says grimly. She takes two steps then glances back. "Do something with this," she says, waving her hand up and down Gabby.

This time she does roll her eyes. "This is my favorite skirt, too," she huffs, running her hands over the tartan mini skirt. But a second later, she's back in the police officer glamor as she follows Riley back to the tent.

Riley is passed a head set the moment she steps into the tent, the officer waving his finger like a helicopter, assumedly to indicate the call is being put through speakers so everyone can hear.

"Hello, this is Detective Riley Espinosa," she says into the small speaker near her mouth. "Thank you for making contact with us."

"Spare us the token niceties," says a raspy voice on the other end. The strange three-dimensional sound as seven angels speak in unison sends shivers skittering down Gabby's spine. "We have our demands."

"Yes?" Riley says tersely.

"We want the parchments stolen from us in return for all the hostages," seethe the Grigori. "And the girl who can read them."

The call ends, the silence after ominous and heavy.

Riley removed the headset with a growl.

"Ma'am?" The officer who called them in steps forward. "What parchments? What girl?"

Riley rubs the bridge of her nose. "I'll find out." With a pointed glance at Gabby, she exits the tent again.

Back beside the black van, Gabby returns to her real self. "Me going inside is fine, but we can't give them parchments." Giving them parchments essentially gives them a roadmap to the obsidian.

"There are innocent civilians inside, Gabby," Riley growls.

"We both know the Grigori won't hesitate in making an example of them."

Gabby pinches her nose in a very similar gesture to Riley's just a few moments ago. "We need to come up with something."

"And fast."

Rubbing her temples, Gabby begins to pace. "They want the parchments. We can't give them the parchments." She stops, an idea hitting her. "Unless we give them the parchments."

Riley's eyes widen. "Did I just hear you right?"

Gabby nods resolutely. At least the detective appreciates exactly the type of dilemma this situation has created—to save dozens of lives, they have to put millions at risk.

"Yes, we give them the parchments. Fake ones."

Riley's eyes are now the size of saucers. "You're going to replicate them?"

"It's the only way," Gabby says, the idea starting to gain momentum. "They'll have to be freaking good replicas, but this way, we give them what they want, we get the civilians out."

"Is that even possible? These aren't any old parchments. They're ancient."

Now, Gabby starts to rub her temples. "It has to be."

"And I have proof it's entirely possible," says a deep voice from behind them.

Gabby spins around to see her father walking toward them. In his hands are seven sheets of thick, aged paper.

"Who's this?" Riley demands.

"Detective Espinosa, this is my father, Archangel Gabriel," Gabby says, trying to understand the satisfied expression on his face. "What do you mean, it's possible?"

He lifts the sheets that to all intents and purposes, look exactly like the parchments. "Tricking the Grigori with fake parchments is exactly something I'd think up. In fact, I did, which is why I had these created over a week ago."

A little stunned, Gabby doesn't answer. Although this is exactly what she wanted, she's not sure how she feels about this.

Her father steps forward, the fake parchments still extended. "We're more alike than you think, daughter."

That's the part Gabby's struggling with. Thinking like him isn't something that sits comfortably with her.

"Except, of course, for your penchant for demons," he adds, obviously trying to lighten the mood.

Gabby's heart plummets all over again at the mention of Colt. At the possibility that her father was right. It turns out, their differences as angel and demon were impossible to overcome. Colt's loyalty to his archdemon lord won out.

Pushing away the thoughts that are shredding her insides, Gabby takes the parchment replicas. "I'm going in."

Riley shakes her head. "I'll send some men with you."

"No." Gabby has to work not to clench the parchments too hard. "Killing Samandriel was intended to bring the Grigori out, I just didn't think they'd do it like this. This is my responsibility to fix."

And she'll be doing it alone.

Her father nods, a small smile playing over his lips. "You never needed anyone in the first place."

Gabby looks away, focusing on City Hall, not really sure that's true but having no choice and find out.

She'll deal with the Grigori.

And get those civilians out, safe and unhurt.

Alone.

32

GABBY

Gabby stands at the rear door to City Hall and adjusts the unwieldy vest she's now wearing. Riley had insisted she wear protective gear even though Gabby repeatedly pointed out it wouldn't do sweet stuff all against the Grigori's powers. But the detective has her own stubborn streak, so Gabby's wearing it even though Kevlar obviously wasn't built for comfort.

A glance over her shoulder reveals her father and Riley watching her from behind a car in the parking lot. It was agreed Gabby would have to sneak in. None of the emergency services personnel are going to be okay with sending a nineteen-year-old girl into a hostage situation that has already seen several people killed.

The irony that her own father thinks this is a great idea isn't lost on her.

Gabby returns her focus to the metal door in front of her. She unlocks it with a wave of her hand and quickly slips in, shutting it quietly behind her. Even then, the *click* feels like a sonic boom. She's never felt more alone. She's about to face the

Grigori. Dozens of lives depend on her right now. Thousands more no matter how this turns out.

She slips the bullet-proof vest off and sits it by the door, admitting to herself she suddenly feels vulnerable without it. Who is she kidding? She feels vulnerable, period. In every scenario when it came to facing the Grigori again, she'd always pictured Colt by her side. Could she have been any more of an idiot?

Shaking off any thoughts of the demon she should've walked away from for the millionth time, Gabby makes her way down the corridor, the parchments tucked in her back pocket. Although every muscle is coiled and wired, ready to fight, the place is eerily quiet. She moves through the hallways, climbs stairs, checks offices, but no one confronts her. She doesn't like how cocky the Grigori are being. They're waiting for her. Almost welcoming her.

Reaching the rear door of the ballroom at the other end of the building, Gabby peers through the crack. Thirty-odd people have been herded into the center and made to sit on the floor, their backs pressed against each other. Several faces are tear-streaked. Several are still crying. Everyone is hunched, the only way they can protect themselves right now.

Not giving herself time to think, especially considering how easily Colt slips into her mind—as if the traitorous demon hasn't left—she pushes open the door. "You wanted me, you got me."

The angels are a blur of movement as they surround her, but Gabby ignores them. She stalks forward as she pulls the parchments out and holds them aloft. "Now let these people go."

Gasps echo through the large room, but one seems louder than all the others. Far more familiar.

Gabby scans the frightened faces who have now all turned to her like she's some sort of savior.

Shit. No.

Her mom is among the hostages.

Of all the days to pay her parking fine...

"Gabby!" her mom cries. "What are you doing? Get out of here!"

She looks away, her heart hammering as she ignores her mother's words. This is a complication she hadn't considered. The need to get these people to safety just multiplied a millionfold.

Laughter echoes through the domed room as seven robed figures land between Gabby and the hostages. No longer nothing more than white light, they've taken earthy figures. Ones that are creepily identical to each other.

"Well, well, well, if it isn't the prophesied angel," one of the Grigori taunts.

"And she seems to know this woman," says another, pointing a pale, thin finger at her mother.

Gabby's pulse is a jackhammer in her veins. The Grigori could use her mother as leverage. They wouldn't blink at it.

"Enough," snaps a third, stepping forward. "You have the parchments?"

Gabby unfurls the scrolled paper but doesn't hand it over. "First you let these people go."

A couple of the Grigori wave a dismissive hand. "Fine," one says. "We'll let them go." A smile twists his pale features. "Everyone except for this woman you know. We will release her once the parchments are examined and you translate them for us."

"And the mayor. We'll keep her too," says a fourth Grigori. "She will also be useful."

Gabby looks around. She hadn't noticed Virginia among the hostages. She finds her a moment later, a little to the side and slumped on a chair. Blood trickles from her nose as she tries to smile…and fails.

Gabby's hand tightens on the parchments. "Fine, but you let these civilians go."

The angels serving the Grigori herd the hostages out the main door, roughly shoving them through the narrow opening. Three remain in the middle of the hall, one holding Gabby's mother prisoner, while another two haul Virginia up from the chair, keeping their hold on her as she sways.

Crap. This isn't going smoothly.

Next thing she knows, the parchments have disappeared from her hand and reappeared in the Grigori's.

Double crap.

Before Gabby can say something so she can buy some time as she tries to figure out this latest glitch, the Grigori turn toward the mayor. "Kill her," they say in unison. "She will be an example of what will happen to the other woman if there are any surprises."

Virginia struggles in the angel's grasp, but she's weak from her injuries and the angels quickly twist her arms behind her back. She arches, her eyes wide as one of them grabs her throat, ready to crush it.

Gabby steps forward, calling forth a fireball in her hand. Except it doesn't come. The air above her palm remains empty

One of the Grigori laughs. "Your powers won't work here, girl," he mocks. "There are runes that prevent angels from using magic."

"Unless you have the neutralizing rune inscribed on your palm," says another.

Which every angel in this place would have, apart from her. Gabby watches helplessly as the angel holding the mayor tightens his hand, a cruel sneer twisting his features.

Virginia pushes up on her toes as if she's arching for more air. "I...can give...you the means to... defeat...her."

Gabby's eyes widen in shock as, with one flick of the Grigori's fingers, the angel loosens his grasp. Seems the betrayals aren't over for today. The mayor just sprinkled another bucketful of salt onto the gaping wound Colt has left in Gabby's chest. The pain is so sharp it has Gabby's eyes stinging.

"Speak," the Grigori snarl.

Virginia drops to the ground as she's released. She lands on all fours, gasping. "The ancient chains that bound a Titan....I have them."

The Grigori's pale faces light with excitement. "Give them to us."

"On one condition," says Virginia as she staggers to her feet. "You'll leave peacefully, and I walk out of here alive."

"Agreed," the Grigori hiss in unison.

The mayor smiles as she straightens her spine, once more looking like she's in control. She glares at Gabby unapologetically. In fact, she holds her gaze for long moments.

And that's when Gabby remembers.

The chains. Virginia gave them to her. She'd said then they'd need to be used when the time came. Gabby's hands clench as she wraps her head around this change of events. If she had her magic, maybe she could conjure them. If she had her magic, she could blast her way to them in her locker. But she doesn't. Not with the runes in place.

A glance at her mother, who's silently watching this all unfold in a terrified daze cements the decision. If Gabby has to fight her way to them, she darned well will.

"This way," Virginia says, heading toward one of the marble panels that line the walls of the ballroom.

As she approaches it, Gabby notices something for the first time. Camouflaged among the swirls of light brown marbling is the symbol of the obsidian. And if she wasn't looking at it with such surprise, then she wouldn't notice the subtle wave of Virginia's hand as she stops in front of it. Two things happen.

The panel opens inward like a door.

And the runes etched on the wall to Gabby's left glow bright for a split second before vanishing, leaving charred black circles where they were.

Actually, make that three. Power rushes through Gabby, filling her in a way that has her realizing how empty she'd been all the years she's lived without acknowledging them. She breathes in deep, welcoming them. Then, she waits.

Virginia disappears into the darkness the panel has revealed and the Grigori follow. The moment the panel closes again, Gabby attacks.

She leaps, extending her wings midair and lands in front of her mother. She hurls the angel stupid enough to put his hand on her and he slams into the wall several feet away. Gabby's mom screams but Gabby doesn't have time to figure out whether it's because of Gabby or the angels now swarming toward them.

Remaining in front of her mother, Gabby strikes, kicks, and strikes some more. Any angel foolish enough to get close to her quickly discovers their error. One collapses with a punch to the throat. Several more decorate the walls in every direction. Four are felled with a sweeping roundhouse across their faces.

The moment Gabby gets a chance, she sends a fireball high up where it explodes like a firework, lighting up the whole room. Almost immediately, the large doors to the ballroom burst open and her father's angels swarm in, clashing with Samandriel's angels. The grunts and cries of battle quickly fill the air.

"This way," Gabby calls to her mother, determined to get her to safety. She has no doubt the clones are under orders to keep her alive. The Grigori need her to read the parchments. It's an advantage she's going to use to get her mom out of here.

She punches and kicks her way through the throng of angels fighting angels, keeping her mom close. When one ducks and weaves, getting far closer than any of the others, her mother squeals with fright. Hating the sound of her mother's fear, Gabby snarls. One pump of her wings and she barrels into him, snapping his neck. She throws the limp body at three other angels rushing at them and takes her mom's hand as she continues on.

But the determined plowing through the grunting bodies is stalled when Gabby sees what's ahead. Her father has joined the fight. The father her mom thinks is no longer in the picture. The realization has Gabby hesitating, and that's all an angel needs to land a punch in her solar plexus. The air explodes out of her lungs and she doubles over. Not willing to let pain stop her, she instantly rears back up, winding up to power her fist through the angel's chin only to find she's not there.

Her father pummels the angel then hurls her away before Gabby can blink. He throws her a smile as he spins and dispatches another that was running up behind. But there's no time for gratitude. Her father, the archangel Gabriel, is now only feet away from her mother, the human he impregnated and left.

Except then Gabby sees what she didn't notice straight away. A shimmering light covers him, ever so slightly distorting his features. He's cloaked himself! Her mother is no doubt seeing just another angel. Relief courses through Gabby even as she realizes she should've thought to do that. She could've cloaked herself and stopped her mother from learning what she truly is.

Her father rushes past her. "I'll guard your back," he says almost silently.

But Gabby hears it. He's protecting her mother as much as she is.

Seeing an opening, she grabs her mom's hand and rushes forward. The doors out of here are only a few yards away. When a fresh wave of angel clones closes in, Gabby draws in a deep breath, draws her hand back, and slams her fist through the air. A shockwave explodes outward, tumbling the angels like bowling pins and slamming several into walls several feet away. Gabby races forward, bringing her mom with her.

She reaches the doors. "Go. You need to get out of here."

For the first time since this ordeal started, her mother's fear fades. "I can't leave you here."

"In case you hadn't noticed, I'm managing."

Her mom's eyes trace the expanse of Gabby's wings, blinking. "I..."

Gabby's heart clenches. She's going to have some serious explaining to do. "Go," she says more gently. "I need to know you're safe."

Her mom nods. Swallows. Then turns and slips through the doors.

Ignoring the lump lodged in her chest, Gabby turns back to the fighting. There's someone else she needs to save. Launching into the air, she flies over the fighting, registering that her father's angels are getting the upper hand. She lands on the other side of the room beside the panel Virginia and the Grigori disappeared through. A press of her hands on the obsidian symbol and it glows bright then opens. Gabby steps through and it closes almost instantly, cutting off the sounds of battle.

She finds herself in a room where every wall is lined with wooden cupboards of every size. There's no time to investigate, even as Gabby remembers Virginia telling her this secret area houses magical artifacts, because there's another door ahead, faint voices coming through it. She strides toward it and the voices become louder.

"Where are the chains?" one of them roars.

"She's stalling," growls another. "But not for much longer."

The threat in the words is undeniable. Virginia led the Grigori in there to buy Gabby more time and get the civilians out. It's time to repay the favor. Gabby flings open the door, finding one of the Grigori holding the mayor by the hair.

"Let her go."

The other six move forward, forming a line between Gabby and the trapped mayor. "We don't fear you," they hiss.

"Really?" Gabby asks mockingly. "Because last time we had a little chat you ran like the cowards you are."

She conjures a ball of celestial fire, allowing it to burn brightly as it encases her hand. She's actually looking forward to using it.

Except the Grigori throw back their heads and laugh coldly, the sound even more creepy in the way it's replicated exactly between them. "Stupid girl," one spits. "You think we would come here unprepared after what happened?"

Gabby flares the ball brighter and bigger even though their confidence undermines her own. "I doubt I could even start to unravel what goes on in your crazy minds," she snaps.

"We've created wards to absorb that fire of yours. It cannot hurt us."

Shocked, Gabby watches as the ball fizzles out as if it was just doused.

Skata.

She takes a step forward. "I'll fight you with everything I have," she vows. "Release the mayor."

The Grigori chuckle condescendingly. "We have no need to fight. We have the parchments."

"With no way to translate them," she reminds them caustically.

"We will find someone else. There are others, admittedly harder to find, but not impossible," says one.

"And no doubt far less argumentative," adds another.

"As for the mayor, she lied to us, and for that, she will die."

Gabby goes to move, her hands hot fists by her side when they simultaneously raise their hands.

"Move, and her death will be a slow, painful one."

She freezes, anger grinding through her veins. All she can do is hope her plans have worked...

The Grigori close around Virginia, their faces twitching with excitement. Except nothing happens. They glance at each other. But still nothing. Simultaneously, their gazes fall on Gabby. "What have you done?" they shout.

"Do you really think I wasn't prepared?" she sneers. "The moment I began working here, this place became a beacon for you." Which is what she intended. "Not only was I here, but so was the mayor, someone who was becoming more and more of a threat to you. The whole building was warded long before you arrived."

The Grigori take a menacing step forward, their lips curled as hatred burns in their eyes.

But Gabby holds her ground. "Your magic won't work here."

A blast of energy rockets the Grigori holding the mayor backward. She steps away, adjusting her suit jacket. "Especially in here, my secret chambers." She waves her hand and several runes flare bright gold on the walls.

A roar of rage echoes through the air, the fury almost bringing color to the Grigori's colorless skin. Yet, they don't move. Gabby can almost see the gears working overtime in their head as they try to plot their next move.

"You will be punished for this," they hiss in unison.

"With the army that's being decimated by my father's angels?" Gabby asks archly. "I was hoping you'd come," she adds, unable to let the opportunity to rub this in pass. She hadn't banked on the hostages, but the innocent civilians are safe now. "Your obsession with the obsidian was your undoing. With Samandriel gone, you knew your hold over the cult was weakening, especially with Leopold in custody, doing time for the very murders you committed. So you formed an alliance with the faction."

"The faction that's been searching for the obsidian for centuries?" asks Virginia derisively. "You actually thought Malcolm would share the obsidian with you?"

The Grigori bristle at the disdain in her voice, or maybe it's at their naivety. Not that it matters. Gabby saved the best for last.

"And do you really think the parchments I handed over to you are real?"

The Grigori stiffen. Scowl. Then a low rumble ripples through them. Their need for violence is palpable.

Yet, without their powers, they're nothing but seven emasculated angels who have no choice but watch their failure unfold.

Gabby senses their intention to attack, their fury too explosive to be contained. She quickly conjures the chains Virginia gave her. "I had these all along, by the way."

One powerful throw and the chains molded to bind a Titan wrap around the seven Grigori. They scream with rage as it wraps around them, then thrash so hard their bodies are a blur.

But it's useless. They're trapped.

The door behind her is flung open and Gabby's father and his angels storm into the room. "You'll be going to the Pearl City to answer for your crimes," she says, not taking her eyes off the struggling Grigori, sweet satisfaction thrumming through her blood. "And this prison will last much longer than your last one."

This time, there won't be a well-meaning human like her aunt who will inadvertently release them.

Her father comes to stand by her side, his head held high as he regards the seven ancient watchers of Eden still trying to fight the inevitable. "You did well, daughter."

Except, as her father's men move in to drag the evil bastards away, any flush of victory quickly drains. Gabby blinks, conscious she's surrounded by either her enemy, or those she doesn't completely trust. There's no one to high five. To celebrate with. To kiss with abandon.

She frowns, trying to shake the melancholy away. She won. The Grigori are imprisoned.

Yet no flush of triumph fills her veins. The victory is tainted. All she can feel is the deep, piercing ache in her chest.

Despite it all, it feels like she lost.

MARKED ANGEL

Evil is thirsting for power. And to divide the only two who can stop it.

An angel and a demon have done the impossible—fallen in love. And the powers that oppose it are many.

Yet Gabby and Colt can't help but gravitate toward each other. Their hearts tell them everyone else is wrong. They just have to prove it.

Even when the obstacles seem insurmountable. There's a traitor in their ranks. A new threat known as the Skeleton Man. And a secret faction thirsting for dark power.

What's more, their enemies don't just want to bring on the apocalypse. They want to tear Gabby and Colt apart. Their impossible connection is a threat. A connection that's their most powerful weapon of all.

GRAB YOUR COPY HERE
mybook.to/MarkedAngel

HAVE YOU READ THE KEEPER CHRONICLES PREQUEL?

**As an exclusive for my subscribers,
you can download it for free!!**

When Sierra sneaks out, determined to escape her over-protective family, she stumbles across a young man covered in blood. His last words are a plea. *Find the Grail Keepers. Warn them.*

Ryder is the young cop who was last seen with the murdered victim. Sierra doesn't trust him, no matter how drawn she is to him. Except it turns out they're both looking for the same thing—the Holy Grail.

They're quickly drawn into a dangerous hunt involving cryptic clues, a mysterious stone, and a Grail that hasn't been seen for centuries. One that leads to more questions than answers. Can Sierra trust her impulsive emotions? Should she believe Ryder's words or the truth she sees in his eyes? And ultimately, should she follow her heart?

Especially when every decision will decide the fate of countless lives.

CLICK HERE TO DOWNLOAD FOR FREE!
https://BookHip.com/TTBMTTV

Also by Tamar Sloan

PRIME PROPHECY SERIES

He failed to shift like every one of his ancestors.

Until he met her.

KEEPERS OF THE GRAIL

The legendary Holy Grail is real.

Yet everything known about it is a lie.

KEEPERS OF THE CHALICE

A vampire. A huntress.

A cure that will change everything.

KEEPERS OF THE LIGHT

Angels and demons have battled for millennia.

Their inevitable war has begun.

KEEPERS OF EXCALIBUR

A fated love. A cursed wolf.

A supernatural war only they can stop.

DESTINED DEMIGODS

Love that defies the gods.

Powers that define destiny.

ELEMENTAL GAMES

Elemental powers. Deadly Games.

No escape.

THE SOVEREIGN CODE

Humans saved bees from extinction...and created the deadliest threat we've seen yet.

THE THAW CHRONICLES

Only the chosen shall breed.

ZODIAC GUARDIANS

Twelve teens. One task.

Save the Universe.

About the Author

Tamar hasn't decided whether she's primarily a psychologist who loves writing, or a writer with a lifelong drive to make a difference. She must have been someone pretty awesome in a previous life (past life regression indicates a Care Bear), because she gets to do both. She divides her time between helping families and writing emotion driven YA stories set in amazing imaginary worlds that surprise even her.

The driving force for all of Tamar's writing is sharing and connecting. In truth, connecting with others is why she writes. She loves to hear from readers. Find her on all the usual social media channels or her website, www.tamarsloan.com where can download one of her books for free.

(Seriously, I LOVE hearing from you guys!)